A FRAGILE MERCY

DOUG SINCLAIR

Storm
PUBLISHING

Ebook ISBN: 978-1-83700-035-7
Paperback ISBN: 978-1-83700-036-4

Cover design: Blacksheep
Cover images: Shutterstock

Published by Storm Publishing.
For further information, visit:
www.stormpublishing.co

ALSO BY DOUG SINCLAIR

DS Malkie McCulloch Series

Blood Runs Deep

Last to Die

A Deadly Flame

A Cold Heart

For my Uncle Tommy and Auntie Winnie, who taught me to always "let it go". I miss you both.

ONE

So much blood. It can't all be his, can it?

But he knows it is.

He hears the moaning sound again and, again, realises it's him.

He sobs. Nobody here to witness him cry like a girl. To see him in this state. No one to help him. Where's Frankie? He needs an ambulance. He thinks he might die, and it enrages him. He doesn't deserve this. Those fuckers ruined his game. They deserve what they got, but he doesn't.

He refuses to die in such an undignified way. It'll be all over the internet. They'll revel in his ignominy and mourn him in equal measure.

No. Not him. He's a someone, not like the fucking nobodies that did this to him.

He'll live, and he'll continue his game.

But he'll escalate. Watch them suffer.

They think they're hurting now? They have no imagination. No idea how much worse he can make it for them.

His sight dims. Eager shades crowd the periphery of his vision. He rages, tries to crawl to the door. Agony sears him again, makes him gasp then scream his fury to the empty room. The room he ran his game from.

Fuck. His stash. He mustn't let anyone find it. The toys he used to torment his playthings. So much fun, listening to them whine and cry and beg.

A distraction from himself. Until now.

He tries to crawl across the floor to it, but collapses, the agony of his injuries too much.

Darkness gathers. Shadows creep into him. It's unjust. His star is on the rise, his trajectory assured after so many years of toil and self-debasement. The brilliance of all he's achieved and still intended to achieve, coming to long-deserved fruition.

He rages against the dying of his light.

He clutches his ruined flesh to staunch the bleeding. He can survive this. Just a few hours. Frankie loathes him but she'll help him, needs him more than he needs her. It wasn't always that way, but he'd played her even better than the others.

She'll save him and hate herself for doing it.

He'll survive this.

But so much blood...

TWO

Malkie watched the door. His eyes burned until he remembered to blink.

He saw movement through the frosted glass panel. Thompson? No, Steph. Too short to be Thompson. And besides, only Steph wore that kind of jacket. Made her look like a farmer, or an academic, rather than the petite Police Scotland Rottweiler he'd come to know and love.

And respect. More than anything else. Or maybe fear? Bit of both.

He shook himself, forced his mind back to his waiting game. Steph sat down again. Heads huddled close. Hands gesticulated. A small Rottweiler fist slammed on the table.

Thompson leaned forward, looked desperate and pleading.

This was killing him. Not nosiness. Worry.

On only two occasions could he remember Thompson ask Steph for a private meeting, and both times had been because the same utter arsehole had reared his stupid, vicious, mouth-breathing head and tried to cause her damage. He reminded himself: Steph always looked ready to skin him alive when he called that sorry excuse for a man her stepfather.

Dean Lang. As much a waste of oxygen as Malkie had ever

met, which was saying something given the knuckle-draggers he met on a daily basis in his capacity as the longest-serving – by choice – Detective Sergeant in Livi CID. Apart from a brief episode in management as probably the most reluctant DI in the history of DIs, long enough to tell him he'd always been right to resist any kind of promotion.

On a daily basis. Did he really just let his mind think those words? *Every bloody day*, he scolded himself. None of that corporate shite from him, thank you very much.

The office door flew open to slam against the inside wall. Steph charged out, her face crimson and her lips muttering a string of uncharacteristic expletives he'd only ever heard from her recently.

She stopped by her desk to grab her jacket. As she turned away to head for the door to the outside, she paused, took a huge breath and put Malkie out of his misery.

'He's dead. The miserable fucker has gone and died. I'm not suspended but management eyes are on me, Thompson says.'

She stomped off, kicked a wastepaper basket halfway to the windows around the outside of the open-plan station desk space.

Thompson appeared.

'I thought that went well, don't you?'

Malkie heard no humour in her voice. 'How?'

'Passed away in the night. Doctors said it could have happened any time, he was so badly injured.'

'Passed away? In his sleep?'

'Well, in a coma with tubes in every orifice and a machine breathing for him, but I take your point.'

'Nae justice.'

Thompson sighed. She lowered her voice and leaned close; she had a degree of professionalism to maintain. Or at least to be seen and heard to maintain.

'We can only hope the last thing to go through his mind as he hurtled four storeys down onto that car was sheer, unadulterated terror.'

'Amen to that.'

Thompson arched an eyebrow. 'Amen?'

'As I often say, sometimes I wish I believed in God so—'

'You can believe in a devil waiting for people like Dean Lang?'

'Exactly.'

Thompson pulled a chair over, and they sat in silence for a moment.

'So, is she going to be suspended? That cannae be right, can it?'

'No. No suspension. All she has against her is Lang's claim that he saw her fleeing the scene of her biological—'

'Don't say that. Please. And never to her. You mean Barry Boswell.'

'Not when Steph's not here, and certainly not when it's becoming official, Malkie. That relationship matters now.'

Malkie held his hands out in grudging acceptance.

Thompson nodded her acknowledgement of his agreement. 'So, it's Boswell's word against hers, but I still worry.'

Malkie picked up a pen just to throw it back on his desk. 'Me too.'

Thompson raised her eyebrow again.

'She's changing, boss.' He checked his watch. 'Sorry... Susan.'

Thompson waited. She'd want to know Malkie's opinion unprompted.

'She's swearing like a bloody trooper recently. And that's my job round here.'

They shared mutual smiles, but both were weak and fleeting.

'And she's no fun anymore. I mean, we all know she has a vicious wee gob on her at times, but she at least had a sense of humour. Drier than a...' – Thompson lifted just one eyebrow – 'than an HR health and safety briefing, I was going to say. But that edge we all love was always there. That's gone now. Like all the joy has been sucked out of her. It's bloody heartbreaking.'

Susan's expression told him what he already knew, that she found the change in Steph as distressing as he did.

Malkie sat up, rubbed his hands together.

'OK. Fuck it. Sorry. This can't go on. What can I do?'

Thompson hesitated for a second. 'Nothing, Malkie.'

He opened his mouth to complain, but she held a hand up, very much in superior officer mode again.

'The best thing you can do for her is nothing. You'll be allowed nowhere near the investigation into Lang's death, and any interference on your part can only jeopardise her case.'

'Her case? Seriously?'

Thompson's distress emanated from her eyes.

'We can't just ignore the complaints made by Lang about her, or the video taken by that pedestrian of her attacking Lang after—'

'Attacking, my arse, boss. He's lowlife and asked for it. He deserved a kicking, was just lucky Steph has more self-control than I'll ever have.'

Thompson let his outburst pass, allowed him to realise for himself what he'd just said.

'Aye, alright. Fair point.' He pinched his eyes, held his head back, tried to ease a tightening of his neck muscles he knew could lead to a headache.

'And it goes without saying you're to go nowhere near Barry Boswell, of course.'

'Aye, I know.'

She studied him for a few seconds, and he stood before his temper could overcome what passed in his case for good judgement. They'd nearly been more than friends during their cadet days, and she knew him almost as well as Steph did, and that never failed to piss him off.

She stood too and laid a hand on his shoulder. 'Just be there for her, Malkie. That's what she needs from you, right now.'

He turned back to his PC before his mouth could say something that might stretch even their long relationship. He noticed that an alert had popped up, a familiar and often dreaded icon and message that all coppers knew heralded a new shout, a call to do their civic duty for the good people of West Lothian.

They glanced at each other. Malkie sighed and reached for his mouse. Thompson leaned over his shoulder as he read.

'Attempted murder. Blah blah. Uniform on scene. Blah blah. Victim en route to St John's. Blah blah blah. Who's Sebastian Beauchamp?'

Thompson's expression soured. She rubbed her hand down her face and heaved a long-suffering sigh.

'He's a highly-regarded secretary to the Scottish Shadow Cabinet. Justice, I think. And tipped to rise much further. This one is going to get political, mate.'

'I suppose I should know him already, aye?'

'Aye, you probably should, Malkie.'

THREE

Malkie whistled to himself as he approached a pair of huge, glossy-black iron gates that marked – with an *in your face* kind of ostentation nobody could miss – the entrance to the luxury home of Sebastian and Francesca Beauchamp, on a private road off of Mannerston Holdings near Blackness, a semi-rural stretch of the choicest land anywhere in West Lothian. Most properties along the various lanes off Mannerston Holdings were traditional-build, modest bungalows, although worth a fortune thanks to the breathtaking proximity to Blackness Castle at the end of the promontory and the view out across the wide, grey, expanse of the Forth Estuary to Fife. Some of them would be occupied by modest-earners, despite the sizeable value of their properties, and many of them would hate the monstrosity that now sat before him. He loathed it on sight. Conspicuous wealth always turned his stomach, mostly because he suspected people who lived in homes like this either came from unearned, inherited money or took it from others in ways that would seriously piss off little people like him.

Two Uniforms, neither of whose names he could remember right now, stood in the entrance, holding back – and looking mightily hacked off with – four obvious journalists, two with mobile phones stuck at their mouths and each accompanied by a camera operator with technology perched on their shoulders that probably cost more than Malkie made in a month.

When the Uniforms had spotted Malkie pull up, they had seen an opportunity to throw their Police Scotland weight about, as if they were still green enough to believe your typical journalist would pay the slightest attention. They pushed the journos to the side of the driveway, less than politely, and held them back as Malkie drove in.

Camera flashes through the side windows threatened to trigger him, to drag back memories of the night almost a year before when his mum died. There had been flashing lights all over the place back then too. All of them shades of blue, and none of them came close to saving her.

He felt fingers touch his arm. Detective Constable Louisa 'Gucci' Gooch. He saw a warning furrow her brow, so he patted her hand and smiled.

'I'm fine, Lou. Promise.'

She removed her hand but looked far from reassured.

They pulled up at the entrance to a massive mock-Gothic manse, all pillars and marble lions.

Perceived class bought with new money. I hate these people already.

A white SOCO van stood to one side, the back doors open, and someone in a paper onesie – looked female from the size and posture – rummaged around in various boxes. A third Uniform – PC Davie Semple – stepped down five marble steps to meet them.

'Morning, sir. I mean, Malkie. Morning, Gucci. Beauchamp is at St John's. Looking grim, the paramedics said. He's been stabbed with the neck of a broken bottle.'

Malkie heard more behind the words, held Semple's gaze and raised an eyebrow.

'In the groin. Several times, they said.' Semple shuddered. Malkie sighed.

Bollocks. Not just a burglar then.

He mounted the steps, but Semple stopped him.

'The wife's in there.' He pointed to a massive glass frontage that looked to extend round the corner of the property. 'The whole ground floor is taped off. And by the way, she doesn't like her name being pronounced like Beecham. She insists on it being said the French way.'

Be good, old man.

He found her sitting in a rattan chair in a conservatory that could accommodate the whole of the lochside cabin Malkie and his dad called home. Everything in the room screamed money, just like the outside. Sweeping beds of orchids and other flowers he couldn't begin to name. Towering fountains of dark-green plants with wide leaves and thick, fleshy stems. He spotted an expensive-looking automated irrigation system suspended from the roof. And it was warm. Muggy, even. This wasn't a conservatory; it was a hothouse like the ones in the Edinburgh Botanic Gardens his mum used to take him to during the school holidays.

'Mrs Beauchamp?' He pronounced it Beecham; he didn't plan to risk it more than once, but he wanted to see if the lady of the manor had as big a stick up her arse as he always expected from people with new money.

She scowled at him and tutted.

Yep. Massive stick.

She opened her mouth, he assumed to correct him, so he spoke over her.

'I'm Detective Sergeant Malcolm McCulloch and my colleague is Detective Constable Louisa Gooch. Have you had a family liaison officer assigned to you yet?'

Beauchamp bristled at Malkie's blunt tone, and he had a word with himself. *This much money means connections and they can lead to arse-kickings. And her husband's maybe just been neutered, more to the point.*

'I was told one is on the way. Someone called PC Theresa Carmichael. She should be here later this morning.'

'That's good. I know her and she's excellent. An incident like this can be immensely stressful. DC Gooch and I are here to see the scene of your husband's attack and liaise with the SOCOs, then we'll need to ask you some initial questions. Will that be OK?'

Beauchamp stood and without another word walked past them toward the door to the outside. Malkie touched her on the arm to stop her.

'I don't think we need to put you through seeing it all again, Mrs Beauchamp. We can manage on our own, thanks. And besides, until the SOCOs – the forensics people – finish up, the whole lower floor, and I would guess access to the upstairs, will be restricted. The FLO will help you arrange alternative accommodation for tonight. Hopefully no longer than that.'

She looked at him like he'd shit in her handbag.

'If you need it, that is.'

'We have a two-bedroom annex apartment at the foot of the garden, which will suffice temporarily.'

Of course you do.

She let out a loud and performative sigh as she returned to her chair.

Gucci stepped past him to the outside. They stopped at the SOCO van to suit and boot up, then PC Semple signed them in to the house.

Wide, double-width doorways led off each side of the immense downstairs hallway. On the left, they saw a drawing room or a sitting room or whatever toffs called it and – Malkie struggled to take this seriously – an actual library, complete with ceiling-height shelves crammed with dusty and stuffy-looking books in leather bindings, and not a paperback in sight. On the other side of the hallway, doors led to another drawing or sitting room and to a kitchen the likes of which Malkie had only ever seen in his mum's magazines. The ones she always told him helped her 'dream-build'.

He swallowed a lump of bitter memory and felt Gucci's eyes on him.

At the back of the hallway one door stood closed, but another opened into a small study, complete with a green-leather-topped desk and more bookshelves. The space was busy with forensic activity, in the SOCOs' own slow and deliberate way. Malkie recognised a bear of a man named Bruce, even in his onesie. The Scottish Police Authority's Forensics Services had to buy sterile scene-wear made specially for him.

'Morning, Bruce. Morning, er, everyone else, whoever you are.'

He grinned but even with only their eyes visible, all three – Bruce plus one male and one female – made no secret of their opinion of Malkie's brand of humour.

Bruce stood and stepped to the doorway. As he moved, Malkie saw the blood. So much of it. Smeared on the floor and the wall and down a curtain.

'Fuck's sake.'

Bruce glanced behind him then turned back. 'Indeed. The victim was stabbed repeatedly in the groin. This much blood suggests copious bleeding, obviously, from what can be a highly vascular part of the body, but I would suspect his femoral artery wasn't cut. He'd have bled out before the ambulance got here if that had happened.'

'And when you say that part of the body *can be* highly vascular, you mean...'

'I mean that part of the body can be highly vascular. At times. You know I can't draw any further conclusions at this stage, Malkie.'

Malkie chewed this over before risking the question he couldn't not ask but which could make the political implications of Beauchamp's position in the Scottish Shadow Cabinet problematic, to say the least.

'Were there any signs of sexual activity?'

Bruce sighed. 'You'll need to ask the paramedics.' He gave Malkie the customary SOCO *that's all you're getting for now* look.

'When can we get in?'

'Sooner than you'd think.'

Bruce waited for Malkie to meet his gaze.

'We've been told to expedite this one.'

Malkie heard the undertone in Bruce's comment and scowled.

'I bloody bet you have.'

He and Gucci returned to the conservatory. Mrs Beauchamp's scowl looked to have grown in ferocity during the brief time they were away.

'Well?'

Malkie stopped in his tracks, halfway to an empty rattan chair across from Mrs Beauchamp's and flashed her a look. It had no apparent effect except to make her scowl harder.

Stroppy cow, aren't you? Not so much distressed as... What? Inconvenienced?

He sat without waiting to be asked. Gucci pulled her notebook and pen from inside her jacket and turned to a new page. She'd have learned this from Steph because Malkie rarely even knew which pocket held his own.

'Mrs Beauchamp.' He pronounced it correctly, allowed her a small self-satisfied nod.

'We can't get into what I assume is your husband's study until the SOCOs have finished their work, so the best use of our time right now would be to cover some initial questions. Would that be OK?'

She nodded. 'Yes. Whatever I can do to help you catch whoever did this awful thing.'

Malkie resisted an urge to glance at Gucci to see if she seemed to react the same way as he did. *You'll never win any acting awards, Mrs Beauchamp.*

'OK. To begin with. Who found Mr Beauchamp and when?'

'I did. We dismiss the staff at weekends unless we're hosting. We like our privacy.'

Malkie detected not a trace of the emotional leakage that recalling such a viscerally upsetting discovery often triggered.

'And when?'

'A few minutes after eight this morning. Most mornings, he knocks on my bedroom door as he heads for the kitchen to make breakfast. When he didn't do that, I checked his room. His bedclothes were undisturbed and he wasn't there. When I found the kitchen empty and no sign of him in the grounds or in here, I tried the only other place he would be. His study.'

She took a moment, her eyes downcast. Malkie fought his own unconscious prejudice, reminded himself that her stern and unemotional demeanour might be a result of a lifetime of smothering privilege and expectation, and not necessarily because the woman had something to hide.

'He was lying against the wall, clutching his... Clutching himself, and sobbing.'

Malkie's mind itched.

'Sobbing?'

Beauchamp's eyes snapped up to his, anger burning in them now.

'I said *sobbing*, Detective.'

Malkie studied her for a second; her displeasure seemed genuine. But also without any apparent confusion at a man who – he'd been told – had been stabbed repeatedly in his most private parts and not moaning or screaming in agony, but sobbing.

'Was I not clear enough, Detective? Of course he was in agony and it sounded like it, but he was sobbing through his cries of pain. Wouldn't you if someone did that to you?'

Malkie dragged himself back from his habit of picking at single words. Columbo he was not, as Steph reminded him regularly.

'And you didn't hear anything? Last night, I mean?'

She threw a sharp warning glare at him. 'I take medication. It makes me sleep very soundly.'

Convenient, Mrs Beauchamp?

'Can you think of anyone who might? Do that to him, I mean?'

She deflated, as if finally accepting that Malkie and Gucci had a job to do.

'There must be dozens of people who bear him a grudge, yes, even though he's not a cabinet minister yet, still a SPAD for now.'

Malkie nodded but didn't admit he had no idea what a SPAD was.

'And no personal issues with anyone?'

She looked at him in disgust. 'How bad a personal issue could he have that would deserve that? What kind of people do you think we are, Mr McCulloch?'

Malkie held his hands up to placate her.

'I apologise for upsetting you, Mrs Beauchamp, but we have to explore all possible avenues.'

She sat back in her chair, crossed her legs and folded her arms. The interview was over.

Outside, beside his car, Malkie stared back at the house and drummed his fingers on his lips.

'Special Adviser.'

He'd forgotten Gucci was there.

'Eh?'

'A SPAD. Special Adviser. Advises the cabinet ministers who take all the glory for good choices and blame cockups on their SPADs. They're pretty much anonymous and invisible, otherwise.'

'This wasn't political, Gucci. And it wasn't a burglar. Or linked to money.'

He sighed as he voiced what she must be thinking too.

'This was personal. And I'd bet my pension sex was involved, somchow.'

FOUR

[Patricia] We need to talk.

[Patricia] Hello? Someone answer me.

[Patricia] Fuck's sake, anyone?

[Zoe] What? I was in a meeting.

[Teri] Me too. I can't drop everything at any time. What can't wait until Wednesday?

[Zoe] Patricia? You demand we answer then you disappear? What's going on?

[Patricia] We need to talk. Before Wednesday. It's urgent.

[Zoe] I'm tired and I'm hacked off. It'll need to wait.

[Patricia] It can't.

[Teri] You're scaring me. What's happened? Are you OK?

[Zoe] Patricia?

[Patricia] No. It can't wait.

[Patricia] I killed him.

[Zoe] Who?

[Patricia] You know who I mean. Who else?

[Zoe] That was you? Seriously? What the fuck?

[Patricia] You already know?

[Teri] Of course we know. It's all over the news. No details about how though. What did you do, Patricia?

[Patricia] I hit him with a wine bottle. Smashed it over his head. Then I…'
[Zoe] Patricia?
[Patricia] I was so sure. He wasn't breathing. Oh God. What if he does die? There was so much blood. He's going to die. I know he is. And it's my fault.
[Zoe] OK. Calm down. Let's all stay calm.
[Patricia] Calm? Really? You don't do calm well, Zoe.
[Teri] That's not helping, Patricia. We'll hear you out, see if we can help you. Of course we will. Isn't that why we started this?
[Teri] Hang on a minute, Patricia. You can't just drop something like that on us and expect us to reply at once. I mean, what were you thinking? What did you do?
[Patricia] I killed him. I think.
[Zoe] You think? Fuck's sake, Patricia.
[Teri] All right. Calm down, everyone. I can't get into this now. Not even this. Tonight OK, Patricia?
[Patricia] Yes. Please. I'm so scared.
[Teri] OK, I'll message Amber and open the call at 22:00.
[Patricia] Thanks. I'm sorry.
[Zoe] Don't thank us yet.

FIVE

'Fuckin' sham. No doubt about it.'

Gucci shrugged and turned the corners of her mouth down, as if reluctant to disagree openly with him.

'Say it, Gucci. Whatever you're itching to.'

She studied him, seemed to weigh him up.'Could be.'

'Could be? It's bloody obvious. Their type always are.'

She sighed, cast a pained expression on him.

He buckled. 'OK. Point taken. They might be the exception, but that Mrs *Beecham* plus all of this.' He waved a hand at his screen. 'Looks very like it, doesn't it?'

Gucci shrugged again, this time in apparent grudging part-acceptance of Malkie's considered and internet-informed opinion.

He picked the choicest morsels from the public profile website on his screen. He felt confirmation bias trying to kick in but he tried to maintain at least some objectivity.

'She's out of the country three weeks of every month, earns five times what he does apparently; no kids, never holiday together.'

Gucci looked confused. 'How does all that indicate a sham marriage?'

Malkie held his hands out as if the answer should be self-explanatory. 'A cold and allegedly passionless globe-trotting and mega-influential woman like her who has never been known to even kiss him in public. Separate bedrooms as evidenced by her comment that she checked his room that morning. And a man who, by some accounts, is so sexy he could have his pick of any young and gorgeous SPUD he wanted? If there's love there, I'll eat my warrant card, Gucci.'

'SPAD.'

'Eh?'

'SPAD, not SPUD.'

'Whatever. My point is, in all these search results...' He scrolled down several screens of soundbites and photos. 'I see nothing to indicate any affection between them. Nowt. Ergo, sham marriage. Or at least one that started cold and functional and went downhill from there.'

Gucci chewed her lower lip before speaking again. 'OK, fine. I can accept that maybe their marriage wasn't the cosiest, but I suspect I know where you're going with this and I don't think the connection is a valid one.'

'Wrong. Understandable, given my past performance, but not this time.'

'Wrong how?'

'I don't think she's involved.'

She held her hands out to admit he'd read her correctly. 'Good. I agree.'

'What happened to *Beecham* was an act of fury. Personal. Someone hated him. Someone passionate in all the wrong ways.'

'Agreed.'

'And I don't think Mrs *Beecham* is capable of feeling passion. I could be wrong, I suppose. I was wrong about something, once. It was a Thursday, if memory serves. But not this time. She's cold. Incredible self-restraint, I suspect. The kind that would take revenge for whatever her husband did to deserve... that... with detachment and calculation. I just can't see her losing the rag with anyone, for anything.'

He took a breath.

'Finished?' Gucci sounded more like Steph than Malkie would ever be comfortable with.

'Aye. You can lay into me now. In Steph's absence.'

Gucci had opened her mouth to do just that but mention of Steph's name closed it again. They sat in uncomfortable silence.

'Will she be OK, Malkie?'

He took a moment. The easy thing to say would be *she'll be fine, Gucci* but she'd never believe him and she – more than most people – deserved honesty from him.

'I don't know, Lou. On one hand there's only circumstantial evidence against her along with some forensics that she was in the fucker's flat. Sorry, Lou, I mean the bastard's. And that's easily explained by the fact that she already confirmed she was perfectly justifiably in Lang's flat on several occasions. But we all know how mud sticks, and even if… When she's vindicated and any suspicion blown to hell as it should be, there'll still be a permanent flag on her career record. And we all know that no matter how much HR claim they're there to support us, the Division's most valued resources, their real function is to protect the reputation of the Force. And aye, I know we're not allowed to call it the Force anymore but I'm too old for all this recent modernisation shite.'

Gucci didn't bother to suppress a chuckle. 'Not since April 2013, Malkie. That's not recent.'

'Good point. Well made. Shut up.' He smiled back, wary from previous close calls with a Political Correctness Disciplinary to leave not a scrap of doubt he'd made his comment with affection.

She rolled her eyes at him; Steph's influence had so much to answer for. 'So, we have no idea, then?'

'None. Common sense is always at the bottom of the priority list of any corporate drone, isn't it?'

Thompson chose that moment to open her office door and wander over. A DI didn't usually get a private space, but she had moved a filing cabinet with enough of her stuff in there to make the point moot and ill-advised as a topic of any conversation. She left the door open ninety per cent of the time, closed it only for conversations of a sensitive or embarrassing nature, mostly involving Malkie but more recently – and worryingly – with Steph.

'What about Beauchamp?'

'Nothing noteworthy so far, ma'am.' Malkie winked at Gucci.

'Guv, Malkie. Or Susan when there's just a couple of us.' She smiled at Gucci, who beamed back at her, no doubt happy to be included in any small but select circle.

'We're checking out social media while we wait for the warrant to poke about in *Beecham*'s life.'

'It's being processed, shouldn't take long. But did no one tell you the SOCOs found a filing cabinet crammed full of his personal documents? Bank statements, phone bills, professional correspondence, that sort of thing.'

Malkie had a word with his inner idiot, which – as usual – won.

'No, boss. Nobody told me.' He glanced pointedly at Gucci. She scowled and opened her mouth, but Malkie talked over her.

'We'll get all over them as soon as they arrive. I was only planning to eat and sleep tonight, anyway.'

Thompson raised an eyebrow, and Malkie couldn't miss the warning in it.

'I mean, we all appreciate the urgency involved in this case. Nasty way to be attacked. Painful. Personal, possibly. And him such a high-profile man.'

Thompson fixed him with a warning look. 'And there it is.'

Malkie feigned innocence. 'What, guv?'

Thompson and Gucci shared a look.

'I'll agree that *Beauchamp*'s profile – and his wife's – will feed an eager public interest in this one. So, we need to be seen to be taking it seriously, but other than that no special dispensation will be made.'

The emphasis on the pronunciation of Beauchamp's name left Malkie in no doubt he was on a shoogly peg if he didn't fall into line on that one. He raised an eyebrow, hoped Thompson would buckle on her claims of assumed objectivity in the investigation.

She did. 'At least as far as my investigation goes. But you know me well enough to toe that line anyway, right? Right?'

After a shared look, the words 'Yes, guv' came from Malkie and Gucci, almost in perfect sync.

Thompson groaned, then sat. 'Fuck it. Clear it quickly and don't piss anyone off, understood?'

'Yes, guv.' Again, in perfect stereo.

All three sat in silence as Malkie scrolled past more comments and photos of both Beechams – Beauchamps, he reminded himself. He paused to zoom in on any which might confirm his belief in the vacuous nature of their marriage. Neither Gucci nor Thompson would miss his silent pointing-out of just how cold and dispassionate the couple were considered by most so-called celebrity journos, but they said nothing.

Thompson's mobile rang. She answered, murmured a few vague comments, then hung up.

'St John's. Update on Beauchamp.'

Malkie felt a lump drop into his stomach.

Thompson stood and pinched two fingers in her eyes.

'Too much blood loss. Organ failure. They called it fifteen minutes ago.'

As she walked back to her office, she stopped and turned.

'You realise MIT will be all over this, aye? Someone with Beauchamp's profile?'

Malkie had expected this but had dared to hope otherwise. 'Do we know who?'

Thompson looked more reluctant to answer that question than she had about Beauchamp's demise. She cast her eyes around the open-plan Livi office before speaking again.

'Let's hope it's not *him*. And you'd better let me warn Pam and Steph.'

Malkie and Gucci shared a look. Both were only too aware of

how DS Pamela Ballantyne had hitched her career to her previous DI, Gavin McLeish, before finding out too late what an utter arse he could be, and the damage even a slight association with him could do to her.

'Fuck,' he suggested.

SIX

'You're kidding. Please tell me you're kidding, guv.'

'I wish I was, Steph. It's not certain but it's possible. I thought I should call to let you know.'

'Can't we get that pair that took over the Lillian Crosbie Case? McGowan and Campbell? They weren't annoying at all.'

'I know, but we have no say in it. If we get him, we get him. We'll just need to make it work.'

Steph couldn't find words; she knew as well as Thompson that McLeish would ask for this one. He'd not pass up a chance to lord it over his ex-colleagues. Oblivious as he'd always seemed to be to the rank and file's utter disdain for him, his thickness of skin and certainty of his own professional brilliance was something nobody believed he'd ever be disabused of; the man was just too self-deluded.

'You've told Malkie already, aye?'

'Aye. He took it about as well as you'd expect, but like I said, we may get lucky. He might be assigned elsewhere at the moment.'

'And DS Ballantyne? Have you told her?'

'Not yet, she's on night shift today. But you know she's changed her tune about him, don't you?'

Thompson's tone suggested she was reluctant to reveal information Steph might not yet be party to. But not very.

'Only vague rumours. Has she said anything?'

'Nothing very specific. Just a subtle change in her demeanour whenever McLeish's name comes up in conversation. And never in a complimentary way, surprisingly.'

'Should you be talking about a fellow DI like that, guv? I mean, regardless of what a venal and slimy wee shite he is. Professionalism and all that?'

Steph heard Thompson's sigh so clearly she knew she was meant to.

'He's chasing a DCI position already, last I heard. And considering he exhibits all the behaviours the shiny, new, corporatised Police Scotland seem to value over old-fashioned traits like empathy and teamwork and respect for colleagues, I fear he'll get one.'

'Fuck's sake. Sorry for using language, guv.'

'No need to apologise, Steph, but you've given me a perfect segue into the other reason I called you.'

'Segue?'

'Aye, segue. Malkie would say something incredibly witty like he doesn't speak Welsh, but don't change the subject. How are you? Considering?'

Steph had never heard her superior officer sound so uncomfortable. Like she'd rather have her fingernails pulled out than have this conversation. Steph decided there was nothing to be gained from making it as painless as she could for them both.

'I'm surprisingly OK actually, guv.'

'Bollocks. It's me you're talking to, Steph.'

Steph chuckled. 'Fair point, but I think I'll be fine. When I got home and calmed down, I stretched out on the sofa with a glass of Chardonnay and a Jim Croce album on and reminded myself that whatever evidence there is linking me to his death, most of it is circumstantial. So, if I have faith in my esteemed colleagues to get to the truth of the case, I should end up cleared, albeit with a dirty great black mark on my record for having even been suspected of killing the bastard. And although I think that will take me a while to get over, until it stops triggering shame and disgust in me that even I know is emotional and irrational, I *will* put it behind me, one day.'

'Steph, nobody, and I mean nobody, believes you could let yourself lose control so badly you'd do something like that. Comments I've overheard at the watercooler have – pretty much without exception – been of the "Seriously?" or "That's just stupid" or "Not Steph, no way" nature. Everyone who matters knows you don't deserve this, and we all agree whatever your HR record says on the subject is Grade A bollocks.'

Steph struggled with a triggered wave of self-recrimination she worried might never completely leave her.

'But I let it happen, boss. I put myself in those situations, against all good judgement. I went to his flat that night. I met him for coffee. I should have been better than that.'

She allowed tears to fill her eyes. She wanted Thompson to know how painfully aware she was of her own stupidity.

'Stop that, Steph. We're all fallible.'

Steph had never heard Thompson's voice carry so much concern. It almost broke her, threatened to overcome her usually solid hold on herself. She could find nothing to say without risking embarrassing herself.

Thompson defused the moment with the sensitivity only Steph and Malkie ever got to see. 'Even self-important pricks like the ever-perfect Gavin *Fuck-Me-I'm-Brilliant* McLeish.'

Steph laughed and snorted. She grabbed a tissue from the box on her coffee table to blow her nose.

'That's better. McLeish is an arse and you're twice the copper he'll ever be and even a dead Dean Lang will not bring you down. Is that clear?'

'Yes, guv.' She couldn't stop a wave of affection from sweeping through her. 'I appreciate the call. Thanks.'

'You're welcome. You are, after all, one of my most valued resources. But...'

'But what?'

'You never heard me say any of this, right?'

'Yes, boss.'

'OK. Try to come in tomorrow. I know desk duties are rotten but shutting yourself away is no solution to anything. Cheers, Steph.'

She hung up before Steph could reply.

It took Steph's mind all of twenty seconds to gravitate back to Lang, the man she'd called her stepfather her whole life. He'd claimed only recently that Lang's best mate, Barry Boswell, had raped her mother but refused to elaborate. Only now did it occur to her – if Boswell was her biological dad, why did her mum say her real dad died in a car crash shortly after she was born? To avoid just the kinds of questions that Steph – she was ashamed to admit now – should have asked many times over the years.

Finding out she was the result of rape had pushed Steph closer to a breakdown than ever before, and only Malkie's supreme effort at sensitivity and support had pulled her back.

She kicked out at the coffee table and yelped in pain as her bare toes slammed against the hard wood.

'Fucking bastard fucker.' She screamed with so much rage she scared even herself. Hadn't that been the failing in her that had laid her open to all the shite she was in now? She'd lost the plot when Boswell had appeared from Lang's bedroom, looking pathetic and pleading for a fair hearing from her. She'd attacked him in public, on a busy street outside a town centre coffee shop and in full view of a public only too eager to point their cameraphones at her as she barely stopped herself from hurting the bastard.

One of her defining traits, her non-negotiable control of her temper and her lifelong refusal to react to any insult or provocation regardless of how personal or offensive, had fallen by the wayside over the past few months, since she discovered what a filthy excuse for a human being she'd inherited half of her genes from.

She cried. A weakness which before today no one but Malkie had ever been allowed to see, and even then only once, in a sleazy pub patronised by people so similarly desperate and broken she felt no shame in allowing herself that brief surrender to despair.

She reached for her half-full gin glass and downed it in three long, slow gulps. She resisted, for now, an urge to drink what remained in the bottle.

It entered her mind how Malkie regularly bemoaned his famous loathing for all forms of booze. Not from any puritanical belief that would be all wrong coming from Malkie, but simply because he hated the taste of every alcoholic drink he'd ever tried. He held out hope, though, that he'd find some kind of drink which he could, if not enjoy, then at least stomach so he could – he imagined – find temporary solace in drunken abandon. She added an item to her mental to-do list: help him find some kind of alcohol he could actually enjoy. Maybe she'd enjoy getting well and truly rat-arsed with him on the too-frequent evenings when the job pushed them both too close to hanging up their warrant cards and switching to some other, less damaging career.

No. She wouldn't give in to despair. That wasn't her. She would not become that person.

She forced herself to her feet and took the bottle through to her kitchen – messier and dirtier than she'd ever allowed it to get before, she noticed – and poured the remaining gin down the sink.

In the bathroom, she recoiled from the mirror. How had she let herself go so much? Greasy and flaky skin, her hair unwashed for three days, her fingernails chipped and grimy. Had she even brushed her teeth that morning?

'Unacceptable, Lang.'

Who was it who famously said '*This, too, shall pass*'? Didn't matter. It applied.

But McLeish?

What kind of shit show could come from even a temporary return of that clown to Livi CID?

SEVEN

'Why are we talking this time? Why are we not messaging? Patricia? What's your latest in a long line of crises? If you tell me it's like when you thought that guy with the sunglasses spent an entire bus journey staring at you then turned out to be blind, I swear I'll—'

'Oh, good grief, Zoe. Give her a chance, will you?'

'Fuck's sake, Teri. You know as well as I do how bad this could be for us. Me more than all of you. And she must know that, too. Even she's not that naive.'

'I'm not naive. I'm just... I've got reason to be afraid.'

'Don't let Zoe rattle you, Patricia. You know what she can be like.'

'What the fuck's that supposed to mean? You mean how I'm the only one here that has the guts to speak up about fuckers like him? Like how I'm the only one of us who wants to do something to make him suffer as much as he deserves to but you lot are too scared of your own bloody shadows to do it? Is that what you mean, Teri? Is it?'

'Go easy on her. You're upsetting her.'

'Oh, sorry. Am I upsetting Little Miss fucking Snowflake? You and Amber are as pissed off as I am about this, Teri. Don't deny it. And where is Amber, anyway?'

'No idea. How would I know?'

'If she's smart, she'll be distancing herself. If he does die, what the fuck are we supposed to do? Turn the Snowflake here over to the cops? What if they find out what we were *planning* to do before she went and jumped the bloody gun? I mean, what were you thinking, Patricia? We had it all thought through. We've all invested time and effort, and we were close to going for it, and now you go and shoot your bolt and fuck it up for all of us, you stupid, stupid, wee Snow—'

'Stop shouting at me and don't call me that. I had my reasons. I couldn't wait. I hoped I could—'

'Christ's sake, she's crying now. We're fucked. All of us. If the cops connect her to him, she'll connect us too. I've got a hell of a lot more to lose than you two, but you were too damned scared to stick to the plan...'

'Zoe. Please. Stop. She knows she screwed up. She's sorry, aren't you, Patricia?'

'Fuck that. Not enough. You could drag us down with you, Patricia. Do you even realise that. Oh God, seriously? Tears again?'

'Zoe. Shut the hell up. Let her speak.'

'Fine. Talk to us, Patricia. Because I'm struggling here.'

'I went there to try to reason with him. That was all. I hoped even he had some scrap of decency I could get through to if I told him the damage he's been doing.'

'Unbelievable.'

'Zoe...'

'He... He pretended to care for me, to feel sorry for me. I even considered going along with it, see if I could maybe connect with him somehow, get him to see me, all of us, as human beings rather than... playthings.'

'And? Enough with the agonised pauses, Patricia. What happened?'

'He punched me. In my stomach. I think he would have hurt me worse if I hadn't grabbed the wine bottle. The rest of it is a blur. Next thing I remember is seeing him on the floor and blood and him not breathing. I ran. Oh God, he looked dead. I should have called an ambulance, but I was so scared.'

'Maybe you should have, Patricia, but you were terrified, right? No, Zoe, let her speak.'

'I was petrified. I was already afraid to go there in the first place. I didn't have a clue what I was going to say to him. I just knew I needed to make him stop, before...'

'OK, Patricia – no, it's fine, Teri. I'll calm down. I apologise. Before what, Patricia? Before we did what we all agreed to do to him? What you agreed to? Did you think you knew better than the rest of us? Was that it?'

'No. I was almost more afraid of what we were going to do than I was of him. I mean, how many more people might we hurt, Zoe?'

'OK. Point taken. But what about the others?'

'What others?'

'We can't be the only women he's been doing this to. Maybe even other men. He's happy to screw over both sexes, and he'll fuck anything warm too, from what I've heard. Who else might he hurt if we don't stop him?'

'I suppose so. I never thought about that. I'm sorry.'

'OK. I just... You know I nearly lost everything? Before? I can't help myself. I just get so furious I can't contain it. Teri gets that way too, don't you?'

'You know I do, but we're all here for each other. Right?'

'Aye. Sorry, Patricia. Why don't you tell us what happened again. Give us lots of details. Sounds to me like you have a strong case for self-defence, and he's not dead, which is a blessing. Fuck's sake. I never thought I'd be happy to hear a loathsome fucker like Sebastian Beauchamp isn't dead. I must be mellowing.'

'Go on, Patricia. You're in a safe space, just me and Zoe. And we love you. Don't we, Zoe?'

'Of course I do, you daft mares. Tell us again, Patricia. Let's get our heads round this so we can prepare for what's bound to come our way. The *polis* will want to be all over it given the bastard's career and his profile.'

'You mean they'll be told they need to be all over it?'

'Yes, Teri. That's exactly what I meant.'

EIGHT

Malkie lifted his eyes at the sound of the door to the custody suite opening. Steph walked through and he bolted to his feet.

She fixed him with a look and he sat again. She'd want no fuss, no questions or at least none voiced out loud in the office. He hoped she'd be open to quiet discreet concern on his part, but the past few weeks had him doubting how much even he could get away with asking.

She sat at the desk next to the one that Malkie continued to mark out as *his* with carefully curated clutter and mess and coffee-mug stains. He'd ignored repeated reminders from management that all desks were bookable by all officers in all areas of the open-plan station. *Hot-desking* they called it. *My bloody desk*, in his opinion.

He waited as Steph worked through the motions of arranging her jacket on the back of her chair, laying her police-issue notebook on the desk and aligning it with her keyboard, and logging on.

When she settled, he rolled his chair over. Two heads popped up, prairie-dog style. Gucci and DC Rab Lundy, the only other officer apart from Malkie still languishing at a junior detective rank long past the age at which they should both be *doing better*. They looked wary, and Malkie had a word with himself. *Now is not the time for one's foot to develop one's habitual affinity with one's mouth, old man.*

Steph sat with her head supported in one hand while the other steered a mouse pointer around her screen, aimless and – Malkie could tell because he did it himself too often – designed more to present an illusion of concentration than real productivity.

She must have sensed his scrutiny. 'Be careful, Malkie. Please.'

He felt sadness envelop him. That his colleague and closest pal needed to warn him to watch his mouth shamed him. He thought long and hard before risking opening his legendary careless gob.

'Welcome back, DC shithead.'

She smiled despite herself.

'Thanks, DS arsewipe.'

They whispered their affectionate greetings because such a level of familiarity was considered unsuitable for the junior rank of any DC. Although the seemingly effortless way Steph performed like a DS or higher left no one in any doubt that for her, it was a temporary state of affairs. Malkie didn't just believe he'd have to address her as *guv* one day but looked forward to it, even though calling her that would piss her off something rotten. He harboured no doubt she'd hang him from a custody-suite cell door by his gonads if he ever pushed his luck and called her *ma'am*, but he also knew he'd have to do it at least once.

And so, normal relations resumed.

'You OK?'

She mulled before answering. 'I will be.'

He squeezed her arm and returned to his own desk; anything more expressive here in the workplace would only embarrass them both.

He nodded at Gucci, who smiled back at him in relief.

Thompson appeared in the open doorway of her self-proclaimed office, noticed Steph, and approached her desk.

'Good to see you back at the coalface, Steph. Plenty for you to do, even stuck in here.' She bent forward a tad to check she'd got away with her possibly unwelcome recognition of Steph's current working restrictions, straightened up again. 'Maybe with your support on info and intel Gucci might exceed even her usual amazing performance.'

Rab held his hands out, an offended scowl on his face.

'You too, Rab. I know you like to help out between trips to the coffee machine.'

All present grinned except for a scandalised Rab.

Thompson turned to Malkie before Rab could think of a dazzling response. 'I know I'm being foolishly optimistic, but do we have anything noteworthy yet?'

Malkie pushed back from his desk.

'Gucci. Bank accounts? Phone records?'

'In progress, boss. I got the usual push-back and warnings about how long it would take, no doubt because of Beauchamp's public profile, but his bank accepted, eventually, that being charged with Obstructing The Course Of etc. etc. would look a lot worse in the news than any unfortunate associations with the man that might come to light. Usual game we have to play with the usual jobsworths. And I'm waiting for phone records. No good reason for the delay, just the way mobile phone companies can sign you up for twenty-four months of debt in a second but take an age to give anything back. Even to us *polis*.'

Malkie gave her a look of mock surprise. 'DC Gooch, I do believe your outlook on life is becoming a tad cynical. Please don't let any of that rub on me, thank you very much.'

She opened her mouth to respond but Malkie turned to Rab.

'Anything on social media that grabbed you, Rab?'

'Gross, but no. I tend to agree with your *early* assumption that his marriage to Francesca Beauchamp was less than lovey-dovey, seems it was more like a partnership. You know, rich and powerful man and his trophy wife, except that they had it the other way round. She's the real big deal. He's never let the fact that his position in the Scottish Shadow Cabinet is just a junior one get in the way of throwing his weight about, but he's the trophy husband, if anything. Handsome, allegedly, and on a promising public career path, but she's the real earner and the press never let him forget it. As for people with potential axes to grind with him, no shortage. For a man who was supposed to be only a junior minion—'

'A SPAD they call them, Rab. Special Adviser.' Malkie beamed at everyone, stupidly pleased with himself. Gucci rolled her eyes.

'As I was about to say, even though he was only an adviser to Peter King, Minister for Justice, he was very vocal, liked to pad his role every chance he got. He was hauled over the coals by his suitably indignant boss and vilified in the press a few months ago for publicly suggesting that right-wing nutters in England had some valid grievances that *might* be shared by our own home-grown right-wing nutters. I've asked the Parliament liaison office to comment on how bad that got, whether he received death threats or anything like that.'

Malkie stared at him. 'I think that's the most I've ever heard you say in one go, Rab. Well done, mate. But yes, he's obviously very much the dependant in their relationship. And don't think I missed your reference to my *early assumption*, by the way. We all know you meant *premature*, but my instincts, again, were bang on, weren't they?'

Rab shook his head as if deciding some battles were never worth fighting. He lowered his attention back to his desk.

Thompson failed to hide a smile. 'Post-mortem results tomorrow morning. Lin Fraser told me she didn't appreciate the Chief Super just happening to wander into the mortuary this afternoon and chewing the fat. She said it took him all of thirty seconds, after *hello* and *how are you*, to say *Oh, are you doing that Beauchamp chap?*

'He didn't actually ask her to expedite the PM, did he?'

'No. Lin made clear her views on how little she cared about the potential political fallout from such a high-profile murder. In her own, inimitable, fashion but in different words.'

Malkie grimaced. 'I wish I'd been there to see that. But if I had been, the Chief Super already has me on his radar.'

Thompson laughed as she stood. 'As usual, keep me informed,

aye? I have an appointment with the DCI. Probably wants to impress on me the urgency of this case. Of course, I fully intend to blame you lot for giving me nothing of note to report, but I'll get it in the neck anyway.'

'That's why you get paid the big bucks, boss.'

She turned back toward her office without dignifying Malkie's dig with a reaction.

Malkie scanned the case notes again. He hated this part of any investigation. Gucci and Rab had their minds deep in research and background, but until bank and phone records had come in and been analysed and the preliminary SOCO report had been received, he didn't have anything to get his teeth into.

Just as he decided he might as well browse some more social media garbage about their victim, Thompson appeared again.

'Heads up. MIT is here. In record time, too. Sebastian Beauchamp must have had some pretty influential friends.'

Rab grunted. 'More like his wife did, boss.'

Thompson shrugged, noncommittal.

Rab wasn't finished. 'Please tell me it's not him.'

She grinned at Malkie. 'Bernie warned me when she saw him approach the front door. Told me to get you out of the office, but I think I'll stay and watch.' She grinned, and Malkie wished they were alone so he could express himself with the candour he itched to.

The door to the reception area opened, and he walked through.

DI Gavin McLeish.

Puffed up and strutting and basking in what only he could perceive as a triumphant return to his old stamping ground. He'd been recently promoted to MIT despite a catalogue of rumours and incidents that would embarrass a more self-aware copper.

Malkie groaned. *A walking, talking, fucked-up example of how to get ahead these days.*

Gucci and Rab stared at each other, then at Malkie. Steph stood, grabbed her jacket and headed for the door to the custody suite and the station's rear entrance. Malkie heard her mutter, 'No.

Not tonight. Not that fucking arsehole.' She shared a look with Thompson as they passed each other. Thompson touched her arm and whispered something to her.

McLeish reached their desks. He beamed at everyone except Malkie, who he granted only a disappointed look. He nodded at Thompson, who returned a bare minimum nod to satisfy professional courtesy.

'Good evening, all. It's lovely to be back in Livi.'

Malkie resisted an urge to punch the smug fucker. Instead he held a hand out and fixed a chummy grin on his face that would fool no one.

'Welcome back, sir. Good to have an officer of your calibre and experience to assist us local plods with such a delicate case.' He widened his already ridiculous grin even further, leaned forward, and raised his eyebrows as if to encourage a response.

McLeish ignored Malkie's outstretched hand and his face turned red. He failed to mask the supreme effort it took him to bite down on whatever vitriol Malkie's gurning kisser had ignited in him.

Malkie glanced at his empty hand and pulled a sad face as if disappointed not to have his gushing welcome acknowledged, then headed for the rear entrance himself.

As he passed Thompson, she scowled at him, but he'd known her too long and couldn't miss the glee in her eyes.

'Well done, Malkie. Another deployment of your legendary diplomacy skills. You'll go far, mate.'

'Fuck him. And the horse his cowboy arse rode in on. Boss.'

NINE

Malkie met Pam Ballantyne at the back door. As he stepped out for some air, he stopped her from entering to start her shift.

'We need to talk, Pam.'

'Forensics said the end of this week, Malkie. Prints section are swamped so I can't chase them any more than I have already on that lighter the Fire Investigator found. Not for a cold case. Not even for your mum's death.'

She threw her head back, closed her eyes. 'Damn it, my bloody mouth. Sorry, Malkie.'

'No. It's not that, Pam. I'll admit Dad and I are dreading what you might find but at the same time we're hopeful, if that makes sense? And aye, we all know what the forensics workstack is like these days, so I've warned him not to expect any quick resolution. Callum Gourlay has retired from the Fire Investigation Unit, but he's been chasing me for news too. He feels terrible that he missed it, even though the fire gutted the whole house and destroyed pretty much every scrap of evidence with it. I'm just trying to be patient, if only to not distract me from my current caseload.'

'I'll push them as hard as I can for you, mate.'

Malkie swallowed an uncharacteristic pang of affection for his normally prickly and abrasive colleague. 'Thanks, Pam. I appreciate you saying that. But it's something else I need to tell you.'

Ballantyne studied Malkie's face. 'What's happened? Has someone been hurt on a shout?'

'Worse. You'll have had the alerts about Sebastian *Beecham*?'

'You mean Beauchamp?' Malkie saw a gleam in her eye. Humour from Pam Ballantyne suggested he really was rebuilding bridges, at last.

'Aye. Him. He's died. Blood loss, organ failure, etc.'

'And? I know he was thought to be headed for high office but he's only a junior SPAD at the moment. Why the ominous tone, Malkie?'

'MIT are here already.' He could get no more words out.

Ballantyne's face turned pale but her eyes blazed. 'Please tell me it's not him.'

Malkie shrugged. 'Sorry, Pam. He's in there now and being every bit the arse he always was.'

She walked away and leaned her back on the brickwork of the building. Malkie joined her.

'You OK?'

She closed her eyes and rested her head against the wall. Malkie half expected her to start braining herself on the hard stone.

'No. Of course not. Good God, what did I do in a previous life to deserve him, Malkie?'

'We all make mistakes, Pam.'

'Thanks, but hitching my career to him wasn't just a mistake; it was blindingly bloody stupid, and everyone knew it. But I was stubborn. How could I have thought I could weather his attitude and his catalogue of screw-ups and not end up ridiculed by association?'

'*Alleged* catalogue of screw-ups. And his last one was more of a spectacular fuck-up than a mere screw-up, wouldn't you say?'

She smiled, but it was weak. 'Fair point. He's obviously been better at covering his arse than he ever was at exercising good judgement in the first place, but he nearly got you killed when he collaborated with the Fieldings, didn't he? That squaddie they framed for a hit and run?'

'Walter Callahan. He would never have shot me.'

'I meant our lot.'

They smiled at each other; smiles laced with sadness and weariness of the damage the job did to them all. He pushed thoughts of that fiasco away but knew he'd relive it for the rest of his days.

'DI McArsehole is attached to my *Beecham* case, so as long as you ask Thompson to keep you well away from it, and you avoid him in the office, let's hope we can wrap that one up quick so he can sod off again to polish his DCI application.'

'Seriously? McLeish, a DCI? God help us all.' Her tone betrayed the depth of her disgust at that prospect.

'Sorry. But aye. He seems to think *Major Investigation Team* is a more fitting job title than being just one of us little people in ordinary CID. Arse.'

She pushed herself away from the wall. 'I'm going in.' She grinned. 'Haud ma' coat, pal.'

Malkie laughed. Out loud. 'Go get 'im, girl.'

He realised what he'd said and both his and her smiles disappeared. She stared at him for a second, steel in her eyes.

He felt his stomach lurch.

She grinned. 'You're too easy, Malkie. Is your middle name *Gullible*, aye?'

Malkie allowed Ballantyne to precede him through the door to the CID area. McLeish spotted her and beamed at her. Then he spotted Malkie behind her and his grin disappeared.

'Pamela. How lovely to see you.' He reached for her hand. She shook it but said nothing.

McLeish looked around him, a possible rare moment of self-awareness; no one had seemed particularly effusive in their greetings. Apart from Malkie, whose gushing sincerity would have fooled nobody.

He concentrated on Ballantyne again. 'How are you? I've been hearing good things about you on the grapevine.' Malkie didn't miss McLeish's pointed glance at him as he said that.

'So, are you working anything interesting at the moment? Are you attached to Beauchamp's murder? Management will want their best people on that one.'

A pointed silence dragged on for several seconds.

Thompson stepped forward between Malkie and Ballantyne. 'The two best DSs in J Division are assigned. DS McCulloch is leading on Beauchamp and DS Ballantyne is juggling most other jobs to allow DS McCulloch to concentrate on such a high-profile case. We look forward to MIT's assistance. Will you be joined by other MIT resources?' She peered beyond him to the empty half of the office.

'Only me for now. DCI William Donaldson will lead remotely via updates from me, but I'll be his man on the ground, as it were. And I look forward to working with your officers on what will, I agree, be a challenging and delicate case.'

No one could miss his glance at Malkie on the word *delicate*.

Malkie smiled. 'I appreciate that. Sir.'

McLeish glared at him for a second then turned back to Thompson.

'My office please, DI Thompson?'

'You can take meeting room 1 for the duration of your time with us.'

He turned, again, to Ballantyne. 'We can catch up later, OK?'

Ballantyne's eyes looked dead. 'Sir,' she managed, and Malkie noticed the fingers of her right hand twitch into a small fist.

McLeish and Thompson walked off, McLeish leading, Thompson casting them all a look of dread as she followed him.

After a brief shared glance with Pam, laced with mutual loathing for the man, Malkie wandered to his desk and Pam to hers. He noticed all eyes were on him, and sighed.

'What can I do, guys? MIT assigns them, we work with them. That pair we had on the Lillian Crosbie case were good. Him? We'll all just need to grin and take his shite. Rest assured, I'll find it as challenging as you will.'

Before they turned back to their desks, Malkie pointed a warning finger at them.

'But you never heard any of those unprofessional comments from me, right?'

'Yes, boss,' Gucci and Rab chimed in parallel again.

Malkie scanned his email inbox and cheered up. Forensics had messaged him to advise that the preliminary SOCO findings had been uploaded. He fired up HOLMES and opened the case file.

He was delighted to learn they had identified one of two different prints from the neck of the wine bottle used to kill Beauchamp.

'Heads up, team. We already have an ID on one of the prints on the wine bottle.'

Gucci and Rab shared an amazed look, then rolled their chairs across to peer over his shoulders as he read off the details.

'Remi Quinn. Nineteen years old. Lives in West Calder with his sister Patricia. He's had a few arrests for Breach Of The Peace and one for assault on us *polis*, aggravated by Autism Spectrum Disorder.'

Rab tutted. 'Level two. Means he needs significant support and may never be able to live independently. Poor sod.'

Malkie made a mental note to find out why Rab would know that. 'His sister is registered as his primary carer, and he's received only suspended sentences on condition he was released into her care.'

He turned in his chair. Rab and Gucci had to wheel themselves back.

'Damn it, troops, you can read the file on your own PCs like I can.'

They stared at him. Rab opened his mouth to complain but Malkie waved his comment away.

'Sorry. Lot on my mind. I apologise.'

Both nodded, gracious and sympathetic.

'Now arses back to your own desks and start on this Quinn guy. Including mental health history, obviously.'

'Yes, boss.' Again, in unison, as if they practised it.

Malkie updated the file to assign the standard actions he knew HOLMES would trigger at the early stages of any investigation. He reread the Forensics Preliminary Report and spotted a paragraph that stated further clarification was needed on the second print, and on the position and orientation of both prints on the bottle. Also the standard SOCO warning not to later quote them on only early findings.

Vulnerable person, mental health issues, single print alongside one other as yet unidentified. Fuck it, McLeish's call.

While he waited for McLeish to mark his territory and establish his seniority over Thompson – in his own self-delusion if not in actual rank – Malkie did some more reading on Sebastian *Beecham.*

Better start saying Beauchamp, old man. McLeish will be looking for every chance he can get to kick your arse.

He found numerous articles on news sites reporting his death and speculating on the cause without a shred of evidence. At least, he hoped no journos had slipped a skint Police Scotland employee twenty quid for a few words off the record that they could later attribute to *a reliable source.*

Beecham's – Beauchamp's – rapid journey up the ranks of the Scottish Shadow Cabinet had been a subject of great interest in political and current affairs channels. As if that wasn't enough for the man, his alleged good looks, his height and muscular frame, his charm and sense of humour, all made him a darling of chat shows and topical news quizzes. All were only too eager to put him front and centre of Scotland's TV, radio and internet culture for several years before his golden boy status became a perceived threat to his superiors. He'd had to start denying journo questions concerning rumours he had his eye on a full

Shadow Cabinet post and government ambitions further down the line.

Pundits were either fascinated by his enviable career or repelled by his occasional reluctance to condemn comments by right-wing nutters and other dog-whistle political candidates.

A chunk of the Scottish viewing public adored him, so many that Malkie despaired. He reckoned the indignant and vocal minority deserved what was coming to them and could only hope the more enlightened populace didn't suffer too much in the brave new world that seemed more inevitable every news cycle.

His internal rant ended at the grating sound of McLeish's voice. He marched into the area between Malkie's, Gucci's and Rab's desks and clapped his hands.

'Right, DS McCulloch. Dare I hope you have something decent to report?'

'Yep.'

'I beg your pardon?'

'I mean, yes we do, sir. ID on one of the prints found on the broken wine bottle neck that was used to stab the victim.'

'To *murder* him, DS McCulloch. That's why you have the benefit of MIT so quickly.'

Malkie bit back a yearning to thank McLeish on behalf of all CID minions everywhere for helping them crack cases that, before the creation of MITs in 2013, they'd obviously floundered on.

He limited himself to a simple and safe, 'Indeed, sir.'

'So, we're bringing this person in for questioning, yes?'

'Waiting for an Appropriate Adult, sir. The lad suffers from mental health conditions, level two autism and we need to ensure adequate professional support is in attendance before we can do any interviewing of the man. We're checking if anyone else, hopefully a family member, lives at the same address who can act in that capacity.'

McLeish looked peeved. 'So? Get on with it, McCulloch.'

A bad feeling began to sour Malkie's gut when McLeish leaned in to study the screen.

'Says he lives with his sister and she's his full-time carer.'

Don't you fucking dare, McLeish.

'He does, but—'

'Then you have your Appropriate Adult.'

'I'd prefer to arrange for a mental health professional to accompany us, sir. His record indicates extreme vulnerability often leading to violence. We should wait.'

McLeish's face reddened. He glanced at Rab and Gucci, then back at Malkie.

'I believe I've made my instructions more than clear, McCulloch.' He loomed over Malkie, who noticed the man's bulk had grown and not in a good way. 'He's a suspect in a murder investigation and strongly implicated by dependable forensic evidence. Bring him in now, or I'll have you replaced as SIO. Have I made myself clear?'

Malkie fully realised he was pushing his luck but couldn't help himself. He refused to stick his head into this particular noose.

'With respect. Sir. As soon as you record that order and log my reservations in HOLMES. Sir.'

He heard Gucci's sharp intake of breath.

McLeish exploded. 'We have a positive ID on a print on the wine bottle used to murder Sebastian Beauchamp. You will bring Remi Quinn in for questioning. Tonight. Just fucking well do it, McCulloch.'

Malkie tore his eyes from McLeish's furious face, saw Ballantyne turn her chair to flash him a barely perceptible shake of her head.

He looked back to McLeish. 'Sir.'

McLeish stomped off again as if he didn't trust himself not to damage his professional facade with a further outburst.

Rab and Gucci's faces told Malkie they felt as he did.

'Late night, boss?'

'Sorry, guys. Lou, with me and grab a couple of Uniforms please. Rab, can you hang on here a while longer and message me when McLeish has recorded this? I'm not bringing Quinn in without mental health support unless McLeish's name is on the order. He needs to log it before Lou and I get there, or we'll need to risk it anyway.'

Rab grimaced. 'It's curry night tonight.'

Malkie waited.

'But any chance to make life difficult for that prick is worth a bit of unpaid overtime. I'll take care of it, but I'm not reminding him again if he doesn't.'

'Fair enough. Thanks, Rab.'

Malkie turned back to his own desk and, with a pained sigh, dialled a number.

'Debs. I'm sorry. Not going to happen tonight.'

'Oh, Malkie. Again? We haven't seen each other for a week. I miss you.'

'I know, Debs. It's work.'

'When is it anything else?'

Malkie couldn't answer that.

'Sorry, Malkie. That wasn't fair of me. I knew what I was signing up for when I ignored my better judgement and gave you a chance.'

'Aye, and I love you too.' The words slipped out before he could stop them. The second time he'd said them to her, and neither time had felt like the momentous utterance that many people thought them to be.

'Can I have that in writing, Detective Sergeant McCulloch?'

'Maybe for your Xmas. If you're good.'

'That'll have to do, I suppose. Now listen to me, mate. You be careful, OK? I've heard all sorts of horrible statistics about how many of you *polis* get hurt doing your jobs, and I don't want you to become one of them, OK?'

'Yes, Debs. I promise.'

'And another thing...'

'What?' He knew what was coming and loved it.

Click.

She'd learned that from his dad, and would be chuckling to

herself. He wished he was there to hear it. But his thoughts turned to the other person he had to disappoint. He dialled her number.

'Jennifer? It's me. Malkie.' He had to take a second; had some small part of him wondered if the word *Dad* would ever creep into a conversation with her? She was in her mid-twenties now, and they'd learned only a few weeks ago that each other existed, so that might be a pipe dream.

'You can't make coffee tomorrow, right?'

He heard not a scrap of disappointment.

'Sorry, aye. Work. Obviously.'

'I have a meeting in the Fiscal's office about an at-risk witness, first thing. Maybe we can meet in the café?'

'Let's see. Cases like this one always tend to grow arms and legs in the first few days, so I can't promise. Sorry.'

'It's fine, Malkie. Call me when you can come up for air and we'll reschedule, aye?'

'Will do. Take care, Jennifer.'

'You too.'

And she was gone. Had he heard a momentary stumble on her part over his name? Did he hear the briefest of hesitations because he wanted to? Was she closer to calling him...?

He couldn't finish the thought.

He dialled again; to let his dad know he'd not be home for dinner, again.

Fuck's sake, all this for no overtime. What kind of a mug am I?

TEN

Steph reeled from the spyglass in her front door.

Barry Boswell.

Rapist, scumbag, and her biological father.

Nausea sluiced through her. She hadn't seen him since the night in Lang's flat, the loathsome creep she'd believed her whole life was her stepfather. Lang had lured her to his home to talk about Steph's recent discovery of her true parentage. He'd wound her up like a clockwork toy, got her good and riled, before signalling to Boswell to come out of the bedroom.

She'd nearly killed Boswell, and Lang later claimed to have recorded the whole episode on a hidden phone. He'd lured her to a coffee shop and provoked her into a rage so complete she'd attacked him in front of another member of the public, also armed with a mobile phone and only too eager to use it.

And now, since Lang had taken a dive from the balcony of his fourth-floor flat onto the roof of a 2011 Ford Fiesta, she'd been put on gardening leave.

And now, her rapist father stood outside her flat.

'What do you want?' she shouted through the door, didn't trust herself to face the man without a physical barrier between them.

She saw him, his face distorted by the spyglass lens, reel from the door as if even her voice promised violence. He gathered himself, held his hands up as if she might wonder if he'd come armed.

'I just want to talk.'

She breathed deep, refused to let this rotten example of humanity provoke her to a point where she might resort to *language*, as Malkie always called it. He'd already remarked on a change in her, and evidence of her weakness had pissed her off, so proud she'd been of her reputation for solidity and dependability.

'Piss off, Barry.' Even saying his name tasted rotten on her tongue.

'Please, Steph. I need to explain.'

'No. Don't make me hurt you again.' She scolded herself inside for resorting to another cheap threat; the kind of comment that an animal like him could use against her.

She peered through the peephole again. Boswell stood with his back to the opposite wall of the stairwell. He looked broken and desolate, but she felt nothing but disgust.

'I won't tell you a second time. Leave. Now.'

She saw him lean into the door until his face became a blur.

'I loved her, Steph. I never—'

She broke. 'Fuck off and don't come back, you rotten piece of shit. I have nothing but contempt for you. You're a lousy excuse for a human being.'

She paced the hallway as she bit down on an urge to open the door and close his mouth for good.

When she'd agreed to meet Lang in a coffee shop, he had – she now knew – intended all along to push her buttons, to provoke a reaction, see her disgrace herself as both a woman and a police officer.

And she had delivered the result he'd wanted. A display of base, animal fury that had been documented by a conveniently prurient passer-by and recorded in full 4K video. Lang had somehow obtained the footage from the man, and had claimed he'd kept a copy somewhere safe. Digital Forensics had found no trace of it on his phone or his knackered and grimy old tablet, only so much porn that it also indicated Lang's complete ignorance of browser security. That revelation had made no impression on Steph, so low was her opinion of the man already.

'Steph? Please?'

She racked her mind. She couldn't risk allowing Boswell to provoke another reaction; she was already under suspicion for Lang's murder. No, she reminded herself. Not a suspect yet. She was a person of interest and nothing more, but she couldn't afford a repeat of her assault on him. She couldn't risk meeting him anywhere public, and she feared what she would do to him in a secluded place. She had only one option, and it turned her stomach.

'Step back from the door.' She saw him do so, eager and hopeful and pathetic.

She fastened the security chain and opened the door four inches, but stood behind it, couldn't bear to face him directly. Boswell tried to peer around from the side as if desperate to display his sincerity but gave up with a heavy and no-doubt performative sigh.

'Thanks, Steph. I apprec—'

'You have five minutes. No more. Say your bit then get out of my life and stay out.'

'Thanks for hearing me out, Steph. I—'

'And stop saying my fucking name. You don't deserve to use my name.'

She put her eye back to the spyhole and saw him running his hands through his hair, his head down.

'I don't know where to start, Ste—. Except that...'

She watched him brace himself and steeled herself not to react in any other way than to tell him to fuck off. And die, preferably.

His eyes lifted to the spyhole.

'I loved your mum, Steph.'

'And yet you raped her.'

'I didn't. I loved her.'

She heaved a breath in, a massive intake of air triggered by a wave of sheer fury that made every inch of her want to rip this despicable man's head from his shoulders. She broke but managed to remain standing. Although she could have opened the door fully and been on him in a second, she fastened in her mind a line she refused to cross, a point beyond which she would not let Boswell's words send her.

She looked through the gap and he recoiled, hopefully afraid his time on this earth was about to end. The tears which now poured from him came over as nothing but self-pitying and perverse.

She squeezed her hands into tight and painful fists to stop herself unfastening the chain and hurting him, possibly beyond any chance of redemption for her.

He lurched toward the front door but turned back. She saw him fumble inside his jacket for something and place it on the floor. She risked a peek around the edge of the door. A bundle of envelopes. His fingers lingered on it before he stood again and fled.

She slammed the door closed and kicked it. She screamed her rage at it, beat it with the heels of both hands until they spasmed with pain. She leaned her back against the wall and slid down to sit on the floor. She sobbed, grabbed a scarf from a coat hook and stuffed it in her face to muffle the sounds of her grief and her fury.

'I'm so sorry, Mum.'

She sobbed, racked with guilt at having passed up a chance to repay all the suffering Boswell and Lang had put her mum through.

She'd let him go unharmed, the man who'd raped her mother and had then allowed Steph to believe Lang was her stepfather throughout her entire life.

This was according to Lang, but were either of them credible?

She felt a headache build, needed copious volumes of gin and to hell with the morning. She made herself stand.

Only now she remembered: what he'd left on the floor outside? Did she want to know? She unchained and opened the door and lifted the letters, tied together with ribbon. Old paper with handwriting in faded ink. She took it inside, untied the bow, and let it fall at her feet. The top one was addressed to her mother. They all were, except one, dated in the weeks before she was murdered.

With a sinking feeling of empty dread in her stomach, she fetched a new bottle of gin and a glass and dumped herself into her sofa to decide whether she was about to turn her life upside down for a second time in three months.

She opened the only letter from her mum to Boswell and dropped the rest on her coffee table, where they sat there in mute challenge, goaded her to read them and ruin her life.

ELEVEN

As Malkie watched the wall clock and waited for Lou to fetch a couple of Uniforms, a box landed on his desk with a thump.

He scowled first at it, then at the bloke in civvy clothing who had dumped it there. The young man grinned. Malkie had noticed him around the office before. With a hipster beard (he believed that style was called), a waistcoat, and drainpipe trousers that Malkie suspected he needed to be cut out of every evening, the lad exuded self-confidence and an eagerness to impress. No, more an assumption that he amazed everyone he interacted with professionally.

'From the Forensics, DS McCulloch.' His grin suggested he thought a thank you would be appropriate, but Malkie was in no mood to indulge him. He should have left for home an hour ago. He was tired and hungry. McLeish had disappeared *to check into his hotel* then failed to return, and while it suited Malkie and almost certainly everyone else, it stuck in his throat.

'Thank you.' He didn't look up at the lad, gave him no smile.

Good training in professional workplace dynamics for you, son.

The civvy wandered off.

'Rab, has McLeish done it yet?'

Rab clicked his mouse and peered at his screen. 'One guess.'

'Fuck's sake.'

Rab looked as disgusted as Malkie felt. He grabbed his jacket and his cigarettes and headed for the rear exit, muttering something about butter chicken.

Malkie cut the seal on the document box and removed the lid. Four ring binders lay inside, the thick kind, each packed with papers. He lifted the top one out and opened it. Bank statements. Hundreds of pages. The most recent listed transactions up to the end of February. He leafed through them, found the earliest was dated the middle of 2022. The second folder contained more, back to 2018.

The third folder contained phone records, again covering more years than Malkie could believe any person would ever need.

Gucci returned. 'Ten minutes. Two are coming in now.'

'Thanks, Lou. Would you say Sebastian Beauchamp's study had the look of an organised man?'

Gucci sat. 'I saw nothing to suggest otherwise, boss. Why?'

He grinned, and her face took on a wary look.

'Just wondered.' He lifted the fourth folder from the box and added it to the first three.

'Phone and bank records. Rab can start on them while we pick up Remi Quinn.'

'Where is Rab, anyway?'

'Went for a smoke. If we pitch in too when we get back, maybe we can all get out of here before midnight.'

Gucci's face darkened. As much as she'd understand that analysis of early intel was an essential stage in any investigation, she needed to direct her grievance somewhere, and right now, Malkie was it.

He shrugged an apology, then headed after Rab. He found him in the rear car park, sitting on a concrete bollard and smoking.

'I'll be five minutes, boss. Needed a ciggie and some fresh air.'

Malkie ignored the contradiction and Rab's complete ignorance of it, waved at him to indicate he should stay seated.

'It's fine, but we're all going to be here late tonight. I need to arrest Quinn and we've got Beauchamp's phone records and bank statements.'

Rab scowled at him. 'Already? Usually takes at least a day to get a warrant for bank stuff.'

'Aye, but Mr Beauchamp seems to have kept several years of phone bills and bank statements on paper. I've only ever known one other person to be that much of a hoarder. Remember that elderly woman who didn't trust computers? She had only the most basic mobile, made phone calls and not much else, and only terrestrial TV, nothing that came in from *those damned satellite things*?'

Rab smiled. 'She was a sweet old bird. Muriel. What became of her?'

Malkie's heart sank as he recalled. 'Ach, dammit. She got mugged in her home.'

Rab stared at him. 'Was she OK?'

'She survived the beating they gave her but died in her bed a year or so after getting out of hospital. Her family said they'd never seen her so frightened and bewildered as she was after that night. Fuck's sake.'

Rab threw his cigarette on the ground, half-smoked, in disgust. 'Fuckers. Did we get them?'

'Aye. But they got off with suspended sentences. Their solicitor argued they came from broken homes and had a diminished sense of right and wrong. Deprived childhoods, alcoholic mothers, absent fathers, victims of drug and gang culture, the usual.'

'What chance do the poor sods have these days?'

'Aye. Fair point, but those two scrotes went right out and did it again. And again. Four more times before they were put away.'

Rab stood. 'Why the hell do we bother?' He ground out his cigarette butt and nodded toward the door to the custody suite. 'Shall we?'

Malkie sighed, laid a hand on Rab's shoulder as he walked past. 'Just see if you can find something to stop his lordship from going off on one at morning briefing. Tell Gucci I'll wait out here. I want to check in on Steph.'

'Will do. Tell Steph... You know.' Rab looked sheepish. For a man who professed ambitions of being a writer, he often ran out of words at the most delicate of times. He disappeared into the building and Malkie walked to the far side of the compound as he dialled Steph's number.

'Yes. Who is this?' She sounded tired, her speech slurred.

'It's me, Steph.'

'Malkie. I'm not in the mood to talk, mate. Sorry.'

'Just tell me you're going to be OK. Tell me I don't need to worry.'

'I'll get through it, Malkie. You know me.'

Aye, that's why I'm worried, Steph.

'Are you on desk duties or on gardening leave?'

'No idea. I think Thompson offered me desk duties, but I can't sit there and watch you all heading off on shouts and me staying behind. I'll take some holiday time if I need to. She'll agree to it. She's always nagging me to use up all the leave days I carry forward every year.'

'Aye, she will. Has anyone been in touch with you in an official capacity?'

'Just my Federation rep, asking the same question.'

'Nobody from Professional Standards, then?'

'No. Not yet. They will.'

'Aye, of course they will. Have you heard anything from Boswell?'

He waited and knew before she answered.

'He came here today. No, I didn't hurt him. No, I don't intend to hurt him. Again.'

'I know you won't, Steph.'

'Do you? I wish I was as sure as you are.'

'You can't afford to allow yourself that luxury, partner.'

Another pause.

'I know. It's just hard. I'm so confused, Malkie.'

'Confused? About what? What have I missed?'

'He brought me something, Malkie. Then he left. Without a mark on him, before you ask.'

Malkie dreaded asking the obvious question, but Steph wouldn't have mentioned it if she didn't want him to.

'What did he leave you?'

It took her long seconds to continue. 'Letters to my mum, from him.'

Malkie waited. This could be one of those situations where Steph had told him he should just shut up and listen.

'He claimed he and my mum were in love with each other. That he never raped her.'

'Fuck's sake. Do you think even he believes that? What do the letters say?'

'I...'

He waited.

'I've only read one.'

Malkie wanted nothing more than a hot chocolate on the deck of the cabin then bed, if only for a few hours, but that evaporated now.

'Do you want me to come over later?'

Another pause.

'No. I don't think I'm up to it, right now. Maybe tomorrow. I'll call you, mate.'

'Do that, or I'll come round anyway.'

'Fair enough, but not tonight. I'm too pissed to do it now. You should try it sometime. Getting well and truly rat-arsed. It's very therapeutic, you know.'

'Ha ha. Comedian. You know I love you, right.'

'G'night, Malkie.'

He disconnected the call then turned to find Gucci and two Uniforms waiting for him.

He joined them and they headed for a patrol van and an unmarked pool car.

He heard Gucci sigh and knew it would be anything but performative; he really was ruining her evening.

'You missing anything important, Lou?'

'My niece's birthday party.' She looked like she wanted to elaborate but didn't.

I wonder if pissing people off isn't just a requirement of the job, but a particular talent of mine too.

TWELVE

They arrived outside Remi and Patricia Quinn's terraced home shortly after nine.

Malkie called Rab. 'Has he done it yet?'

'Nope. Still nothing. Sorry, boss.'

'Not your fault. Anything from Beauchamp's paperwork?'

'Nowt, yet.'

'Fuck's sake. Can you record it, make it clear you're logging it on behalf of the idiot and that you and I and Lou were present when he said it, OK? To protect all of us.'

'Aye. Will do.' Malkie couldn't miss the heavy disappointment in Rab's voice.

'Thanks for this, Rab. I'll make it up to you.'

'I doubt that. You've never tasted my wife's butter chicken.'

'Fair point. Sorry, anyway.' He hung up.

Lou's face told him she didn't need to ask. 'Are we going to risk it?'

'We'll have to.'

They exited the pool car and waited for the accompanying Uniforms to join them. Stevie and Paul, but he couldn't remember their surnames.

Every home on the street had a front garden barely big enough to park a car on, although one had managed to squeeze a massive, gleaming black Audi in at an angle, and set traffic cones – almost certainly nicked – to warn passersby away from getting anywhere near it. He felt for people who lived in two-bedroom terraced boxes and couldn't seem to afford the time or money to keep their front gardens from becoming dumping grounds for old furniture abandoned after the council started charging for bulky uplifts. Until he spotted TVs that looked bigger than his desk at work and reminded himself how one person's priorities could be another's most optimistic wish list.

Malkie faced the Uniforms. 'Who wants to come in and who wants to go round the back?'

Stevie turned to go. 'I'll go. I never enjoy these shouts.'

When Gucci and the remaining Uniform, Paul, nodded their readiness, Malkie rapped on the door. He'd spotted a doorbell, but he believed a hard knock always unnerved people and put them on a useful edge for questioning. Too late, he wondered if that might not be the best approach to arresting someone with known mental health issues.

The door opened, and a young woman appeared. She wore baggy pyjamas under an oversized T-shirt. Her face looked slept in, and a bunch of her short-bobbed black hair stuck up on one side.

Malkie and Gucci held their warrant cards up for her to see.

'Good evening. I'm Detective Sergeant Malcolm McCulloch and this is Detective Constable Louisa Gooch. We need to talk to Remi Quinn. May we come in for a moment, please?'

'Remi? I'm his sister, Patricia. Talk to me.'

The woman's eyes revealed fear, whether from some knowledge that her brother had just murdered a man in a brutal fashion, or from the normal terror most people experience when finding the *polis* on their doorstep and looking like they mean business.

Everyone has something to hide, whether it was untaxed extra cash for baby sitting or an internet browsing history they suddenly realise they haven't wiped in a while.

'OK, Ms Quinn. Patricia. We need to talk to Remi personally.'

He stepped forward but not far enough to cross the threshold. 'I'm afraid we'll have to insist.'

The woman looked like a cornered rabbit, all wide eyes and head darting everywhere but at her unwelcome visitors.

'Madam? Please?' He took another step forward but held a hand out to gesture she should move inside ahead of him. She dithered for another second, then appeared to realise she had no choice. Malkie guided her into the hallway so that Gucci and the Uniform could follow.'

Inside, Patricia cleared a pile of laundry from a two-seater sofa, then sat on an armchair. Malkie and Gucci sat, Gucci relaxed, her legs crossed at the ankles and her notebook and pen in her hands. Malkie sat forward, closed the distance between himself and Patricia.

'Is your brother in? It's him we need to see.'

She stared at him. No words came for long seconds.

'Ms Quinn?'

'He's asleep. Upstairs. It's really not good to wake him before the morning.'

'And that's because?'

'What's this about?'

'I'm afraid I need to discuss that with your brother, Remi.'

She took on the same trapped demeanour again. Her left hand picked at a bare patch on the arm of the chair.

'I can't wake him. You have to believe me. There's a good reason.'

Malkie studied her for a few seconds, gave her time to elaborate, but nothing more came.

He stood and faced Paul. 'Constable, please find Mr Quinn's room and ask him to join us.'

He turned back to Patricia. 'Unless you prefer to bring him down here yourself?'

Tears spilled from her. The fear in her eyes battered at Malkie's over-developed empathy for anyone obviously struggling emotionally. How could she not be conflicted beyond most people's ability to endure? Her behaviour suggested she knew what her brother had done, or at least that he'd done something terrible enough to bring police officers to her door.'Please. I can't. He mustn't see you. He'll—'

'He'll what? I want to be as supportive as I can, but I'm obliged' – *under seriously idiotic orders, actually* – 'to bring your brother in for questioning. If you can go with us as his Appropriate Adult, that would be the best possible plan. If not, we'll need to call someone in and have him taken to a hospital and held there.'

She flashed him a sharp and knowing look.

'Yes, Ms Quinn. We're aware of your brother's... Challenges. So, please, make this as painless and help us cause him as little distress as possible. But he will have to come in for interview. I cannot leave here without him.'

He recalled his mum defending him against a teacher, all beard dandruff and body odour, who regularly took teenage Malkie's surly and uncommunicative manner personally. She'd thrust all five-foot-three of herself in his face and her ferocity had been glorious to behold. A sister's love for her vulnerable brother must be no less passionate. His appreciation of Patricia Quinn's intense drive to protect Remi made him want to add an '*I'm sorry*', but he knew from painful experience that over-empathising with anyone met during performance of the job could backfire later, with disastrous consequences.

She agonised with herself a moment longer, but Malkie had already noticed her move her hands closer to the arms of the chair; she meant to stand and he had to hope for the right reason.

'Let me wake him. Please. I'm not sure if even I can get him to go with you without him hurting himself or—'

She bit back her next word, looked at them both as if she could beg them to rewind those few seconds of conversation.

'Or what, Ms Quinn? Hurt someone else? Does Remi have a history of violence? To himself or others?'

She stared at the ceiling as if hoping for divine assistance. 'I assume you've checked his record. He hurts people but he never means to. He doesn't know how strong he is. And when someone or something triggers him, he's terrified and he has no chance of catching himself. He's not a violent man, just frantic when he hits the brick wall of people who have no clue what it's like to be him. We tried CBT and it helped a little, but it still happens without anywhere near enough warning for himself or me to talk him down.'

She stopped, heaved in a huge breath, as if nearing exhaustion. 'But it's not his fault, Detective.'

'Please. Go and get him. Would it help if I ask my uniformed colleague to wait outside?'

She considered this. 'Yes. It might still upset him, seeing two strangers in his home at this late hour, but a police uniform will likely trigger him, and I doubt I can control him if that happens now.'

She chewed her lower lip. Malkie noticed her hands shaking. Could her brother's behaviour really have her that afraid? Could the man turn so violent that even his own sister feared an episode of his loss of control? No. Not violent. He needed to understand this, get his head around it. As much as anyone not in the lad's head could.

Patricia passed Malkie to stand with one hand on the door to the hallway, and glanced back. 'Please remember. Nothing he does is his fault. Nothing.'

Malkie nodded his understanding. She glanced at the Uniform, still standing behind her.

Malkie spoke over her shoulder. 'Wait in the car, please. If he kicks off then come back in and help us, but otherwise stay out of sight until I say.'

'Are you sure, Malkie?' He looked torn between procedure and trusting an officer who – Malkie hoped – he respected.

'I know it's off protocol, but if the lad doesn't see your uniform, he might be able to at least get into our car without us triggering him.

'OK.'

Malkie nodded, satisfied, then turned back to Patricia.

'I'm already bending the rules here. Please go and bring him down, Patricia. I can't wait much longer before I need to ask the Uniforms to compel him.'

'OK. I'll explain to him who you are and where you'll be, and then I need to know you'll be where I tell him you'll be. Can you wait in the living room? Not on the stair or in the hallway. Please. It's the only way this might work.' Gucci flashed a look at him and he raised a hand to let her know he felt the same. He was pushing his luck. For good reasons, but risky.

Malkie listened to what he could hear from upstairs. Only Patricia Quinn talking in subdued murmurs and sounding tense and insistent. It felt wrong, but she seemed genuine and if her brother was affected half as much by his autism as his record suggested, Malkie was aware how rigid and controlled his life needed to be, and how distressing any break in his routine could be.

They waited and eventually Malkie thought he heard movement on the stairs, but the sounds stopped again.

As he started to worry – and he could see Gucci had passed that point already – they heard a scream that chilled Malkie and had him fearing another in a long line of well-intentioned but reckless fuck-ups. They rushed into the hallway, found it empty. It came again, a howl of pure distress followed by Patricia Quinn's voice.

'Remi. No. Please listen to me.'

They found her in the back yard with a young man thrashing about like a man possessed. The lad was trapped under Constable Stevie. Half the officer's size but animated by a frenzy that shocked Malkie to his core, and Stevie struggled to keep a hold on him. He managed to get a hand on one of Remi's arms and pulled it away to make room to get to one knee and push his greater weight down and grab the other arm. Remi wailed, a sound that Malkie hoped he'd never hear another human being make. It wasn't rage or violence – a word he'd already promised himself to never again apply to someone like Remi – but utter terror. Tears poured from his eyes, and he sobbed as if all of his worst nightmares now tore at him.

PC Paul appeared at the back gate, and together the two men pulled Remi to his feet and held him while Patricia approached him.

'Remi. Remi. It's me, Remi. Listen to my voice, Remi. Ignore these men, Remi. Listen to my voice, Remi.'

He seemed to hear her and his struggling lessened but only by a small degree. He pulled against the grip of his captors and kicked backwards, but with less energy, less rage.

'Remi. Look at me, Remi. Listen to my voice, Remi. Come back to me, Remi. Hear your name. Be my Remi, darling.'

Malkie noticed how she repeated his name, a way of gaining his attention to talk him down. Patricia Quinn struck him as no amateur at caring for her troubled brother, and a spark of admiration humbled him.

When Remi had settled, Patricia turned to Malkie but kept her hands on his arms.

'The Uniforms. Send them away. Just you two and us, and in your car. No police van. I'm not demanding anything. I'm explaining to you the only way you're going to take him anywhere without him harming himself or something even more awful happening. Do you understand?'

Malkie nodded, amazed at how Patricia's earlier distress had evaporated, replaced by some kind of incredibly focused autopilot.

He took one of Remi's arms. The lad pulled back, but calmed when Malkie gave him a smile born of a compassion he felt so genuinely it surprised him. Remi relaxed, still tense, but somehow curious now, too.

Patricia Quinn stared at them both. She looked stunned.

Malkie nodded to Stevie, who held one hand to a gash on his forehead and seemed unwilling to step away from Remi. Malkie tilted his head toward the gate at the rear of the back yard, and Stevie released his grip. He held his hand close to the boy's arm for a second as if to satisfy himself his superior officer was in no immediate danger, then stepped away.

'You two. Get back in the van and park round the corner. Follow us to the station, OK? And you, get the nurse to see to that head wound.'

The Uniforms nodded, stepped backward through the gate, and crept away.

'Lou, walk beside Mr Quinn, please.'

Gucci took up position and put her notebook away to keep both hands free.

Patricia looked from Gucci to Malkie. 'Thank you. It's not over, but... How did you do that? How did you touch his arm without triggering him. I've never—'

'I don't know, Ms Quinn. I just know I saw a very scared young boy. But I'm still a police officer so I do have to take you both in for interview.'

He resisted a temptation to add, *'For the record, I advised against this.'*

She recoiled from Malkie, then glanced at her brother and forced herself to relax. 'Why me?'

'You tried to help your brother evade a police officer conducting his official duty. That's a criminal act. Lou, please read Ms Quinn her rights.'

Patricia glanced from Malkie to Gucci and back, looked cornered all over again.

As Gucci recited the words of the formal caution, Malkie heard an engine start, then a vehicle travel a short distance and idle. The patrol van should now be safely out of sight of the front of the house.

Malkie allowed Patricia to hold her brother's other arm but didn't release his gentle contact, and they walked back through the house, stopping to allow her to lock up.

Outside, neighbours stood on pavements, watching. None felt any need to peek discreetly from behind twitching curtains; all stood outside for the best possible view, mobile phones held high.

Some laughed and pointed. They heard someone shout 'About time that fuckin' freak was banged up' and Malkie saw Patricia stiffen. Remi didn't react. He looked from his sister to Malkie like a child being led somewhere and not caring where.

Gucci walked to the man who'd shouted, stuck her full five foot seven in the six-foot-tall mouth-breather's face and had a word with him. Malkie couldn't hear what Gucci said, but the ape, who first fronted up to her, seemed to shrink in on himself, and nodded like getting home to his bed tonight had just become far from certain. As Gucci walked back to the car, the man's mates laughed at him, and he barged through them and into a garden.

Steph's special secret training is strong in this one, Malkie smiled to himself.

As Malkie guided Remi into the back seat of the pool car, the patrol van appeared from around a corner.

Too soon, damn it.

He tightened his grip, but Remi saw it, snatched his arm from Malkie's hand and bolted. Malkie got a hand on him, but Remi lashed out backwards and caught Malkie's nose with a solid blow. He felt blood pour but ran after the lad.

He had no chance. The boy was young and – he now knew – fit and fast. Both constables jumped from the van and gave chase. Gucci checked Malkie seemed OK, then sprinted after them.

Patricia Quinn screamed at him. 'You stupid, stupid, man. Oh God, they won't catch him and he'll not last a day on his own. What have you done?' Her words turned to sobs, and she paced the pavement, frantic and furious.

Malkie tried to say he was confident his colleagues would bring him back safely, but blood poured from his nose and into his mouth, and he had to spit several times before he pinched his nostrils and could speak.

'We'll get him, Ms Quinn. He'll be OK.'

She turned a look on him that would have made Steph proud, and despite his best effort, he recoiled in alarm.

'You have no idea what he's capable of when he's cornered, Mr

McCulloch, the damage he might do to himself or others. Oh, you bloody idiot.' She sobbed again.

Malkie recalled the amount of blood he'd seen on Beauchamp's study floor, and Bruce the SOCO's preliminary assessment of Beauchamp's injuries.

Oh, I think I do, Ms Quinn, and I wish I didn't.

THIRTEEN

Minutes later, Gucci and the Uniforms returned without Remi, and with expressions on their faces that spoke volumes about how pissed off they were.

PC Paul glared at Malkie, who harboured no doubt that the man would make very clear his initial objection to being told to wait in the van. Shit would fly over this, and Paul intended to let none of it fall on him.

Stevie looked just as pissed off. 'I'm not taking the kicking for not securing him. Guy went bloody psycho on me.' He touched his forehead again then checked his fingertips for blood. His meaning was not lost on Malkie.

Malkie resisted an urge to tear a strip off Stevie. He'd known a boy just like Remi once, and he'd behaved no better. He'd known Jimmy McGuire in primary school, or rather he'd known of him, because Malkie, like all the other kids, had made his life hell. They'd called him the same thing, a psycho, because he sat staring out the window all day and had a way of working through his lessons that nobody else understood. He would become uncontrollable and – school reports always said – violent when they tried to give him the strap for – again, as his teachers claimed – his constant inattention. Malkie had never found out if Jimmy was autistic, or had ADHD or dyslexia or a cocktail of several neurodivergences, as sensitivity training had helped him to understand. He hated to think he was once a Stevie, and so couldn't completely blame the man.

'He's not a psycho, mate. Poor sod is just a seriously confused and frightened lad and not psychologically equipped to cope with us Plods turning up at his door. We should have waited for a bloody mental health professional.'

And I'll make damned sure management know just why I was forced to bring him in without one.

Gucci gave Malkie a pointed look but limited her comments to the information that Remi had been incredibly fast on his feet and had lost them in a wooded fringe around a nearby public park.

Patricia Quinn appeared from inside her house with a box of tissues and almost threw them at Malkie. He mumbled an embarrassed *Thanks* and set to stuffing his nostrils.

His professional authority degraded as it was, he caught Gucci's eye and nodded towards Patricia. Gucci approached the woman after a dirty look at Malkie.

'Ms Quinn. My colleagues will call in support and start a search for Remi. Let's go inside and talk, please.'

She stared away down the now empty road; the earlier eager audience had decided the show was over and, after pointing and laughing and a few choice comments about *useless Pigs* from anonymous clumps of idiots, had headed back inside. Windows would be left open enough that they wouldn't miss any resumption of the night's entertainment.

Inside, Patricia and Gucci took up their previous seats. Malkie asked for directions to the bathroom. Patricia reached into a pocket on the side of her armchair and produced a packet of wet wipes. She threw it toward him with a glare that Malkie couldn't deny he deserved.

Gucci stepped in. 'Ms Quinn, that was unfortunate...'

Patricia stared at her, incredulous.

'...but our colleagues will find Remi and look after him. They're good at what they do. They'll find him. For now, we need to know if there's anyone or any place you can think he might go? Somewhere he'll feel safe?'

Patricia shot one more poisonous glare at Malkie as he looked for somewhere to put the first blood-stained wet wipe clutched in his hand.

'Not anywhere near here. He never makes friends and we have no immediate living family. He rarely leaves the house.' She took a deep breath. 'Remi has needed full-time care since he was born, and he may never be able to live an independent life. I'm all he has. Our parents both died years ago. He has nowhere else to go and no one he can rely on. He's out there in a world he doesn't know and doesn't trust, and he'll be terrified. I'd like to get this over with quickly so I can go looking for him. If he's hiding somewhere nearby, he might come out if he hears my voice. After you and those uniformed officers have left.'

Malkie checked his third tissue and decided the worst of the bleeding had stopped. He looked around, clutching three bloody wet wipes, then stuffed them in his jacket pocket.

'As my colleague, Detective Constable Gooch says, Ms Quinn, we'll start a search for Remi immediately.' He glanced at Gucci, who pulled her mobile from her pocket and headed for the hallway, ready to leave. 'We'll get him back.'

A suspicious gleam appeared in Patricia's eyes. 'You didn't say why you want to interview him. Are you not supposed to give us an explanation before you arrest someone, if that's what you were doing? Were you arresting him?'

Malkie considered how much to tell the woman. On one hand it was Remi's prints they'd found on the bottle neck, not his sister's. But on the other hand, she was his Appropriate Adult, and he'd guess she had full guardianship over the lad.

'We need to talk to him in connection with an attack on a man late last night. We have reason to believe Remi either knew the man or had come into contact with him at some point, and we need to give Remi the opportunity to explain the evidence that suggests this connection.'

'What evidence?' Patricia's face had blanched and her eyes widened. Had she been less than honest about her brother's lack of friends or acquaintances? Did she already know who the victim was? After all, it had been rehashed in albeit minimal and desperate detail all day by the rolling TV and radio news stations.

'I can't say at the moment, Ms Quinn. Not until I can put my questions directly to Remi. I hope you understand.'

She seemed lost. Her eyes looked to be focused somewhere over Malkie's shoulder, and she fidgeted with one corner of her woollen cardigan.

'Ms Quinn?'

She came back to herself, seemed to have forgotten he was in front of her. She snatched a breath as if surprised to see him sitting on her sofa. She glanced around the room, her eyes desperate, verging on wild.

Malkie stood. 'Ms Quinn? Are you alright? Should I call someone for you?'

What are you afraid of? More than just your brother, I think.

'Has Remi said anything to you today about any unusual event? Did he go out, last night or this morning? Ms Quinn?'

She looked to have drifted off again. Tears welled and spilled. Her bottom lip quivered.

She stood, straightened her cardigan and tucked her short hair behind her ears. She drew herself up, and Malkie braced himself for something significant.

'Detective McCulloch. I killed Sebastian Beauchamp. In his study at his house near Blackness. Late last night.'

She swallowed.

'With a wine bottle.'

FOURTEEN

Why did those policemen come to the house?

They wanted to take me away. Like before. Me and Patty, this time.

Did I do wrong again? Is she in trouble because of me again? What I did? To that man?

It wasn't my fault. He scared me. He shouted at me and he hurt me. I hate people shouting at me. Mum shouted at me all the time. She hurt me, too.

He hurt Patty, too.

He was bad to the core.

Mum always said I was bad to the core.

Patty always got angry when Mum said that. They would fight and shout at each other and the noises hurt me.

I never know when I'm being bad. It's not my fault. It's never my fault. I know people say that a lot when they don't mean it, but I never lie.

The man scared me. He hurt me. And Patty.

Did I do wrong?

Why did those men come to the house? Why did Patty let them try to put me in that car? I don't like cars and nobody warned me I'd have to go in a car. I only go in Patty's car. I know Patty's car. I like it. I know it. It never surprises me.

Patty says I don't always know what's good and what's bad. I try, but I forget.

When I'm scared. Or when people shout at me. Or touch me.

Patty says she understands but I don't think she does.

I don't think anyone does.

That's why they hate me.

They're all so mean to me.

Those boys. Some girls, too.

The people at the clinic don't scare me. They're really good at not scaring me. I like the people at the clinic.

Mum didn't like the people at the clinic. Bad to the core, she told them. They didn't like mum.

It made Patty angry.

I wish Dad had stayed. I don't think he ever said I was bad to the core.

I want to go home. There's nobody here but it scares me.

Like that man. He scared me. He hurt me.

I just wanted him to stop hurting me.

And Patty.

He scared Patty. And he hurt her worse than me, I think.

I'm going to the bridge. Patty will find me there. I think I remember what bus to get, and I have lots of pocket money left. I knew I'd need it one day, so I kept it safe and never spent it.

I'll wait there. She'll find me.

I hope they remember me. I never saw them, but Dad said they help people who get lost.

I hope they'll like me.

FIFTEEN

Patricia Quinn sat on one side of the scratched and grubby table in the interview room. He'd left PC Jenna Hitchin inside with her. Malkie watched the video feed from the tiny cupboard beside the custody suite that housed a desk and chair, and a monitor attached to a single PC. Any detective with the right access level and a valid reason to do so could stream any interview, live or recorded, from any PC, but this glorified closet was the official observation facility. No one-way mirrors here, just an uncomfortable plastic chair and a table even nastier than the one in the interview room.

Patricia sat as if already convicted. Resigned. She did look every inch a guilty party despite the prints ID'd on the bottle being her brother's. If the other ID came back as hers – which could be tested now she'd been printed after being arrested following her confession – then Malkie couldn't decide if that would help or complicate his hunt for Sebastian Beauchamp's killer.

Did she know Remi had killed him and only wanted to cover for him? If so, then as he'd seen happen twice before, her story would collapse in the absence of any genuine, first-hand recollection of the scene or the crime.

Or did she kill Beauchamp and now figured that the *polis* wouldn't have turned up at her door to take Remi away without some kind of evidence, some link to the man she claimed she had murdered?

Nothing's ever easy, is it?

Gucci appeared in the doorway. 'The duty solicitor has arrived and been signed in and briefed. She looks tired and I know how she feels. Ms Quinn's prints are off to the lab, and I've asked them to expedite given we have a confession from a suspect in custody.'

Malkie stood. 'Let her brief in then, Lou. Hopefully she'll want to get back to her bed and won't drag this out.'

Gucci did so. Malkie watched Patricia on the screen; she sat rigid, bolt upright in her chair. When the brief entered and introduced herself, Patricia didn't relax as Malkie expected; she spoke to the woman then folded her arms as if to cut off further discussion. The brief tried again, but Patricia held a hand up and refused to say any more.

Malkie sighed. 'She's not going to budge from her story, is she?'

'Nope. You'd think she *wants* to go down for it.'

'That's exactly what I'm wondering, Lou.'

Malkie and Gucci entered the room and took their seats. Malkie introduced himself and Gucci to the brief, who advised her name was Miriam Lawson and stated her intention to represent Patricia. Gucci started the recorder and recited the tedious admin part of any police interview under caution. They heard the long, solid tone and Gucci nodded at him to begin.

'Ms Quinn, did you get your phone call?'

She nodded, but her expression suggested she'd not taken much comfort or hope from it.

'For the benefit of the recording, Ms Quinn has confirmed. And you've read and understood the Letter Of Rights you were given?'

She nodded.

'For the tape, please?'

'I have.'

'OK. Thank you. Ms Quinn, you've been formally cautioned

because you've claimed you murdered Sebastian Beauchamp. Do you still maintain that?'

'Don't answer that, Ms Quinn.' Miriam Lawson turned to Malkie. 'Was this *alleged confession* made under caution? Had Ms Quinn been read her rights before she made the *alleged confession*?'

Here we go. Bed is a long way off.

'She hadn't. We attended Ms Quinn's address to interview her brother, Remi. He fled the home and it was while I was trying to support Ms Quinn and gain any information which might assist our officers in locating Remi that Ms Quinn, of her own volition and without any prompting from me, confessed to murdering Sebastian Beauchamp. She correctly stated the site of Mr Beauchamp's death, a credible approximation of the time of the attack, and described an item we believe was used as the murder weapon. All of this constituted ample reason to arrest Ms Quinn. She has now been cautioned and is free to repeat her confession on the record, now if she so wishes.'

Lawson scribbled in a notebook, before looking at Patricia. 'I advise you to say nothing more until you and I have—'

'I don't want a solicitor.'

Aw, hell. One of them.

Lawson appeared nonplussed. She sighed. 'I advise against that Ms—'

'Please make her leave. I don't want a solicitor.'

Lawson flashed Malkie and Gucci a knowing and long-suffering look, then produced a form from her briefcase. 'You'll need to sign this to confirm that I've advised you that refusing legal aid is not in your best interests and could lead to you unintentionally incriminating yourself. Then I'll need to get it countersigned by a DI.'

Quinn did so without reading it. Malkie handed it to Gucci, who took it for sign off. She returned more quickly than Malkie expected. He recognised Susan Thompson's signature and assumed she'd come in to support her team with such a sensitive case. He showed it to Lawson, who stood, flashed them her best professional *All Yours* smile, then left.

Malkie took a second. Contrary to reason, a suspect refusing legal representation worried Malkie. In some, it indicated complacency and a belief in their own ability to run rings round your average plod. In others, it could mean deep distrust of a free duty solicitor and a contempt for all aspects of the State Justice System machine.

He feared Patricia fell into another category. He suspected she wanted Sebastian Beauchamp's murder blamed on her solely to stop her brother going down for it. This, again, suggested she might believe Remi could at least feasibly be guilty and she was taking no chances. For her to want to admit culpability and risk a long custodial sentence meant she was prepared to see Remi go into care, based on her comments about her and her brother having no living relatives. Was she aiming for the lesser of two horrific outcomes for the lad? Did she hope he might learn to survive the care system without her while she was in prison?

'Sir?' Gucci's voice.

'Sorry. For the benefit of the recording, Ms Quinn has signed the necessary paperwork confirming she refuses the assistance of the assigned duty solicitor. Ms Quinn, why did you do that?'

'Because I killed him, and I don't want you trying to set my brother up for it. You'll look into his past and find out he's susceptible to uncontrollable outbursts and that'll make him a perfect suspect, won't it?'

Malkie refused to react. The suggestion that he would try to hang any murder on a convenient but innocent man offended him, but he reminded himself this was a woman in about as much distress as he could imagine. And yet she hadn't once resorted to a lazy word like *violent* to describe her brother's episodes.

'Have you found my brother yet?'

'Officers are patrolling the area around your home now, Ms Quinn. We also need to find him because, even before your confession, I'm afraid your brother was already a person of interest in this case.'

'What does that mean? A person of interest?'

'It means we're interested in speaking to him, and I am not being obtuse, Ms Quinn. If Remi might be in serious trouble on his own, then we need to find him as soon as possible.'

'Why do you need him? I confessed. I know who was murdered, where, how, and when. Remi was in bed at home. I told you already; he virtually never leaves the house and once he's gone to his room for the night he never comes downstairs again until exactly eight the next morning. He's severely affected by his autism to the extent that any departure from his routine never goes well. It was me. Charge me then find my brother. It's your fault' – she stared daggers at Malkie – 'he's out there scared and alone. Anything could happen to him. He's like a child, for God's sake, and you've made him run away from the only safe place he's ever known.'

She collapsed forward onto the table and sobbed, massive, distraught wails filled with fury and grief.

Malkie couldn't look at Gucci. He'd answer tomorrow for the fallout caused by his deviation from procedure. If Remi turned up injured or worse, his career could be over, but he'd do all he could to bring the lad in safely.

'Ms Quinn. Can you tell us again what happened last night. And in as much detail as you can, please? I need to get a full and thorough statement from you to fully assess your claim that you killed Mr Beauchamp.'

Her head snapped up, and she looked from Malkie to Gucci and back again.

And this is where you realise you haven't nailed your story yet. And that's how you trip yourself up, Ms Quinn.

She sat up, straightened her back and settled herself.

'Some time after ten o'clock last night, I drove to Mr Beauchamp's home on the shore road at Blackness. I buzzed the doorbell at the gate and he admitted me.'

'Why were you visiting him? What's your relationship with him?'

She paused and Malkie could almost see her put together whatever she could dredge up that might sound plausible.

'I met him when he came to do a publicity thing at the café I work at. It's one of those places where people can donate cash to pay for a meal for a homeless person. I was on the counter. He spoke to me and he was lovely. We talked, and he stayed on longer than he'd been scheduled to. We started seeing each other. He asked me to keep it quiet because his wife's a big deal apparently. Jealous, too. So, once or twice each month, I went to his house. I couldn't go often because he said she was home most evenings. So, I went there any evening he said she would be out.'

Either you're lying now or he was then. His wife is out of the country more than she's home and she's anything but jealous.

For a moment, Malkie almost feared she could read the doubts on his face. She stopped talking and stared at him. When she continued, she'd become curt and evasive.

'When I went to see him last night, I said I needed to stop going out there. I can't afford the petrol, and Remi has started to ask me questions about why he didn't hear me going to bed.'

She took a breath. 'He was furious. Said I had no right to cancel him. I thought it was odd the way he said it. Not cancel *on* him but cancel him.'

It's called the cancel culture, and I would think he's more used to cancelling other people than having it done to him.

She stared at her lap, and Malkie couldn't help but think the gesture forced.

'He attacked me, pushed me up against a wall, said nobody cancelled Sebastian Beauchamp. I was terrified. He was so strong, and so angry. I know he was going to rape me. I grabbed a wine bottle and smashed it over his head.'

His head? What about his... Fuck's sake. Here we go.

'And then, Ms Quinn?'

She looked confused. 'What do you mean, and then? I ran. I

was terrified. He wasn't moving and there was so much blood. So, I ran.'

She looked at both Malkie and Gucci as if wondering what the hell she could possibly add. Malkie resisted an urge to share a look of dread with Gucci; this had just turned complicated and Malkie hated complicated.

'You ran? You hit him over the head with a wine bottle and then you ran. That's all that happened after he attacked you?'

'Yes. He attacked me. Punched me in my stomach. I panicked. I was terrified.'

'Yes, you said that, Ms Quinn, and you believed the injury you did to his head killed him?'

'Yes.' Her voice rose now, some combination of anger and confusion feeding on each other.

Malkie stared at her for several seconds. He knew Gucci would be thinking the same as he was. He checked the time on the wall clock. 'Interview suspended at 23:17. Detective Sergeant Malcolm McCulloch and Detective Constable Louisa Gooch leaving the room. PC Jenna Hitchin will remain with Ms Quinn.'

Gucci pressed the button and another long tone marked a pause in the recording.

Outside, they returned to the viewing room to study her. They found Thompson sitting there already.

'Guv.'

'Malkie. Lou. I saw you'd pulled her in for questioning and wanted to observe.'

They watched Patricia ask the PC for a glass of water, and Hitchin knocked on the door. A second Uniform answered, then headed in the direction of the kitchen area.

Malkie leaned back in the chair and spoke without taking his eyes from the monitor. 'Not much to say, really.'

Thompson sat in the chair beside him and rubbed her eyes. 'Is she telling the truth?'

Both Gucci and Thompson looked to Malkie.

'Mostly, I think. Not sure about her explanation of why she

went there, but I can believe she didn't murder Beauchamp. Someone else did, after she fled the scene. And the number one suspect has to be her brother, Remi. If she had also inflicted the fatal injuries or at least knew about them, she'd admit it, given her obvious desire to take the rap for it.'

Gucci sighed. 'I'm not getting to bed tonight, am I, bosses?'

Thompson stopped Malkie from answering.

'Sod that. Get off home for some kip, Gucci. You too, Malkie. Put her back in her cell to stew. Have another go at her after morning briefing, in...' She checked her watch and scowled. 'Eight hours.'

Thompson left.

'Get yourself home, Lou. In the morning, we'll discuss whether to charge her for assault and wasting police time for now, in which case she'll know something's wrong with her story. Can't charge her with murder, unless we think she's pulling an elaborate double bluff, i.e. she did it and is claiming she only clobbered him with the bottle hoping we'll believe someone else did him in afterwards. But personally, I don't get the impression she's got that in her. Very few people are actually stupid, but it takes a sharp mind to concoct a story like that, complete with built-in wriggle room. I doubt she could have done that during the short car journey from her house to here.'

He squeezed his fingers into his eyes, ignored how good it felt to close them even for a few seconds.

'No. I don't think *shedunnit*, Lou.'

'Neither do I, boss. Assault, maybe, but...'

'We need to find that boy, Remi, and bloody quick. Alive, hopefully.'

SIXTEEN

'It's ten minutes past. Where the hell is she?'

'You know as much as I do, Zoe.'

'She wanted this bloody call. And the last one. Now she doesn't bother turning up? Fucking cheek, Teri.'

'We don't know why she's not joined. Amber hasn't either. Do you think Patricia was telling the truth, maybe not overreacting after all?'

'I don't know. But she knows we have our own plans, already. And she knows we've put a lot of time and effort into them. Why would she even think she could have talked some reason into that fucker? He's an animal. I mean he was.'

'I have to agree – she seemed to be telling the truth. But then, she's the newest to the group and we don't know her as well as we know each other. Oh God. What's keeping her.'

'Maybe...'

'Maybe what? Or do I not want to know what vile thing's about to come out of your mouth?'

'Maybe it was that brother of hers. He's a mental, isn't he?'

'Zoe. You can't say that. That's horrible, even by your standards.'

'Ach, you know what I mean. She said he has mental health

problems. Needs constant care. Some of his kind can be violent, you know? Unpredictable? Maybe he wanted to protect his big sister, so he went to the bastard's house and did him?'

'I don't think so. Didn't she also say he never leaves the house?'

'Aye, but never leaving the house isn't the same as not being *able* to leave the house, is it? People like him can seem simple but they're really devious underneath.'

'Zoe, how do you get through a day without being punched? Do you talk like that to other people?'

'I say what I mean and I mean what I say. It's just me, Teri. Cannae help bein' me.'

'She's not joining, is she? Neither is Amber. Maybe Amber's emergency ran on into the evening.'

'Aye, right. We'll not hear from her again. She's bottled it. One whiff of the Pigs and she's nowhere to be seen. Just us die-hards, doll.'

'Goodnight, Zoe.'

'Don't be like that. If Patricia's gone and done us all a favour, then we got what we wanted. Better than we wanted.'

'Speak for yourself. I never wanted that.'

'What, you don't think he deserved it? Seriously? He deserved worse.'

'Worse than being murdered? Please tell me you don't really believe that, Zoe.'

'Why? You too chicken to admit it yourself?'

'I'm going to bed. I think we should discuss whether we need this group anymore.'

'Don't you dare. Don't you fucking dare. There's more like him out there. Worse.'

'Teri? Talk to me. We need each other. 'Teri?'

SEVENTEEN

As Malkie chewed on the last sandwich from the vending machine, he mulled over just how shitty a day can turn in no time at all.

First, he got the kind of shout he hates, the kind that attracts attention and pressure from management, and never ends up bringing plaudits or merits regardless of the outcome. The kind that's kept quiet for the sake of some bastard's precious reputation.

Then he – they – got McLeish back. About the worst form of support Malkie could imagine.

Then he had to cancel on Deborah for the second time this week. She had gone easy on him, but he knew she needed his visits as much as he did, anything to alleviate her inability to enjoy what little freedom her injuries allowed her, inflicted when an RAF training helicopter failed with her in it. He needed an escape from the worst of the ugliness that modern society generates in otherwise decent people.

And now, he had a vulnerable and volatile murder suspect on the run because he gave in to his sentimental inner idiot. He gave Remi Quinn a chance to go quietly rather than strong-arm him into the back of a van. He corrected his own thinking; he now believed Patricia when she said her brother was incapable of regulating himself. That his outbursts and previous attacks on people had all been triggered within him, with no ability to stop and reason with his own tormented mind. He was a man filled with confusion, ill-equipped to cope with the kinds of brutality modern life could throw at people. What chance did someone like him have? The poor sod couldn't leave his own home without running a gauntlet of knuckle-draggers helpfully yelling at him that he was a freak and a waste of good oxygen.

Sometimes, protecting the public required more from him than he believed they deserved.

Some of them, he corrected himself. Only some. What had he said the night he sat on his dad's boat at Port Edgar and imagined he could commune with his mum? His job was to protect the best of people from the worst? Something like that.

He believed Remi Quinn to be the former, despite the atrocity that the evidence so far indicated he'd inflicted.

He threw most of his stale cheese sandwich into a waste bin and settled back in his chair to try to catch a few minutes sleep.

'Malkie. Why are you still here at this time? You'll be back on soon, won't you?'

He suppressed a groan, resisted an urge to bark at her, didn't want to give the previously severe and difficult DS Ballantyne reason to revert to type. He'd only recently got to know another side to her and had found himself keen to build those particular bridges.

'Hi, Pam. The Beauchamp case has turned messy.'

'Another one? You do seem to have an affinity for messes, don't you?' She smiled at him, then scanned the open-plan office for observers.

'The guy whose prints we pulled off the wine bottle we believe was used to kill Beauchamp; he's on the run. Please don't ask how that happened.'

She rested her backside against the edge of a desk, folded her arms and gave him a look that expressed no surprise whatsoever.

'His sister then stood in her own front room and confessed to the same murder we want him for, despite the fact that we hadn't even mentioned Beauchamp to her yet. She's in a cell now, and the Super has pulled in several Uniforms to drive around all night until they find him.'

'Have you asked if you can charge her?'

'No. It was obvious – to Lou Gooch as well as to me, before you say something – that her confession was as fake as hell.'

'She didn't kill Beauchamp?'

'Maybe.'

She frowned at him. 'You're making no sense, Malkie.'

'She knew enough details to be convincing: who and where; roughly when; and she was kind of truthful about the weapon. But... She said she smashed the bottle over his head then scarpered, terrified.'

'But Beauchamp was neutered with the broken neck of the bottle.'

'Exactly. So, it's possible she tried to brain him – she claimed he tried to rape her – and only knocked him unconscious, thought she'd killed him and still believes that today, then someone else finished the job.'

'The brother.'

Malkie couldn't bring himself to confirm he believed that, so he just shrugged as if refusing to commit.

'When did her twelve hours start?'

'Around eleven.'

'So, if you don't find the brother...'

'Remi.'

'If you don't find Remi by eleven this morning, what then? Ask to charge her with attempted murder?'

'Nah, I don't think she meant to kill him, more self-defence. She claims she was in fear for her life. I think he was alive when she left him.'

'Hang on, what was she doing there in the first place?'

'Having an affair with him, she says. Anyway, we need those other prints back. We have hers now, obviously. All might become clearer when we get them back.'

'Or murkier.'

'Aye. Thanks for that.'

Pam sat at a desk next to Malkie's, nowhere near the one she usually tried to bag on the other side of the CID area from his. He glanced at her, but she refused to react. After grimacing at some marks or stains on the desk, the monitor and the keyboard, she woke the PC and at least nine or ten beeps came in quick succession. Usually that number of notifications would have Malkie heading for the canteen to fetch some strong coffee before he could face them. Pam seemed untroubled, and – not for the first time – he had to admit a grudging admiration for her. He turned back to his own screen and what felt like the hundredth banal and vacuous celebrity-stroke-society news site of his day.

'Malkie.' Her tone dropped a heavy lump of dread in his guts.

'Pam?' He couldn't turn to her at first, his mind already plummeting deep into Worst Case Scenario mode. She made him look at her before she continued.

'The prints have come back from the lighter Callum Gourlay found at your mum's house.'

Her face had Malkie wanting to run for the door, anything but hear what she had to say to him.

Her eyes shone with more empathy than he could have imagined her capable of.

What the fuck?

'They're Liam Fielding's, Malkie.'

When Malkie returned from the bathroom, his knuckles bruised from punching a cubicle wall and his throat raw from screaming his favourite expletive in all its wondrous forms, he found Pam sitting where he'd left her. She did him the favour – or perhaps she just didn't have it in her – of not deploying a look of fake sympathy that he loathed in so many other colleagues when they tried to *connect* with him. He saw genuine concern in her eyes, whether from some newfound understanding between them or from simple, decent appreciation of the impact she knew her announcement would have on him.

'You OK?' She glanced at his knuckles.

He groaned and it turned into a frustrated snarl. 'Are they sure? They make mistakes sometimes.'

'Fielding's prints have been taken a dozen times, and the one lifted from the lighter was full and clear. It's his.'

He slid down in his chair and laid his head back, closed his eyes like a wee laddie who still believed the bogeyman would disappear if he didn't look at it.

'Sorry, Pam. Bit of a sideswipe, that. It's not enough to arrest him though.'

'No.'

'Do you think management will deem it enough to justify reopening the case?'

She chewed this over for a moment. 'Hard to say, but personally, I would believe so, given your past dealings with the man.'

Malkie scoffed, disgusted at the thought of Fielding being the same species as him. The son and only living relative of a West Lothian lowlife called Jake Fielding, the pair had run the usual string of security firms, haulage, lap-dancing dives, plus a minicab company and a barber shop, neither of which accepted card payments.

Thoughts of the Fieldings revived the memory, again, of how appallingly he let down Walter Callahan and nearly got shot for his efforts. An ex-squaddie with a serious case of PTSD-denial and addiction to foreign-territory deployments, he had driven a minicab for the family, until Jake Fielding, a bigot through and through, learned his precious son and heir to the family businesses, Liam, was gay. He'd run over Liam's secret partner in a blind rage and framed Callahan for it. After a couple of completely fucked-up stunts pulled by McLeish, Callahan had gone off reservation, obtained a gun, appeared at the Fielding home and worked his way through Jake's security goons, although only later did Malkie learn they'd *only* been knee-capped rather than shot dead. Callahan had cornered Jake and Liam in the house and Malkie had to stand in his way to stop the man from committing murder for real. McLeish had tackled Malkie to the ground, and an AFO had put three rounds into Callahan's chest. He'd died in Malkie's arms, and one more catastrophic mistake was added to Malkie's ever-growing mental fuck-up list.

'Malkie?'

He returned to the room, but Walter Callahan's face, bewildered and coughing up blood, remained etched at the forefront of his mind.

Both Fieldings played their part in that poor sod's death. And now, this...

'Malkie?'

He'd drifted again. 'Sorry, Pam. This is tough.'

'I know, Malkie. We all know what happened, and how close you got to vindicating Callahan. You turned a few people's opinions of you around after that case, I can tell you.'

She probably meant that comment to comfort him, and he stopped himself from uttering some scathing and self-indulgent vitriol about what he believed would always be his greatest failure.

He sat up, rubbed his face with both hands, took a deep breath, held it, then released it, long and slow.

'OK. So, what's your next step?'

The worry in her face eased a little, but she'd be watching him. 'I'll discuss it with Thompson in the morning, Malkie.' They glanced at each other. 'Later this morning, I mean. Shouldn't you go home? Get some sleep? You know the briefing might be a bit rough, don't you?'

'Oh aye. That bastard won't pass up a chance to humiliate me in front of an eager audience.'

She tutted, scowled at him. 'Oh good grief, Malkie. When will you stop believing half of Livi CID has a rotten opinion of you?'

'I don't.'

This seemed to confuse her.

'It's probably closer to eighty per cent, I would imagine.' He forced a grin, but it withered under Pam's disapproving expression. Only Steph could have topped the cold he felt emanating from Pam's scowl. And Gucci maybe. And Thompson. And Debs.

Fuck's sake, maybe it's me after all.

'Malkie, stop that.'

'What?'

'You know what. Stop feeling sorry for yourself. You're a decent copper when you extract your thumb from your gob. Try to believe that. Give us all a break.'

'A break from what?'

Her temper finally broke, and the freezing scorn he was used to from her returned. 'From you, you bloody idiot.'

He stared at her, could find no words. She stood with an exasperated sigh, switched off her PC and grabbed her coat and briefcase. As she stomped past him, she muttered to him.

'I'll talk to Thompson after morning briefing. You know I'll keep you informed.'

'Yes, Pam. Thanks, Pam. Message received and understood; you won't catch me interfering, Pam. Promise.'

He thought he heard a whispered F-bomb come from Ballantyne's mouth, but he couldn't be sure.

Time to listen to someone other than your inner idiot, mate?

He resisted a temptation to open the Callahan/Fieldings case file. It would serve no purpose and would only keep him sitting here in the middle of the night. A couple of hours sleep might stop his mouth from earning him a career damaging rebuke in the morning if McLeish was on his usual annoying-as-fuck form.

As he reached for the button to shut down his PC, a stubborn idea forced its way into his mind. He switched to the historic evidence logs and searched for Liam Fielding's previous arrests and which possessions had been taken from him.

Out of fifteen arrests – of which only two led to charges and convictions, both of them suspended – he found three where a lighter was taken. No photos because both of those ended in no further action.

He recalled an evening spent near Hopetoun House on the Forth Estuary, he and Liam sounding each other out, Malkie trying to make him admit he had something to do with Callahan's false accusation and Liam losing the plot repeatedly and protesting that he had nothing to do with it. Liam had been smoking that night. Malkie racked his mind trying to remember how he had lit his cigarette, but nothing came.

'Fuck's sake.' He jumped as he realised he'd spoken out loud in an otherwise empty office.

As he scanned the desks around him, his eyes fell on his own reflection in the night-black windows.

'What are you playing at, you idiot. What the hell could that prove anyway, even if you could remember? You're fraying at the edges, man. People need you now, so you can't be this weak.'

He gathered his belongings and killed his PC. As he turned to head for the rear exit, he caught his reflection again. He scolded himself. 'You do *not* go anywhere near that bastard's home. You need that kind of distraction like McLeish needs *How To Be An Arsehole* lessons.

'And you're bloody talking to yourself again.'

EIGHTEEN

[Zoe] She's been what?

[Teri] She's been arrested. I went round to her house last night, after dark, hoped I could talk to her.

[Zoe] Face to face? I thought we had a rule about that.

[Teri] We do, but we're in extreme circumstances right now.

[Zoe] Fair enough. Was she there?

[Teri] She was, but so were two police cars. One was unmarked and two people not in uniform were in that. The other one was one of those vans with the cages inside, had two uniformed coppers sitting in it. A crowd had already gathered when I got there, so I blended in and watched.

[Zoe] And?

[Teri] The two I'm sure were detectives went in with one of the PCs and the other PC went round the back of the terrace. After about twenty minutes they came out again. There was a young guy being led to the unmarked car. Her brother, obviously. Something freaked him out and he bolted. Three of the coppers went after him but they came back without him. Then they brought her out and took her away.

[Zoe] Fuck's sake, Teri. This is bad. What if she tells them about us?

[Teri] That won't be a problem, will it? All we've done so far is talk. Right?

[Teri] Right, Zoe?

[Zoe] Aye. I've not done anything. Just talk, like you said.

[Teri] Are you sure? I mean, really sure, Zoe?

[Zoe] I went there, to his house. Just once. I parked outside and watched. I had no idea what I was going to do, or even if I would do anything. I just got so fucking furious, I had to see him.

[Teri] For what he did to you?

[Zoe] Aye, the bastard caught me.

[Teri] Stop, Zoe.

[Teri] We don't discuss what he did to us. Remember?

[Zoe] Sorry. Aye. Forgot.

[Teri] I've decided I'm closing this chat down as soon as this mess pans out one way or another. Even if Patricia says nothing to the cops about it, I don't doubt they'll find it anyway. So, I'll keep it open for now, but from now on we say nothing that could be construed as linking us to what Patricia said she did to him. Understand?

[Zoe] OK. What about Amber?

[Teri] Oh, I'm sure you'll find a way to get word to her, with all your connections and your oh-so-convincing lying skills.

[Zoe] I'm sorry, Teri. Really. I just thought I saw a way to really give him and all those other fucking men a kicking, for a change. A way to take some action. To hit back.

[Teri] Zoe, this was never about giving men a kicking. It was only ever about stopping him. I thought we were all clear about our reasons? Were you lying, when you agreed with us on that, too?

[Zoe] No. I just thought we could do more.

[Zoe] Teri?

NINETEEN

Malkie got no sleep all night.

Between hoping his mobile would ring with news that Remi Quinn had been found safe, and the new knowledge that Liam Fielding, of all people, had murdered his mum, his nerves were shot.

Possibly murdered my mum, he insisted to himself.

His caution stemmed not from frequent conversations with Steph about confirmation bias. More from his realisation that once it was established that manky old Jake Fielding had driven the car that ploughed into Liam's partner, Liam never stood a chance. With a father like Jake, he was always going to become the kind of person Malkie and other police officers dreamed of nailing. Malkie himself had itched to collar Liam, and later had to admit he'd *wanted* the man to be guilty. He'd assumed Walter Callahan's innocence based on the bare few minutes of their first meeting, and he'd also assumed Liam's guilt based on nothing more than the family's reputation.

Bad to the bone, he'd thought, and discovering how wrong he was had shaken him at a time when blaming himself, irrationally, for his mum's death already had him on his knees mentally.

He felt the same ugly bias try to push up from deep inside to take root in his mind. He must not assume, based on one piece of, admittedly damning, evidence. He needed to let Pam's investigation run its course. Interfering could only sabotage his chances of winning justice for his mum. However much he wanted to rock up at the Fielding home and break every finger on both of Fielding's hands. As well as recognising that for the career-ending act it would be, he admitted to himself that Liam Fielding could dismantle him in a dark room, one-handed, without breaking a sweat. The man was more muscle than brain and vicious with it.

He heard his dad shuffling from his bedroom to the bathroom. What the hell could he tell him? That his mum died because Malkie had pursued Liam Fielding like a ferret down a rabbit hole, long before the Callahan case? That the wife he'd courted before they left school had died because Malkie had chosen to become a copper? Had that opened him and his family to the risk of revenge attacks from any number of mouth-breathing criminals he'd put away over the years? Had he considered the impact his career choice would have on those he cared about? Did he, even now, continue to court disaster by discovering only last month that he had a twenty-six-year-old daughter? Was he risking Debs' safety by allowing his relationship with her to grow and deepen?

He sat up, his head spinning and anger building in him. He heard his dad leave the bathroom and walk into the main room of the cabin. He stood with a groan, realised he hadn't undressed before collapsing into bed only four hours previously. He heard the coffee percolator gurgling and decided a shower and change of clothes could wait twenty minutes.

'Good grief, Malcolm. You slept in your clothes? Again?'

'Aye. Sorry, Dad. The job, you know.'

'That job of yours needs to stay in the office when you come home. I'm not sure you know how damaging it can be, sometimes.'

Oh, I know, Dad. I really know.

They sat together on the deck, sipped their coffee, and stared out over Harperrig Reservoir. A cold blue sky to the west promised a bright and cloudless day. He recalled so many mornings like this, when he was a sallow and socially clumsy youth. While his school peers – calling them friends had always been a stretch – had spent their Saturdays playing footie or hanging around Livi town centre and pedalling their Raleigh Choppers along pavements so fast they terrorised pedestrians, Malkie had sat here, on this deck, with his mum and dad. They had given up trying to persuade him to *join in* before he turned twelve. At that age, he'd spent most of his weekends on the Pentlands, the range of hills that sat to the south-west of Edinburgh and had been his hiding place from a youth never blessed with an excess of social success. He'd fill his satchel with graphic novels and jam pieces and bottles of banana milk and climb the old Drover's Road, up the Cauldstane Slap, where he'd wander away to the east, as close as he dared to the fenced-off army shooting range. He'd found the sound of distant gunshots both exciting and frightening, but had been drawn to them anyway.

'Malkie. Planet Earth to Malkie. Come in, Malkie.'

'Sorry, Dad. I was miles away.'

'I know. Up the Slap and over East and West Cairn Hills?'

Malkie smiled. 'Aye. Jam pieces and my comics. Good days.'

A shadow darkened Tommy McCulloch's face. He had to find this difficult, too. The home he built and lived a lifetime in with the only woman he ever loved was now no more than an ash-covered patch of land in the Livi Village with a *For Sale* sign at the gate. Buyers had started to show an interest, but neither Malkie nor his dad could bring themselves to discuss actually selling the place. Malkie suspected they would both call this worn and tired old cabin home for the rest of their lives. Well, for the rest of his dad's life; he couldn't imagine Debs, with the life-changing nature of her injuries, being able to live here long term. He had to pray that his dad intended to survive Malkie's mum's death by a good long time. Debs would wait.

His phone rang, and he jumped. Not for the first time, he hated the thing for the merciless way it intruded on his life at the most unfortunate moments. With a sigh, he picked it up from the table. Steph. He came to full wakefulness in a second.

'Hi, partner. How you doing?'

'Can you come over, Malkie? Like, now?' Her voice sounded weak and tired. So unlike the Steph he knew, he felt an overwhelming need to show her that she could rely on him any time, as he'd told her so often.

He glanced at his watch and swore inwardly. Seven fifteen. The drive to the station normally took twenty minutes, so he usually left at seven thirty to arrive just in time and avoid any risk of a boss drive-by before the morning briefing even started. Adding a detour to Steph's flat in Linlithgow would stretch that to an hour or more, not counting time spent with her. And turning up seriously late for the first briefing with McLeish at the helm of a J Division case since they got rid of him was simply not an option.

'Steph. I can't. Not right now. I'm sorry. Can I come over at lunchtime? Or this evening?'

The pause before she spoke again almost broke him.

'It's OK. The job. I know. McLeish. Don't worry about it, mate. Are you OK?'

He could hear she was only going through the motions and probably had no capacity even for his troubles at the moment.

'I'm fine, Steph. I'll be round as soon as I can get away, OK? I promise.'

As the words left his mouth, he regretted them.

'Don't promise, Malkie. Never promise.'

'Do I need to worry about you, Steph? Tell me the truth?'

Another excruciating pause.

'I'll be OK. Talk later.'

'Steph, you're—'

She'd hung up.

He threw his phone on the table.

Tommy had been watching him. 'Is she OK?'

'No, Dad. She's really not. She needs me now and I can't be there for her.'

'The job?'

'Aye. The job, Dad.' *Isn't it always?*

Despite a temptation to call in with some crap excuse that would fool no one, he showered and dressed in record time.

Tommy had a beaker of coffee and two slices of buttered toast in a plastic container waiting for him. 'You need to look after yourself better, son. For our sakes, if not for your own.'

Malkie turned to thank his dad for the minor guilt-trip, but the worry etched on the old man's face stopped any rebuke dead. Malkie was all he had, now.

'I will, Dad. I promise.'

Steph's warning about promises echoed in his mind all the way to his car.

TWENTY

Steph found the courage to reach for the rest of Boswell's bundle of letters, but only after another gin. At breakfast time.

She saw a stamp in the bottom corner of most that indicated the staff at Cornton Vale women's prison had opened and read them before they got to her mum, and she shook, again, with rage at her spending even one day in prison because of the desperate shell of a woman Dean Lang had turned her into.

The only one from her mum to Boswell had almost broken her. In neat, almost childish writing she'd apologised for getting herself imprisoned, for allowing Lang to brutalise her so badly she'd got herself shut away from her daughter.

She swallowed another huge mouthful from her glass to wash down a surge of sour self-doubt, then lifted the top letter from the pile and pulled the stiff, yellowed paper from it.

Two hours later, she realised her cheeks were wet and her gin had lain untouched since she'd started reading.

She couldn't doubt that Barry Boswell had believed himself deeply in love with her mum.

So, why could she not shake – despite his words and her mum's heartfelt single letter back to him – her profound conviction of his guilt, even when claimed by a manky animal like Lang? She read every one again, and on a second reading she found the sinister thread that ran through them all. Boswell's tone in every letter, every sentence, held an undercurrent of what Steph could only call *persuasion*. As if he'd felt a need to convince her that his feelings were genuine. Too many of his insistences that they loved each other sounded equally desperate, like he struggled with some doubt that he deserved her.

What the hell was she picking up from the spaces between his words? Guilt? Regret? As if a part of him he buried deep couldn't hide from what he'd done? And what that made him?

She wondered about a link between that and Lang's death, only days ago. Had Boswell finally found the strength and the rage to end Lang's sorry life? Had he been driven by Lang's recent destruction of any meagre chance of reconciliation with his daughter? Had Lang tricked him into surprising Steph that night by promising to help repair their relationship? How must he have felt when, far from seeming glad to see him, Steph had attacked him and nearly killed him? Could that final betrayal of all he hoped for have driven him to a point he could never have dreamed of in all the years he kept his identity a secret from Steph? A point where his need to make Lang pay outweighed his fear of the man?

She glanced at her watch and the early morning daylight creeping around the edges of her drawn curtains, ignored them both and reached for the gin bottle again, but found it empty. She forced herself from the sofa to the kitchen but found no more booze. She'd not thought to restock to ease her passage through her current circumstances.

She sat again and stared at the letters, now strewn across her coffee table. She wept, as grief swamped her. She was used to seeing the worst that one human being could do to another, but all of this had happened to her mother. Steph could still just about remember her as a young woman full of life and dreams and promises to herself and to Steph. And Lang had ended all of that.

He'd as good as murdered the woman her mum might have become, and the life they might have enjoyed together.

She felt so confused now, reluctant to let go of her hatred of Lang and Boswell, as if only that had sustained her through Lang's attempts to poison her and the life she'd worked so hard to build from her shabby beginnings. Or was her enduring rage at both men born of another factor: a voice that whispered at the back of her mind that Boswell still wasn't telling the whole truth, that he was lying about something by omission.

Yes. There was more that she wasn't seeing. Boswell was asking her to believe a fundamentally different version of events to the story she'd already worked through shock and anger to finally accept.

Did she *want* to believe him? Might that banish the huge chunk of shame and revulsion she'd suffered since Lang's first poisonous revelation to her?

No. She wasn't seeing the full picture. Something sat right in front of her that she couldn't see.

For better or worse she needed to see it. Even if it damaged her beyond repair.

TWENTY-ONE

Malkie reached the station with fifteen minutes to spare. The toast lay untouched on the passenger seat; he hadn't been able to muster any appetite for it.

Inside, preparation for the morning briefing had started. Chairs had been pulled from under desks and arranged in two semicircular tiers around a whiteboard. Some bums were on seats, but other officers still ambled toward the area. McLeish stood, arms folded and feet apart, his customary look of smug superiority plastered over his much-loathed kisser. Thompson leaned back against a desk behind him, studying her phone.

Malkie took the seat Gucci had saved between her and Rab.

'You get any sleep, guys?'

Gucci yawned. 'Not enough.'

Rab nodded but produced a sheaf of bank statements and phone bills.

'Before the briefing starts, I found some good stuff in Beauchamp's files. Regular monthly credits on the last working day of every month; his salary, I assume.' He pointed to a number on a statement that pissed Malkie off no end.

'That's his salary? We're in the wrong line of work, guys.'

Rab checked whether McLeish or Thompson were about to

start the briefing, didn't see either so he continued. 'Each one is followed by an amount back out to what looks like an offshore account, always exactly twenty per cent of his salary. But then here and here and' – he pointed to other entries – 'here. Credits for £200. Always four of them, always for £200 on different dates each month, and always from the same four accounts. Then he makes bank transfers of the whole £800 to that same offshore account. I'll need longer, but it looks to me like they started a couple of years ago with just one payment, then two in the year after that, then four every year up to now. The latest, I think, has only paid in twice in the last two months.'

Malkie chewed this over. He wanted a lead, something to throw to McLeish to get him to back off a bit, if that were possible. This was reaching a bit, but it did look odd. No other credits at all, except for what looked like salary payments, and they all started within the past two years, and all from the same four accounts.

'Keep on them, Rab. Good work.' He paused, couldn't miss a smug look on Rab's face that indicated he'd *done good*.

'What? Amaze me, mate.'

Rab grinned. 'Patricia Quinn applied to remortgage her home. Three weeks ago.'

'Interesting. Was it approved?'

'Still in progress.'

'OK. It's thin, though. We should get the warrant for his bank and phone data tomorrow morning, so hopefully we'll have the data by tomorrow afternoon to do some proper analysis on. Do you know yet who you'll be liaising with in Digital Forensics?'

Rab's grin disappeared, replaced by an annoyed scowl. 'No. Not yet. I've asked twice.'

'OK. Keep at them. Anything from his phone records? Aye, I know, bit early to pick numbers out of a list, but any obvious patterns yet?'

'No. Not until I get the data files and his contacts list from his phone.'

Malkie glanced at the wall clock, racked his mind for anything else they could do that McLeish might pick them up for in just a few minutes.

'Sod it. Good work, mate, and really, thanks for staying late. I do appreciate it.'

Rab and Gucci looked at each other and then at him, their expressions filled with mock suspicion.

'What?'

Gucci nudged Rab, who scowled at her but then sighed in surrender.

'Lou wants to know who you are and where you buried the real Malkie McCulloch, boss.'

Gucci punched him on the arm, and he pretended it hurt far more than her diminutive size made likely.

'You two are hilarious. No, really. Sod off home before I put you both on report for insubordination.'

'Yes, boss. Have you heard from Steph?'

'Aye, and I'm worried about her, Lou. I need to get over to Linlithgow at some point today.'

She nodded. 'We'll cope, won't we, Rab?'

'For Steph? Aye.'

Malkie gave him a light punch on the arm. 'Aw. Thanks, mate. Appreciate that.'

Rab twisted his neck as if suppressing a reaction he might regret.

'Lou, any news on Remi Quinn?'

'No sign of him. No sighting, nothing on CCTV. He and his sister have no family, and neither seems to have any friends we can ask. Remi's never had a bank card so we can't know if he's travelled somewhere. His main assigned social worker is coming in later this morning to advise us.'

'OK. I'll—'

McLeish's voice sounded, loud and demanding. 'DS McCulloch, with your permission we'll make a start? Or do you have somewhere else you need to be?'

Yes, I do. Dickhead.

McLeish opened his mouth again, but Thompson stepped forward.

'OK. Let's kick off. We'll cover the usual agenda items, then DI McLeish and Malkie's team can discuss the Beauchamp case without keeping the rest of us.'

McLeish's face burned, but he stepped back. He attempted a gracious gesture for Thompson to continue but she stepped in front of him and ignored it.

Brilliant. Piss him off even before he starts on us. Thanks, boss.

After the usual assignments, actions and announcements had been covered, Thompson stepped to the side.

With McLeish about to step forward, Thompson nodded at him. 'All yours, DI McLeish. Anyone not directly involved in the Beauchamp case, carry on.'

The rush with which all but three of the audience scarpered spoke volumes. No one stayed to watch McLeish give Malkie a kicking.

Maybe my star is rising after all.

McLeish gathered himself, then nodded toward meeting room one. 'In there, please. Five minutes.' He walked away in Thompson's direction, and Malkie would have sold his left kidney to be a fly on the wall when he reached her.

Malkie logged in to HOLMES, found no updates that got his juices going. The second set of prints hadn't come through yet. Post-mortem had confirmed the obvious, that Beauchamp had been murdered by repeated stabbing injuries to his genitals with the broken bottle. And still no sign of Remi.

Nothing. McLeish would rip him a new one.

When the big man returned he stomped straight into the meeting room without any further reminder. Malkie and his side-kicks stood, shared a look, then joined him.

'Where is Remi Quinn, McCulloch?'

'I don't know, *Detective Inspector* McLeish.'

McLeish glared at him before continuing. 'Why not? He's been missing for over nine hours, and you have nothing?'

'No, sir. I don't. While CCTV operators and mobile patrols search for him, activities which no amount of assistance from me or my colleagues can supplement in any way, we've been researching Mr Quinn's affairs, as per standard procedures.'

McLeish read a document on the desk in front of him. 'And his sister?' His eyes didn't lift from the desk.

'She's in custody.'

McLeish looked up now. 'In custody? Why?'

Malkie stared back. All present would know that nothing should come as a surprise to the man if he'd studied the case file before grilling them.

'She confessed to murdering Sebastian Beauchamp. Last night when I interviewed her at home. She's been cautioned. She refused legal representation and repeated her assertion that she killed Beauchamp.'

'But her brother's prints were found on the broken bottle, were they not?'

'Yes, sir. Sometime this morning, we're expecting identification of a second set of prints, though. Ms Quinn admits only to braining Beauchamp with the bottle. She seems to know nothing about the fatal stab wounds.'

McLeish shook his head.

'When are you going to learn to put your Columbo act aside and see what's in front of you, McCulloch?' she confessed. Does her failure to describe the stabbing wounds change that?'

Malkie braced himself. 'Yes it does. Sir.'

McLeish would want nothing more than a quick resolution to such a high-profile case, for which he would take full credit with a token recognition of the team effort involved. If that happened, Malkie would gladly allow the fucker all the limelight he could handle if it meant getting rid of him again.

'The confession is solid. He shut down Malkie opening his mouth to interrupt. 'Even if it's not complete, a confession from the sister of the man whose prints were ID'd means we're on the right track.'

'But it's only part of the story. Ms Quinn only said she smashed the wine bottle over Beauchamp's head. When I encouraged her to elaborate, she just repeated that she believed she'd killed him and fled. She said nothing about then repeatedly stabbing Beauchamp in the genitals.'

'When will you interview her again?'

'As soon as we're done here and we can get a duty solicitor here, sir.'

'But you said she refused legal representation.'

'She did, sir. But I want to give her a second chance. After I've told her exactly how Beauchamp died. That information might well make her reconsider her position.'

'No. She's refused. I assume she got her Letter Of Rights and confirmed she understood it?'

Malkie bit his tongue. *How can a supposedly grown man reach the rank of Detective Inspector and still carry around so much spite and bile and self-delusion? How the hell does that happen?*

'She did. Sir.'

'All in order unless she proactively asks for a brief after all, then. Anything else?'

'No, sir. Despite DC Gooch and I working most of last night and into the early hours of this morning, there's still a regrettable limit on what we can achieve. Of course, I don't mean to teach granny how to suck eggs. Apologies if I gave that impression, sir.'

He felt Gucci stiffen and could imagine Rab perking up for some choice Malkie-kicking entertainment, but McLeish waved Malkie's sham apology away.

'That'll be all, for now. Let me know when you're about to interview Patricia Quinn again. I want to observe.'

Rab and Gucci made a swift exit but Malkie stopped halfway out of his seat and sat down again. 'Will you want to sit in or watch from the video room, sir?'

'In the monitoring room. MIT is here to support, not to take over the investigation.'

'I'll let you know, sir. As soon as we're ready.'

Malkie left and closed the door behind him. Rab and Gucci spun their chairs to face him.

'He'll not be in the room.'

They nodded their relief.

Gucci voiced what all three would be thinking. 'Can she change her mind about legal representation?'

'She can, Lou. But of course she's more likely to mess up and incriminate herself or otherwise sabotage her chances of a decent defence without a brief supporting her. And only a highly cynical person would wonder if that was something to be desired in the pursuit of justice.'

Both she and Rab looked as if someone had waved shite under their noses.

TWENTY-TWO

[Zoe] Teri? Are you there?
[Zoe] Teri?
[Zoe] Fuck's sake, Teri. We need to talk about this.
[Zoe] Teri! I'm not going anywhere.
[Teri] What do you want?
[Zoe] Thank fuck for that. We need to decide what to do about this.
[Teri] What can we do? We've done nothing wrong. We planned to do something to him, but we never followed through. If Patricia did kill him, and the police find their way to us, we just need to tell the truth, that we started a chat room of local women who had suffered at the hands of toxic males, and leave it at that. As long as we say nothing about what we planned to do to him, we can't be implicated.
[Zoe] And Patricia? What about her?
[Zoe] Teri? What about Patricia?
[Teri] You weren't very concerned about her yesterday.
[Zoe] Fuck off. That's not fair. She'd just dropped a bloody bombshell on us. I was reeling. So were you.
[Teri] No, you were furious and scared. All you care about is that none of what she's done comes back to you. Don't start pretending you care because we've always known you were as much a misandrist as any man was ever a misogynist.

[Zoe] What's a misandrist?

[Teri] Oh good grief, Zoe. Really? A misandrist is someone, a woman or a man, who hates all men. You didn't know that? You're the most militant of all of us and you don't know what a misandrist is?

[Zoe] Fuck off. I might not have a degree and talk posh like you three, but I'm not stupid.

[Teri] You just decided you hate all men without actually bothering to educate yourself and come to reasoned opinions? You just want to castrate everything with testicles, right?

[Zoe] That's not fair. I don't hate all men. I don't hate my family.

[Teri] Seriously, Zoe? You stabbed your dad in the back. With a fucking corkscrew.

[Zoe] How do you know that?

[Teri] I'm sorry. That was unfair of me.

[Zoe] How do you know?

[Teri] I researched all three of you. I had to. I'm the admin of this group, so anyone who might be toxic to it, I had to reject them.

[Zoe] Have you ever rejected anyone?

[Teri] Yes. I have.

[Zoe] Who? And why?

[Teri] It doesn't matter, Zoe.

[Zoe] Would you have rejected me if you knew me as I am, now?

[Teri] It doesn't matter, Zoe. You're one of us now, and we look after each other, right?

[Zoe] Would you have rejected me?

[Zoe] Answer me.

[Teri] Possibly.

[Teri] Zoe?

[Teri] You OK Zoe?

[Zoe] Goodbye Teri.

[Teri] Zoe?

TWENTY-THREE

'Any word on Remi Quinn, Lou?'

'No, boss.'

'Bollocks. OK. You ready?'

'Yes, boss.'

Rab's head appeared over his monitor. 'How come you never ask me to help you interview suspects?'

Malkie ignored an urge to tell Rab the truth – that his gob was the only one in Livi CID more expected to utter the worst possible comment than Malkie's. He fished for a reason that would sound credible without pissing him off.

Gucci saved his arse, again. 'Sorry, Rab. I asked Malkie if I could do as many interviews as possible. I need the experience. Is that a problem for you?'

Rab chewed this over. Malkie suffered no illusions that he actually wanted to take on more duties. He was well known for being perfectly happy on his arse and single-finger typing on his keyboard if it got him out of actual exercise. If he was now expressing an interest in helping to interview Patricia Quinn, it would be because he enjoyed watching a car-crash interview rather than from any professional development urges. Rab didn't fail to confirm Malkie's opinion of him.

'Fine. I just wondered, is all.' His head disappeared behind his monitor again.

Malkie and Gucci shared a look and Malkie risked a finger to his lips, as if she wouldn't already be aware how irritating a Rab Lundy huff could be.

They headed through the door to the custody suite.

'Did you warn DI McLeish, boss?'

'Ach. Forgot. Never mind.'

Gucci stopped, gave him a look that would have done Steph proud, which only served to remind him that he still hadn't gone to her when she needed him.

'I'll tell him.' She disappeared back through to the CID area in the open-plan part of the office.

Malkie ambled around to the front of the charging bar. Sergeant Martin Reid was on the desk today. He and Malkie had known each other for long enough to remember *old-school policing*.

'Malkie.'

'Marty.'

Malkie grinned and tipped a nod toward the door into the booth and Reid leaned over to open it from his side.

'Forgot the code again?'

'Rarely need it, mate.'

He gazed around him, at the trappings of a Police Scotland custody and charging desk. Three seats at three keyboards and monitors, although he'd never seen more than two in use at any one time, and only then on a Friday and Saturday night when the flotsam and jetsam of Livi nightlife was scraped off the streets and brought in to waste time that officers could otherwise spend scraping even more up.

He took a seat. 'Can we get Patricia Quinn in interview room one please, Martin?'

He typed something into his PC. 'Solicitor?'

'She's waived.'

'Oh dear. One of them.'

'Actually, she's not a typical *one of them*.'

Reid raised an eyebrow.

'She's not the kind of arsehole we get sometimes that thinks they're untouchable or that they can't be caught out if they just *No Comment* every question. No, it's almost as if she wants to be convicted. Because her brother's prints are on the murder weapon.'

'Nasty one, that. Brought tears to my eyes when we booked her in.'

'Aye, horrible way to go.'

They settled into a companionable silence. Reid continued with his admin while Malkie took the chance to close his eyes, if only for a few minutes.

Too soon he heard a knock on the plastic screen that protected the desk sergeant from physical attack and mouthfuls of saliva gobbed at them on a regular basis. He groaned and stood.

He and Gucci waited for a Uniform to fetch Patricia and lead her into the interview room. As they headed that way themselves, Malkie muttered to Gucci, 'You know, Lou, usually I look forward to dropping a bombshell on a suspect. I know, I take my job satisfaction from all the wrong sources. But this time I'm not going to enjoy it.'

'Why, boss?'

'Because she worries me. I don't think she murdered Beauchamp. Assaulted, yes. Murdered, no. I'm not even sure she has it in her. Her story about him assaulting her and her being forced to smack him over the head with a wine bottle rings true to me.'

He wanted to ask Gucci if she shared his doubts, but he'd been making a serious effort recently to have confidence in his professional abilities and his copper's instincts. And besides, she didn't deserve to be put on the spot like that.

They saw McLeish appear from the main office space, bless them with a dismissive look and disappear into the video monitoring cupboard.

When they walked through the door Patricia stood up, her eyes frantic and her hands clutching at air by her sides.

'Have you found him? Is that why you want to talk to me?'

Something occurred to her, and tears spilled. 'Oh God. Is he OK? Please. Tell me. Is he OK?'

Malkie held his hands up in a futile attempt to calm her.

'No word yet, Ms Quinn. I assure you, we'll update you the minute we hear anything. We have officers out in patrol cars and civilian staff scouring CCTV cameras and every other source of information we have access to.'

She sat and rested her head on her arms on the table. She sobbed, quiet and miserable. Malkie wondered whether it was even fair to interview her under these circumstances, but the custody clock was ticking. He had no doubt he'd be OK to charge her with assault at least, possibly attempted murder, but the time limit still worried him.

Lou performed the preliminary recording actions: date, time, location, persons in attendance. When the long and bloody irritating tone eventually stopped, Malkie began, but with a deep feeling of discomfort.

'Ms Quinn. We'd like to go over your recollection of that evening again, please.'

She lifted her head. Malkie saw exhaustion. Had she slept at all? She hadn't been considered a suicide or self-harm risk, so she hadn't had to put up with two Uniforms sitting on hard chairs, bored out of their minds, watching her all night through an open cell door. He made a mental note to himself to scan the footage from the cell's CCTV camera.

'Again?'

'Please, Ms Quinn. It's necessary.'

She stared at him, wiped the wetness from her cheeks then leaned forward, elbows on the table.

'I went to Beauchamp's house, late. I planned to tell him I didn't want to see him anymore. We opened a bottle of wine—'

'Do you remember what kind of wine?'

She glared at him. 'No. We had a glass each, then I told him I wanted to end our affair. He—'

'Why?'

'Why what?'

'Why did you want to end the affair?'

She looked confused for a second. 'I just didn't feel the same way about him anymore. Why does that matter? The important fact is that he took it badly, got aggressive, tried to rape me, and I smashed the bottle over his head. He—'

'The wine bottle.'

'Yes,' she snapped, and he knew he was achieving his primary aim of rattling her. Hard to keep a story straight when pissed off at the person you're telling it to.

'Can I continue?'

'Yes please, Ms Quinn.'

'I grabbed the bottle and—'

'Yes, you said that already.'

'Oh for God's sake. Do you want to hear this or not? Why aren't you out looking for my brother? Do you not realise how vulnerable he is? Anyone could—'

'We'll find him. What did you do next?'

She glared at him, possibly starting to wonder if she'd made a mistake dismissing the duty solicitor.

'He was dead. He wasn't moving, his eyes were closed and he wasn't breathing. So, I ran.' She swallowed. 'I need some water.'

Gucci nodded at the Uniform standing by the door, who opened it and headed for the staff kitchen.

'You ran. It's a long way from Mannerston Holdings back to your home?'

'Where?' Her eyes widened, and she looked like she'd just realised the hole she'd opened in her story.

'I mean, yes. I parked at the end of the lane.'

'Why?'

She took a moment, and Malkie knew she was starting to unravel. He felt dirty and unworthy in his charade. He needed to get her to finish her increasingly feeble story, give her the best second chance to present her version of events, then put her out of her misery. Or rather, pile more on her.

'I don't know. In case his wife was home?'

'Are you asking me or telling me, Ms Quinn?'

'Telling you. I wanted to make sure her car wasn't parked outside his house without revealing myself. That lane's a cul-de-sac, so any car driving along it would be noticed.'

'I'm confused, Ms Quinn. Beauchamp knew you were coming that evening, didn't he? Would he have allowed you to go out there if his wife was home? And earlier you said you wanted to end the relationship because of petrol costs and Remi noticing your absences, but now you say you just didn't feel the same way about him?'

She looked from Malkie to Gucci and back. She chewed the skin on the knuckle of a forefinger. Just as Malkie hoped she'd crumble and confess to having concocted at least some of her story, the door opened and the Uniform returned.

She took the tumbler of water he handed her but drank slowly, and Malkie knew she was thinking hard, desperate for a way to fix her story.

'Why did you call him Beauchamp earlier, Ms Quinn?'

'I didn't.'

'You did. You said you went to *Beauchamp's* house. Not Sebastian's house. Beauchamp's house. I'm sure I heard that correctly, didn't I, DC Gooch?'

Gucci nodded. 'You did, sir.'

Patricia gaped at them. Malkie needed to wrap this up soon. Attempting to knock a suspect off his or her story was an accepted interview technique for identifying and exposing contradictions, but for some reason he felt bad trying to actively trip this woman up. He was convinced she was doing nothing worse than protecting her brother, and he needed very little to make him believe that, given Remi Quinn's prints on the bottle. He felt certain that the second ID would come back as her prints, so he saw little justification in continuing to let the woman embarrass herself.

He couldn't bear to drag this out any longer.

'Ms Quinn. Sebastian Beauchamp didn't die from a blow to the head.'

She reeled. At the same time her expression turned wild and bewildered. Malkie watched her process this and saw a feral gleam appear in her eyes.

'You're lying.' She sounded desperate, unconvinced by her own accusation.

'We wouldn't lie about that, Ms Quinn.'

'But you are. I saw him. He was dead. I killed him.'

'Why would we try to trip you up while you're confessing? It would make more sense for us to accept your version of events verbatim so we can close this case off quickly and easily.'

She stared at him. Hostility battling with what looked like a plea for him to believe her story despite clearly knowing she'd been caught out. No, not caught out. She'd genuinely believed she had killed Beauchamp. Which left only one other plausible explanation: *now* she was covering for the brother she'd just realised might have committed murder.

Every way Malkie looked at it, he came to the same conclusion. She had believed she'd killed Beauchamp, but her reasons for being there in the first place stank of pure fabrication.

As much as he hated to do it, the time had come to reveal the terrible truth. Maybe then, they could make some progress on why she went there that night.

'Mr Beauchamp was stabbed, repeatedly, with the broken neck of a wine bottle, Ms Quinn. In his genitals.'

She shook her head, slowly and disbelieving at first, then furiously.

'No. You're lying.'

Malkie knew he had no choice but to continue.

'Also...'

Her face took on an appalled look and Malkie feared she might throw up.

'We found Remi's fingerprint on the neck of the bottle. I'm sorry, Ms Quinn, but if you have any idea where your brother might be, you *must* tell us now.'

He watched her process this information. Bewilderment turned to denial, then to despairing acceptance as, he assumed, she decided he wouldn't make such a statement without being certain of his facts. He felt for her. Any relief she might have gained from discovering she hadn't killed Beauchamp after all lasted only seconds before being swamped with the implications of evidence she couldn't believe Malkie would fabricate.

Remi, her brother, had killed Beauchamp.

Malkie watched her world fall apart in awful, unbearable slow motion.

She stood so quickly she knocked her chair over. Then she dropped like a dead weight to the floor with a sickening thud as her head struck concrete.

TWENTY-FOUR

'Martin. Ambulance, please. Urgent.'

Gucci didn't wait for Martin to respond but returned to help Malkie tend to Patricia Quinn.

'Heart attack, Lou?'

Gucci placed two fingers to Patricia's neck. 'No. Her pulse is strong and regular, but racing.' She laid the back of her hand on Patricia's forehead then her neck. 'She's cold and clammy and her breathing is fast and shallow. I think she's having a major anxiety attack, but we can't take any chances, obviously.'

'Of course. Let's get her into the recovery position, and someone get her some water. A jugful. Cold. And a towel.'

McLeish appeared, his expression more irritated than concerned.

Fucker would go far up the greasy pole if he wasn't too self-serving and sociopathic even for Senior Management.

Malkie held on to Patricia's shoulder to stop her rolling onto her back and loathed himself. He recalled his dad, on the lawn outside the now-destroyed family home, trying to fight Malkie off to crawl back into their burning house on broken legs to rescue his wife, Malkie's mum. He'd had to hold the old man down until an ambulance crew took over, and he'd felt just as cruel as he did now, despite there being no other option.

Had he really needed to spring those facts on Patricia? Yes, he had. She was a suspect, guilty by her own admission of assaulting Beauchamp at the very least, and possibly of attempted murder. Her story about an affair made no sense given the way she'd referred to him by his surname, so huge questions remained over why she *had* gone there? His instincts told him the reason for her visit was not pleasant.

She stirred, interrupted a train of thought Malkie was happy to derail for now.

'Ms Quinn. You fainted.'

She frowned and reached behind her head. 'What happened?' Her fingers came back with a trace of blood on them. Not enough to indicate a serious bleed but enough to mean she'd hit the floor with some force, so she'd need to be checked out at St John's.

Malkie heard McLeish mutter an expletive as he walked away. He'd be irritated about the amount of extra paperwork coming his way as SIO, and even more pissed off that the interview had failed to deliver a clear result.

Fuck him.

Patricia tried to sit up. Malkie pushed her back down, gently but firmly. She tried to roll onto her back and Malkie let her, but kept a close eye on her.

'What happened?' Before he could answer she snapped at him. 'You think Remi did it.'

He stared at her, didn't try to continue the interview. Couldn't, under the circumstances.

'We can talk about that after you've been checked out, Ms Quinn. An ambulance is on the way.'

'No.' She tried to sit up and Malkie eased her back to the floor again. 'Stay there and lie still until the ambulance gets here.'

Gucci handed him a tumbler of water and a wet towel. Malkie wrapped the towel around her neck and lifted her head so she could sip the water.

When she'd had enough she looked up at him. 'Thank you.'

Malkie smiled down at her. There would be time for him to play Bad Cop again later.

'Please find him. If he did... do it, he would only have been protecting me. He's vulnerable, and he has serious self-control issues because of his autism. He's not responsible for his actions when something triggers him. Please find him.'

Malkie let her talk, confined himself to nodding his understanding. Regardless of her dire situation, she remained a suspect in at least an assault that could have proved fatal.

He heard new voices in the custody suite and two paramedics appeared, a man and a woman. They walked in, calm and measured, and took over. Malkie stood and stepped back, happy to look away from Patricia's distress.

The medics examined her blood pressure and oxygen levels and shined a pen light in both eyes.

The woman spoke first. 'No immediate signs of concussion, and the bleed on her scalp is superficial, doesn't suggest a really serious blow. We'll take her in for observation, but I'm not overly worried at the moment.'

'Thanks. Shall we go and do the paperwork?'

Malkie felt a surge of relief, and not only because of the potential fallout had she suffered a more serious injury. She nodded and her colleague took over. Outside, they signed the necessary forms and assigned a Uniform to accompany her. He'd have a long and boring few hours ahead of him. Malkie had heard too many Uniforms moaning about four-hour waits in A&E because some idiot had swallowed so much booze they'd injured parts of themselves they couldn't even feel. Arse-covering Police Scotland protocol dictated that Uniforms had to wait with them for triage and treatment with other late-night walking wounded before being escorted back to the station for booking in. Malkie couldn't imagine a more scandalous waste of police time.

When Patricia had been helped into a wheelchair and trundled out to the ambulance, Malkie and Gucci braced themselves for McLeish's undoubted disappointment at their apparent failure to conduct a simple interview without sending his suspect to hospital.

McLeish didn't disappoint.

'Great result, McCulloch. Brilliant. By the time she's seen and treated, we'll be lucky not to exceed twenty-four hours, so we'll need to put a convincing argument together for charging her with assault at least, and hope the Fiscal's office doesn't chicken out of letting us hold her given what you've put her through. Do we have *anything* concrete to tie her to Beauchamp's death other than her ridiculous story? Anything at all to reach the charging threshold for his murder?'

'No. Sir.' McLeish would not have missed the fact that Malkie's response had been squeezed out between gritted teeth.

'Fuck's sake, McCulloch.' He rose and stomped away to his temporary office and slammed the door behind him.

Aye, we get the message, you performative twat.

He realised Gucci was watching him. He sighed and waved away the look on her face. 'Don't worry, Gucci. You did everything by the book. I think I did too, but if I didn't, you were only assisting.'

She looked less than comforted.

He glanced at his watch. 'Chase up that second print on the bottle, please. I need to be somewhere.'

'Yes, boss.' She sounded miserable.

His drive to Linlithgow took twenty-five minutes, then he spent another ten finding a parking space and walking a quarter mile back to Steph's flat. He'd texted her before leaving the station but received no response.

When she answered her door Malkie recoiled from the state of her, and from the smell of gin on her breath. She looked tired and groggy, but – worse – broken, as if all capacity for joy had been sucked from her. He reached for her, but she turned and left him to follow her inside.

She seemed evasive, reluctant to let even him in, and he soon discovered why. He'd only been in her living room twice before, enough to know that the mess he saw confirmed just how right he was to be worried about her. Pizza boxes and other takeaway cartons sat strewn on her coffee table, and an empty gin bottle lay on its side beside a glass containing three dried-out slices of lemon. She'd drawn heavy blackout curtains over every window and the gloom weighed on Malkie as much as the stale smell.

'Fuck's sake, Steph. What's happened?' He stared at the mess as if that alone was reason enough to assume the worst.

She gazed around the room then seemed to slump into herself.

'I can't seem to care anymore, Malkie.'

So unlike her, it broke his heart.

She stretched out on her sofa and draped an arm over her eyes. Malkie swiped a hand at her feet. She lifted them to let him sit, then rested them on his lap. He laid his hands on her ankles, as much physical comfort as he dared, given his limited knowledge of her present crisis.

Only now, from his position on the sofa, did he see the dozens of envelopes and hand-written letters spilled on the floor and under the coffee table. He leaned forward and tilted his head to read the names on them.

'I'm guessing *Joyce* was your mum's name?'

She followed his gaze to the floor and grimaced. 'Oh, you spotted them, did you?'

'Despite your best efforts at tidying up, aye.'

Her mouth turned down at the edges. Malkie figured she'd know his teasing was meant to put a smile on her face, but she looked incapable of mustering one, even for him.

'Boswell brought them. Left them outside my door.'

'Why did Boswell risk writing letters to your mum?' His mind had already started formulating theories, as any copper would, and most of them went somewhere he wasn't surprised would have screwed her up.

'He claims he never raped my mum. Says he loved her, and she loved him. But his letters... I think he knew what he'd done, that being in a relationship with her didn't give him the right to... Not without her consent.'

Malkie raised his eyebrows, an expression of how much he appreciated the weight of Steph's statement. As she'd advised him on several occasions, he kept his gob buttoned and waited.

'The letters are all stamped by the mail-room staff at Cornton Vale. I think they only went one way because Boswell couldn't risk Lang seeing anything she wrote back to him.'

Tears welled in her eyes. Malkie ached to reach for her, but figured she'd signal him when she was ready for such an uncharacteristic leaning on him.

'While she was inside, she was forced to go through rehab. Apparently it was as brutal as we always hear it is, but she found strength I never knew she had and in only a few weeks she believed she could beat it; her one letter to Boswell sounded so hopeful I can't bear knowing what happened to her in there, just days after she sent it.' She laid her head back and wiped her eyes with the heels of her hands. She breathed out a long, desperate moan of grief she seemed to have been holding inside her. Possibly because she feared she'd never stop crying if she started.

Seeing her like this was torture almost as painful as when Malkie's mum died, and he felt just as helpless.

'They were planning to move away, all the way to Thurso. Boswell had a cousin there, dead now. They hoped Lang wouldn't follow them.'

Steph's eyes smouldered with rage, but it was smothered by grief.

'Mum was shivved three days after her last letter to Barry. I know why he never tried to punish Lang for putting her in there in the first place: he was still terrified of him. And it's likely that when Lang set us both up that night, the look on Barry's face wasn't what

I thought it was. I assumed he was desperate for my forgiveness after I found out he'd raped her. I think Lang had found out about Boswell being my real dad and promised him a reconciliation. And I nearly killed him. Oh Christ, Malkie, even after how they both treated my mum, what did I do? I'm so confused.'

Tears came now, wouldn't be refused. She sat up, turned around, and folder herself into him. He held her, said nothing, felt her hang on to him so tight he feared she'd bruise his ribs. After a while, her anguished sobs stopped. She relaxed into him, and he stroked her hair.

'How's the Quinn case going? Are you... You know? Handling it OK? It sounds like a difficult one.'

Malkie doubted she really cared about Patricia or Remi Quinn, but she'd worry how such a case might affect him, knew how easily he could fall into over-empathising and damage himself as he invested too much in helping others. He'd never deserve her.

He laid his head back and closed his eyes, dreaded sharing the sordid details of what he feared would turn into one of the most cruel and unjust cases he'd ever investigated.

'Ach, it's a stinker. I find Patricia Quinn's claims credible enough to believe Beauchamp was a Grade A bottom-feeder, even with holes in her story big enough to drive a bus through. But she's starting to accept that her brother is culpable, and I'm worried neither of them will survive what's coming. You know these cases where doing what's lawful feels the exact opposite of what's right?'

When she didn't answer, he glanced at her.

She lay, her eyes closed, her breathing deep and slow, exhausted – he guessed – from a sleepless night raging against Lang and the damage he did. That and her misguided disgust at allowing herself to be played so absolutely by the man.

He laid her back on the sofa, covered her with a throw which had dropped on the floor, and eased a cushion under her head.

He knelt beside her, stroked her hair some more to ensure she didn't wake up too much. Without planning to, he leaned in and kissed the top of her head. Grief swamped him, and he nearly cried himself.

He left her looking at peace, and hoped she'd wake feeling the worst of the crisis behind her.

As he reached his car, he knew he needed to clear his mind, maybe take some time off, be there for Steph as the friend she deserved. And for that to happen, he needed to find Remi Quinn and get him somewhere safe.

Only one person could help him do that.

TWENTY-FIVE

Malkie found a Uniform seated outside an A&E cubicle, working his way through a plastic cup of what looked like vending-machine tea and a sandwich. He placed them to one side when he saw Malkie, who waved him back into his seat.

'Has she said anything?'

'Not a word since we left the station.'

'Any estimate of when she'll be fit to be returned to the custody suite?'

'Another hour or two, they said. Something about the pharmacy being out of some drug they want to give her.'

'OK. I'll have a wee chat with her.'

The Uniform looked uncomfortable. 'Without a brief?'

'She refused legal representation.'

'Really? Why?'

'No idea. Yet. You finish eating, mate.'

He sat again, but looked wary, and Malkie reminded himself to watch his bloody mouth, brief or no brief.

She raised her eyes when he parted the plastic curtain and stepped through, but it seemed an immense effort for her. When she saw it was Malkie she shook her head and turned away, slid down under her blanket, facing the wall. Malkie sat.

'How are you feeling, Ms Quinn?'

No answer.

'Ms Quinn? I'm not trying to trick you. I'm just concerned. That looked like a hell of a thump when your head hit the floor.'

'Worried I'll sue?' She sounded bitter and miserable.

'There'll be a report filled out and the video of your interview will be examined, but we did nothing outside of the standard protocols. You passed out, and we didn't cause that. Stress did, Ms Quinn.'

She stayed silent for long seconds. 'Have you found Remi yet?'

He braced himself for piling yet more misery upon the poor woman.

'I'm afraid not. We've knocked on doors all around your neighbourhood, but no one claimed to have seen him. We're waiting for a couple of households to let us know if they find anything on their Ring door cameras, and we hope to get those responses within a couple of hours. Apart from that, we're continuing to monitor street and train station CCTV around and in Livi, and bus video recordings. It takes time I'm afraid.'

As soon as he said this, he braced himself for her to kick off, but she remained still and quiet. After a second or two he heard her sniff. He pulled a handful of tissues from a dispenser on the wall and handed them to her. She took them without a word. He saw her wipe her eyes as well as her nose, and a surge of pity threatened to undermine his best attempts to remain objective. He knew less about her than he did about Sebastian Beauchamp, and no number of society and showbiz articles about him and his wife could constitute evidence to back up Patricia's description of his alleged behaviour the night he was murdered. He'd been stung before, falling for *damsel in distress* syndrome only to find out later he'd been played.

'Will they be gentle with him when they find him?'

Malkie considered lying to her but felt a need to maintain his professional neutrality. 'I can't promise that. Sorry. If he resists arrest, if he turns violent – sorry, if he becomes distressed – then the arresting officers will do all they can to minimise injury to him and to themselves, but...'

'But you saw how he became at the sight of a uniform.'

'He's dangerous, Ms Quinn.'

She turned on him, nearly fell off the side of the trolley as she lunged at him. 'He's only dangerous when other people make him dangerous.' Her face had turned red and her eyes furious. 'He's never laid a finger on me at home. He's as gentle as a lamb as long as his routine isn't broken. He attacked some little bastard from down the street last year, but only after he woke up to find I'd gone to the corner shop.' She seemed to regain some calm as she told her story. 'When he panicked because I wasn't home, he went looking for me. And that was braver of him than most people ever need to be, Detective.'

He itched to tell her to call him Malkie, but she was still a suspect linked to a murdered man.

'When he passed the home of that nasty little boy, Andrew Harris, Harris and his pals stood around him and yelled horrible things at him. When Harris picked up some dried dog turds and pushed them into Remi's face, he lost it. Harris ran crying to his mum like he always does, but Remi caught up with him that time. If Harris had fallen face up, Remi could have killed him. Harris's mum told everyone she watched the whole incident from her doorstep and swore Remi attacked her son for no reason.'

She sighed, seemed to slump into herself. 'That incident gave most of the rest of the street a green light to hate Remi just because he was different. None of them ever approached him directly again, but we couldn't walk from our front door to my car without one of them yelling the most vicious and hurtful things.' She seemed to drift for a moment. 'What lets people be like that? Turning on someone who already suffers more than they'll ever know and making him a target for all of them to hate out of spite because of their own sad and nasty little lives?'

She seemed to realise she'd shared her feelings with the copper who would probably charge her with assault, and her brother with murder.

She lay back and faced the ceiling again, pulled her blanket up around her neck.

Malkie would get nothing more from her for now.

'I'm going back to Beauchamp's house, Ms Quinn. If there's something there that might corroborate your story, I want to find it.'

Her eyes flashed briefly before she could regain her feigned and unconvincing absence of concern.

'What?'

'Nothing.' She looked away again.

You're really not helping yourself, lady. But then, it's not yourself you're worried about, is it?

'Ms Quinn, contrary to what you might think, the vast majority of police officers are not interested in charging any convenient sucker for the sake of an easy life. We hunt for the right person, and we find evidence to make our charges stick because we believe we've identified the guilty person. Far from *fitting people up* or taking the path of least resistance, we're actively suspicious of spontaneous confessions, especially when they're factually flawed.'

He'd hoped she'd react to that but got nothing. He left her to her misery.

What the hell just occurred to her? Something she doesn't want to talk about. Time to annoy some SOCOs again.

He found Beauchamp's home still taped off and SOCOs still beavering away. Scene Manager Josh Lamb confirmed that their search of the ground-floor hallway outside the study and the upstairs had been concluded, and that Malkie would be allowed to access the crime scene as long as he got suited and booted and touched nothing.

Suitably lectured, he obtained a hooded paper onesie, gloves, shoe covers and face mask from a bored-looking young bloke sitting on the back edge of his open SOCO van.

At the entrance to the house, a Uniform signed him into the scene, and he made straight for the study.

Two SOCOs remained. The core work of dusting and printing everything, removing samples of every stained carpet or curtain, and bagging every object had been completed. Beauchamp's desk might well be removed intact for examination in the lab, and he hoped they had Big Bruce on shift today.

He stopped at the door until one of the SOCOs looked at him with a question in her eyes.

'May I enter?'

'Yes, but you know the rules?'

'I do. Thanks.' He stepped inside.

A huge blood stain, covering a square metre of the luxurious, cream-coloured carpet and still tacky in places dominated the scene. What was it Bruce had told him the previous day? The part of Beauchamp that had been wounded could be highly *vascular*. Malkie hadn't experienced many occasions of *high vascularity* in his adult life until a few months ago, and he cringed to imagine anyone stabbing him there.

He noticed that one of the SOCOs had placed their open kit box on a chair against the wall on the opposite side of the room from the huge stain on the carpet.

'Can I assume that chair's been processed, aye? May I sit there, keep out of your way?'

'Aye, that'd be good, thanks. No, I'll move it.' She stepped over, closed the case and moved it to a bare patch of floor where Malkie saw sealed bags containing smaller items of evidence. He sat and studied the scene. For what, he had no idea.

As his eyes wandered around the room, he tried to form an impression of Sebastian Beauchamp.

Every book on the floor-to-ceiling shelves looked to be of the leather-bound and stupidly valuable kind. He saw the names of many classic novels on the spines, along with others he suspected sat there to be seen rather than to be read. He knew nothing about Beauchamp except what he'd seen on news sites and watched on

TV. Him and his trophy wife, or was it her and her trophy husband? What was it Gucci had said? She was the real earner in the marriage but the circles she walked in eschewed publicity so she was assumed by many to have married him for status. If that were true, he had to wonder how pissed off she must be at losing him, regardless of what depth of marital bliss they shared.

Every piece of furniture looked to be mahogany, polished to a deep shine and immaculate, devoid of scratches or marks. Except for the corner of the desk where, he had been told, shards of the wine bottle had landed and then fallen onto by either Patricia or Beauchamp.

He fastened his attention on the right edge of the open doorway, then scanned, slow and meticulous, every square inch of wall and every item of furniture.

His eyes reached the left edge of the first bookshelf. Every book sat with its spine flush with its neighbours, as if Beauchamp kept a spirit level and ruler handy to ensure the perfection of his display of conspicuous but faux intellectualism.

Careful. You still know just the reputation, not the man.

He lifted his eyes from the books themselves, to the space above them, between their top edges and the shelves above. What the hell did he think he was going to notice? Was he so desperate to find evidence to back up Patricia Quinn's claim that Beauchamp was a sexual predator?

He recalled how Patricia had called him *Beauchamp*, not *Sebastian* or *Seb* or any other pet name a lover would prefer. Was he reaching? Probably, but that would never stop him from doing it, and Rab Lundy, of all people, had unknowingly validated Malkie's habit. Everyone in CID had found, to their immense surprise, that Rab attended night classes in creative writing. The only officer in J Division other than Malkie still to languish at a sub-DI rank in his forties. A man who never missed a chance to sulk and never used five words when an unintelligible grunt would do, and he wanted to be a writer. He'd let slip that he recognised a quote from *The Count of Monte Cristo* during a previous case, another one that had left Malkie near-broken.

He'd confided to Malkie that he used a technique for brainstorming his stories that involved taking any idea and jumping as far into the realms of fantasy as possible, then work back until the idea became credible but still retained an ability to surprise.

So now Malkie adapted the technique. He imagined empty spaces lurking behind the rows of books hiding some juicy morsel, a belter of a clue that would spin the case around and fire off whole new avenues of investigation.

But he refused to look. If he did, one of the SOCOs would ask what he thought he'd spotted that they – God forbid – might have missed, and he would struggle to justify his interest without embarrassing himself with Rab's off-the-wall theory.

As he sat, he felt his eyelids grow heavy. He'd had only four hours of crap sleep in the past two days and had to acknowledge that he wasn't as young as he used to be, as bloody obvious as he always thought that statement was. He straightened in his chair, shook his head and started his scan of the room again. This had worked before. Only once, but it did work.

What are you afraid I'll find, Ms Quinn?

TWENTY-SIX

Steph decided to give it another minute. She needed to be more than careful. This could lead to the end of her career or worse.

The flat across the landing had been pounding out wall-shaking hard rock at about a million decibels when she arrived. That kind of selfish behaviour normally pissed her off. Right now, she wanted it to start again.

It did.

Thrash metal now. She had to assume that the residents beside, above and below had learned to their cost not to complain. She'd grown up in a place like this. The shitty end of Britain's spectrum of grubby ghetto housing developments. She'd escaped, but never stopped feeling for people who couldn't, those too scared or old to challenge the brutality of those who preyed on them. *Survival of the fittest* took on a whole new meaning when it came to the food chain of your typical sink estate. More *like survival of the shittiest*. Malkie and she had discussed, often, their shared failure to comprehend what happened in the brain of a person that allowed them to terrorise and brutalise and even murder the old and infirm, those confined to wheelchairs or beds that were in turn imprisoned in the lowest-cost council accommodation that reached the bare minimum standard laid down in law. West Lothian didn't contain any seriously high-rise blocks of flats such as were found in big cities like Edinburgh or Glasgow or London, where so many people demanded their entitlement to free housing that the only way to expand the stock was upward.

She'd had to climb the four floors to Lang's flat because in the best tradition of buildings like this, the lifts stank of piss and worse, were strewn with used needles, and – the reason for Steph's climb – never worked. She had no idea what even the most feckless and bored vandals could do to completely kill an elevator, but somehow they'd managed it.

She didn't recognise the song now playing in the flat opposite, although she struggled to think of it as music. More a wall of enraged and psychotic sound screamed by people whose vocal cords she doubted would still function by their thirties. But she found a pattern and waited for the track to cycle around to a repeated crescendo. At the peak of the ear-bruising racket, she forced the blade of her screwdriver between the door and the frame, at lock level, and heaved on it. The wood, as secure and solid as anything else in places like this, splintered and fell away with barely a noise. She entered and pushed the door closed behind her.

At first, nothing appeared out of place. The SOCOs had completed their work quickly, the SIO on Lang's case unwilling to spend a great deal of taxpayers' money on a scrote like him, although no employee of Police Scotland would ever do the local journos the favour of voicing that opinion on the record.

Lang had taken a dive off his balcony and landed on the roof of a 2011 Ford Fiesta parked four floors below. SOCOs had found no transfer evidence of anyone other than Lang himself, Barry Boswell, and her.

She crossed to the balcony, saw dustings of print powder on most surfaces, although she knew that in this dim light she'd be seeing only a small fraction of the work Forensics carried out here. The balcony door turned out not to be locked. She stepped out onto the frosted glass and steel balustrade and looked down. No sign remained of the more intensive search and analysis that had gone on around Lang's bloodied and broken, but still twitching body as firemen eased it off the top of the car with more care than the bastard deserved.

Back inside she closed the door again, returning everything she touched or moved to its original position without having to consciously think about it.

She couldn't stop her mind from replaying that night. Lang sprawled on his sofa, relating the most poisonous accusations that Steph's youthful precociousness and her academic success had served to shame her mother right into his arms, and he'd kept her hooked on cheap drugs and booze, almost as if she were nothing but a plaything, a pet to torment. Lang couldn't have timed Barry's appearance in the bedroom door better, at the peak of her fury. She had nearly killed him. Lang had pulled her off of him.

She sat on the sofa, despite her revulsion at the stains and crusted food plastered to it in various places. Her eyes fell on the cabinet that held a TV, a satellite box, a DVD player and – of all things – an ancient VHS video recorder. She saw no tapes stacked beside it, only DVDs, nor anywhere else in the living room.

Why did this scratch on her brain so much? It came to her: home movies. He had bought a VHS video camera when they were new technology, in the days when he still earned a wage. She stood, opened cupboards and drawers, found no tapes.

Why would he keep the player if he'd switched to DVD?

She entered his bedroom, saw grimy and worn bedclothes, the pillows still stained with his night sweat. She couldn't stop the thought: her mum had slept in this bed with him, and he'd defiled her in this room. She felt tears well and wiped them away with the heels of her hands.

She opened more drawers and cupboards but found nothing. At some point she realised she'd stopped replacing things as she went and now had no chance of remembering where everything had been. Although she was confident the SOCOs would not re-examine the flat at this stage of the investigation into his murder, she knew it would lurk in her mind that she'd allowed herself to become so careless.

She found it under the bed. A shoe box. Dusty and grimy, like everything else in the place. She took it to the living room and laid it on the same coffee table she'd jumped over to attack Boswell, that night.

She found her old school reports inside, now faded and yellowed and the paper brittle. Under them, one of her primary school class photos which looked well-thumbed. Finally, a VHS tape.

Her breath caught in her chest. She removed it from its cardboard case. On the label, in what looked like a woman's careful script in blue ink, it read *Xmas 1998*.

Shaking, her stomach churning, she grabbed a TV remote control from the table and pressed the red power button.

Nothing. Idiot. Lang had been so persistently in debt he'd had a key meter forced on him. She found it in a cupboard in the hallway, and as expected, saw a line of zeroes flashing on the LCD display. Nothing on earth would stop her watching what was on this tape, but not here. She hadn't owned a VHS machine for decades and she didn't know anybody who might have one gathering dust somewhere.

She argued with herself but knew the outcome would be predetermined.

She unplugged the video recorder and stuffed it, the tape and the cables into a holdall she'd found under the bed.

She took one more circuit around the flat. Lang had threatened to expose her attack on Barry using some hidden video camera or phone, but she'd never believed him. She reasoned that anything like that would have been found by the SOCOs or Tech Forensics, so Lang had either lied or hidden it elsewhere. The fact that the tape in the shoe box hadn't been taken as evidence surprised her, but she was glad of the mistake.

. . .

Back in her flat, she dosed her jangling nerves with a long glass of re-supplied gin, then an immediate refill. It occurred to her that modern TVs might not have the old red, white and yellow plugs that hung on the end of the cable. She looked but already knew she'd find her TV to be too new for such archaic connections.

She yelled a wordless shout of frustration, then remembered her cheap old TV from her student days. She found it in her box room, under a pile of document crates containing her course notes from Tulliallan and heaved a sigh of relief when she saw the three ancient video sockets on the back.

She plugged the old set in and connected up the video recorder, then – her heart in her mouth – she pressed the power button on the front of both appliances and held her breath while they took long seconds showing only single LEDs before snow appeared on the TV and the video recorder clunked and whirred then flashed a cheery *Hello* on its garish blue segmented display. She pushed the tape in, felt the machine take it from her and swallow it. She prayed the ancient machine wouldn't chew it up, took a long, deep slug of gin, and pressed the play button.

The TV switched to the inputs and an image appeared, grainy and blurry with bands of snow travelling slowly from top to bottom as the machine found the right tracking position.

Her mum's face backed away from the lens. In her mid-twenties but looking thirty years older, her features thin and sallow, her eyes glistening but shadowed, her teeth yellow.

Steph cried, then. In the privacy of her own home, she felt no shame, no accusations of weakness from her own rigid sense of self-control. Her mother deserved a daughter who felt grief as intense as this even so long after her death. Steph realised she grieved not only for her mother, but for the childhood she never got to spend with a mum she loved and respected and could depend on. She hated Lang all over again for robbing her and her mum of any chance of a life they should have been allowed to look forward to. Her inability to even consider any possibility of Boswell's innocence stopped her from including him in that. Regardless of the letters or his reaction on the night she nearly killed him. Her instincts told her he was lying. Possibly even to himself, but lying nonetheless.

What is it? Something I should be seeing but am missing. Wake up, damn it.

In the video, when her mum stepped to one side, an infant Steph appeared, perched on her Uncle Barry's lap, laughing and playing with some toy Steph had liberated from wrapping paper that long-ago Xmas morning, her second she guessed from her pudding-bowl haircut and her pudgy wee face.

She smiled, even as tears poured out of her and down her cheeks. She rocked backwards and forwards, wrapped her arms around her as if afraid she'd fall apart, and moaned to herself. She leaned to one side and grabbed a cushion, clutched it to her chest and laid her head on another, then smiled and cried through to the end of the tape.

Near the end of the sixty-minute running time, she noticed Lang, slouched in his armchair, a can of cheap lager in one hand and a roll-up in the other. He glared at the domestic scene, his face sour and poisonous. When toddler Steph approached him with her new toy held proudly out to him, he lifted his newspaper from his lap and ignored her. She stood for a second, unsure and awkward. Her mum picked her up and hugged her, and glared daggers at Lang's newspaper as if she could pierce the thing and impale him on her disgust. She turned to carry toddler Steph back to her seat and saw Boswell look up at her and manage a weak and bitter-sweet smile. Then, unseen by Lang, he flashed the man a look that promised violence. She doubted she'd seen such hatred in a man's face before, despite the job bringing her into regular confrontation with the worst that human biology could create.

When Lang lowered his paper Boswell didn't recover well, and Lang flashed him a look that dared him to speak his mind. He glanced from Boswell to Steph's mum, and Steph had to wonder if the way he appraised them both might have marked the moment Lang realised Barry was interfering with his 'property', the moment that spelled the end of her mum's hopes for any kind of life worth living.

Cold fury ran through Steph's veins. Too late to kill Lang herself, and that – she feared – might never let her sleep easy again.

She watched the whole tape twice more.

Steph's second Xmas. As yet oblivious to the extent of toxicity in her dysfunctional family. Boswell and her mum clinging to what happiness they could, at least for a short time.

The letters. Faded and grubby and creased as if held tight in miserable hands. She checked her mum's sole letter again and saw she'd misinterpreted one key sentence.

When the significance hit her, her blood ran cold and she threw up two glassfuls of perfectly good gin.

TWENTY-SEVEN

When he spotted it, he kicked himself. Two onesie-clad heads turned, and he realised he'd sworn under his breath.

'Sorry. Just remembered... Something.'

The SOCOs shared a look then returned to their work.

On one shelf sat five polished mahogany boxes with no lids, looked like the kind used for storing letters and trinkets, personal stuff. Parts of various odds and sods stuck up above the rim of each box. He'd spotted a row of books he recognised: foreign travel guidebooks. He knew the brand because he and his parents had never gone on an overseas holiday in their lives without researching their destination and learning at least the basics of any languages they expected to need. They were almost square in shape, designed to slip into the pockets of cargo pants, as he believed they were called. His eye had picked up, without his brain needing to get involved, that they seemed to stick up about three inches higher than he'd expect given his estimate of the depth of the boxes. He told himself they could just be sitting on other books laid flat, but something bothered him about it.

He stood and got a warning look from one of the SOCOs. He held his hands up, promised to be good but crossed to the boxes anyway. He couldn't see the bottom of the box with the guidebooks because its width was filled. He agonised over whether to ask a SOCO to lift the books out. If he'd found something he'd score some major Brownie points, get McLeish off his back to some degree, and maybe even boost the investigation.

He sat again, chickened out, didn't fancy adding another tale to the ongoing collection shared amongst his CID colleagues, Uniforms, civvy admin staff and probably the cleaners too.

He tried to continue his scan of the room, but his eyes kept darting back to the box of travel guides.

Fuck it.

He rose again and earned himself a tut, a sigh and a pained look from the same SOCO as before. He stood in front of the box, wrapped one arm around his gut and propped his chin on a hand. He waited, relied on the care and diligence with which SOCOs did their jobs, constantly conscious of the legal and personal consequences of missing something.

It took less than a minute. The SOCO who had issued him a stern warning earlier joined him. 'What?' Her voice carried an edge, now, laced with irritation or worry or both.

'That box. Would you mind lifting those books out please? I'm not allowed to touch anything.'

She stared at him, and with only her eyes visible, she seemed wary. 'Why?'

'An educated speculation formed from attendance at many crime scenes and reading many Forensics scene reports.'

'You mean a hunch?'

'Aye.' He grinned at her.

Her eyes smiled. She pulled the box forward on the shelf and lifted the books out.

Bingo. His first glance suggested the inside of the box was shallower than the outside.

'Indulge me. The ones either side too, please?'

She did so, pulled an assortment of what looked like travel souvenirs from one, and sets of documents tied with ribbons from the other. He checked both, made an obvious effort to lean over without touching them.

Both looked deeper than the suspect one.

The SOCO looked too, then turned to Malkie with dread in her eyes.

'You don't think...'

'I do.'

'People still do that?'

'Oh, aye. Still very common,' he lied.

She pulled the box from the shelf and laid it on a paper sheet spread out on the desk. They both noticed a tiny strip of ribbon, no more than a centimetre long, sticking out where the bottom of the box met the sides. She produced some plastic tweezers and tugged on it.

The wood lifted.

Malkie's heart raced.

They looked at each other then back into the box. Malkie leaned further and the SOCO gently pushed him away again. She lifted out the false bottom.

Underneath was a set of wooden slats, interlocked to form a lattice, like his dad had in his tie drawer before... He shut that thought down. He was getting better at ignoring the memories, a habit he needed to cultivate to be able to do his job, but which always felt like some kind of betrayal.

In four of the nine sections lay small mobile phones and black notebooks. Each phone looked basic, not the kind of palm-stretching monstrosity that many of his more ambitious and image-conscious colleagues owned. McLeish had one, and it even folded out. Malkie failed to understand who the hell could need that much screen space on a phone.

'Detective? Hello?' She held one of the notebooks in her hands, open to the first page.

He returned to the room.

'Sorry, miles away. This is a bad one.'

'I know.'

Something in her voice chilled him. He read the page, without thinking about touching it.

Not sure where this will go, but I'm so fucking bored. My first one. First of many, if it turns out to be as amusing as I hope. Angela. Secretary. Got video of her at an office party, enjoying a career-enhancing shag with me. Took me four attempts over a month to seduce her. Cried like a fucking baby when I showed her, begged me to delete it. Will start her on fifty a month, see how it goes. Don't need the money but hell, we have to get our kicks where we can, right? Fuck all about my job ever turns me on anymore, and the wife does nothing but lie there looking bored when we do it these days. Bitch. Fuck her. She gets her regular fixes of society sycophancy and status, I get some kudos from marrying into money. So much fucking money. For what? Selling other people's jobs out from under them. Not that I give a fuck about peasants losing jobs, but she gets all that cash for doing such a cracking job. Bitch.

Anyway. Let's see how this one goes. I already have video of another uppity wee cow, Amber; maybe do her next. She's got money. But then, I don't need money. I need a hobby.

She leafed through the rest then the first few lines of another. Malkie didn't bother to read them in detail; enough words jumped off the pages to tell him they all said more of the same. He bit down on an urge to punch something. He couldn't afford yet another arse-kicking, certainly not for compromising the forensic integrity of a crime scene.

He and the SOCO shared a look, and he couldn't tell if she felt more or less revulsion than he did.

'Any chance you can expedite this please? It's obviously a potential game changer.'

'Of course. Sorry we missed it.'

'No problem.' Another lie. It was a howler of a setback, but he hoped she would apply some internal pressure to expedite in order to reduce any flack she'd get for her cockup. 'No need to mention that I spotted it, OK? Just say you noticed something off yourself, aye?'

'No. I'll record it fully and accurately.'

He suspected she dreaded having to report a colleague's miss, but he admired her professionalism, so he kept that assumption to himself.

'Do me a favour, DS McCulloch?'

'What?'

She leaned in close and whispered, 'Whoever killed this fucker, shake them by the hand. For me.'

He squeezed her arm and nodded, then left. He allowed himself a brief recognition of a good result on his part, and resolved to remember it, to give himself a break and some credit for a change.

TWENTY-EIGHT

I think I'm near the bridge now. It's been a long time. Patty would know but I'm not sure. I'm never sure. About anything.

The bus is too full. I nearly couldn't get on, and I had to sit beside someone. Had to or I won't get there.

I hope it's still there. It's been a long time.

Mum stopped taking me on holiday with her. She asked Patty to go but Patty wouldn't. She stayed with me. I love Patty.

Where is she?

It's so cold.

I don't like being cold. It scares me. I saw it on YouTube. Mount Everest. Even colder than here. People died. Some of them are still up there. Why don't they bring them down? Not fair to just leave them there. Nobody likes being alone.

I don't have my special winter coat, the one that Patty bought me, with the stretchy cuffs and the big hood. I like it. It's like lots of pillows. I remember the day I got it. I was happy that day. She made sure I knew I was going into town to buy a coat and where and she asked me what colour I wanted. I don't think I let her down that day. I was brave. She forgot, and asked me if I wanted an ice cream, but she didn't warn me about that before we went into town. But I was brave, and I don't think I embarrassed her.

Where are you, Patty? Did you forget me already?

Mum hated when I forgot things. She called me bad to the core.

I don't think Mum's brain worked like mine. She never seemed to forget anything. But she got angry when I told her she never said what she thought she said to me, so I think she did forget things sometimes.

Patty never forgets anything.

But she's not here.

Has she forgotten me too? Even her?

I wouldn't blame her. People say I'm different, but I know what they mean. They mean difficult.

Bad to the core.

I'm cold. Cold to the core as well as bad.

There are people eating fish and chips where we used to stop for dinner.

The fish and chips is great here and I'm hungry. But there are too many people. I can't go in. They'll look at me.

The man who drove the bus looked at me.

I hate people looking at me. Except Patty.

I think he was a nice man, and he looked worried about me. He asked me if I was OK.

I didn't answer him and he looked sad.

I should come with an instruction book.

Where are you, Patty?

I'll wait for you. Not far now, I think.

They'll be there, won't they?

TWENTY-NINE

Malkie called in and learned Patricia Quinn was back in the custody suite. He told Gucci to have her ready for interview as soon as he reached the station.

When he arrived, Gucci wasted no time. 'I'll get her moved to an interview room, boss.' She picked up her desk phone.

'Thanks, Lou. Then I need to talk to you. You too, Rab.'

'Development, boss?'

'Yes, Rab. A deeply unpleasant one. Lou, get her ready please.'

He checked his watch. Less than six hours to charge or release her or provide compelling enough evidence to request an extension. He needed something. He slipped his shoes off and stretched his legs out. He felt like every muscle and joint in his body was tense and aching.

When Gucci ended her call, she told him, 'Room one. Ten minutes. Boss?'

'Sorry, Lou. Miles away.'

She glanced at the wall clock. 'Counting the hours?'

He smiled at her. 'Something like that, Lou. OK, gather round.'

They looked intrigued to find out what Malkie couldn't discuss openly in a CID office, of all places.

He took a breath, felt dirty even relating what he'd discovered.

'Sebastian Beauchamp was seducing and blackmailing women. Four that we know of from his notebooks.' Rab's face turned sour, Gucci's so dark and intense Malkie found himself promising never to piss her off.

'OK, so obviously this sheds a whole new light on Patricia Quinn's case. If we find her number on any of those phones, then she was just one of five.'

Rab leaned forward, rested his elbows on his knees and looked at the floor. 'And it gives her one hell of a motive.'

'Aye. But it may also strengthen a case for self-defence. If Beauchamp was blackmailing her, it's not a small leap to assume a man capable of that would also happily assault a woman, particularly one who threatened him.'

Gucci nodded. 'Let's hope so. Sorry, boss. Struggling to stay objective. Fucking vile bastard. Oh God. Sorry.'

'No problem, Lou. I expect we all share your opinion of the man.'

'Fuck, aye.' Rab looked ready to punch something.

'OK, you're both up to date. I need to have a think about how to handle this, what to ask Patricia when—'

Gucci's phone rang and Malkie swore under his breath.

Perfect fucking timing.

Gucci listened then hung up. 'Too late. She's ready.'

'Before we go in, any word on Remi Quinn?'

'Not as of half an hour ago.' She clicked some icons on her screen. 'Nope. Nothing yet.'

'Fuck's sake. How does a lad that young and insular and troubled disappear so completely that even the entire police and council technological snooping framework can't find him?'

She shrugged. 'Maybe he has help?'

'I thought about that, but correct me if I'm wrong – you and Rab have found nothing to suggest either Remi or Patricia has regular friends? The kind he could have asked to shelter him? And even if he did, any friendship close enough to agree to protect and care for someone as troubled and volatile as Remi? That's something you guys wouldn't miss.

'Rab? Care to join me?'

'No thanks, boss.' He nodded at Gucci. 'Patricia will need familiar faces to persuade her to cooperate.'

'Good point, Rab. I didn't think of that.'

Rab scrutinised Malkie and seemed to decide the piss wasn't being taken, on this occasion.

Malkie put his shoes back on after a discreet reminder from Gucci, and they headed for interview room one. He didn't bother calling McLeish. The walking ego trip had said he wanted to observe this morning's interview. He said nothing about any others.

Patricia took all of a half second to jump to her feet when Malkie and Lou opened the door.

'Have you found him?'

Fuck, I hate this.

'I'm sorry. No.'

She exploded. Kicked her chair away and charged at him. He caught her and let today's attending Uniform get her under control and guide her back to her chair. All the way, she screamed at Malkie.

'This is your fault. I told you it was a stupid idea to arrest him. I told you he was vulnerable. He could be in all sorts of trouble. It's a bloody horrible world out there. I told you.'

The fury in her last words silenced everyone. She dropped her forehead to the desk, sobbed and muttered 'I told you' repeatedly.

Malkie could have explained that he'd wanted to interview Remi at home first, and gently, but had been ordered by a grade A moron to bring the lad in. He refused to allow himself that luxury. Maintenance of professionalism mattered, even when it protected liabilities like McLeish.

Lou and Malkie sat, but he stopped her from performing her usual recording admin tasks.

'Ms Quinn, I need to ask you if you're sure you feel OK to continue, and if you've changed your mind about legal representation after what I told you about the manner of Mr Beauchamp's death.'

She remained face down, and Malkie had to strain to make out her words. 'I want to continue, and without a lawyer. Please, just get on with it.'

Malkie nodded at Lou and she did the necessary on the recording equipment.

'Ms Quinn, I want to ask you about something we found at Sebastian Beauchamp's home today.'

Patricia looked up. Had she expected him to lead with the groin-stabbing bombshell? She swept stray hair from her face and adjusted her police-issue sweatshirt but said nothing. Malkie detected no sign of awareness in her, and feared she knew nothing about his discovery. If that was the case, then her story about going there to end an affair started to ring truer, but not by much.

'In a box on a shelf in Mr Beauchamp's study we found some mobile telephones and notebooks, four of each. They'd been hidden under the false bottom of the box. What can you tell me about them?'

He watched some spark of realisation cross her face before she suppressed it. 'Nothing. No idea.'

He studied her. His instincts whispered to him that she was telling half of the truth as she believed it.

'So, that wasn't the reason you went to his house?'

'I told you, I went there to end an affair I'd been having with him. Nothing more than that. I can't imagine why he would have mobile phones hidden.'

'Will we find your number on one of those phones, Ms Quinn?' He couldn't miss it, and he knew Gucci would have seen it too. Her pupils dilated and she looked away, at the surface of the desk. Most armchair crime experts knew the theory that looking up and to the right meant you were lying, but proper coppers knew it was bollocks. Or rather, was so unreliable as to be a waste of time. But she looked away, broke eye contact, which did suggest evasion.

'Are you sure, Ms Quinn? You looked, just then, like maybe you remembered something?'

She refused to lift her eyes from the desk. 'No. I know nothing about them.'

'Does Remi have a phone, Ms Beauchamp?'

Her eyes remained down but he saw her look sideways. 'No. It wouldn't be good for him.' She swallowed, hard, on her last word, and Malkie remembered how much he hated this part of the job.

'I can understand that, Ms Quinn. Social media is a filthy swamp these days, isn't it?'

'It is for Remi and people like him.'

Malkie gave her a moment. He pushed a box of tissues to her side of the table, and she grabbed some to dab her eyes.

'And there's no chance he could have bought himself a pay-as-you-go phone that you don't know about?'

'No. I don't even ask him to get milk from our local shop, and he never leaves the house without me. Even when I take him out it's a major organisational exercise. I need to tell him where we're going and how we'll get there, and why we're going. I can never take him for a spontaneous McDonald's or an ice cream. Words like *spontaneous* are invalid when it comes to Remi's life. He's better than he used to be, but...'

'Lifelong challenges?'

'Yes. He might never be able to lead an independent life, and he's certainly not capable of travelling anywhere at short notice that he hasn't been to before, and...' She stared straight at Malkie. 'Murdering someone, Detective McCulloch.' The steel in her eyes spoke clearly of her frustration and anger.

'How then did Remi's prints get on the broken bottle, Ms Quinn?' He asked the question as gently as he could.

'I've been thinking about that. In that cell. All those hours. I remember now, I took the bottle to Sebastian's house. Remi must have picked it up that evening, before he went to bed and I left.'

'You took the wine?'

'Yes.'

The words *I remember now* always rang false when uttered by a suspect. They never seemed to realise that it didn't provide the protection they hoped it would. He could imagine her forgetting what was said between them, but not that.

'You forgot that you bought a bottle of wine and took it with you to Beauchamp's house?'

'Yes. I forgot. You were harassing me, asking me too many questions. I got confused.'

'What was the name of the wine, Ms Quinn?'

She stumbled over this, but only for a second. She had been doing a lot of thinking in her cell.

'I didn't take any notice of the label. I just picked one that looked classy and wasn't the cheapest. I was preoccupied at the time.'

'Where did you buy it?'

'In Tesco.'

'Did you pay cash or by bank card?'

A look flashed across her eyes; she spotted one trap at least. 'Cash.'

'Did you keep the receipt?'

That look again. 'No.'

Malkie's bullshit detector rang loud and insistent.

'That's fine. We can verify this by looking at Tesco's CCTV footage or their checkout logs. What time did you buy it? Approximately will do.'

Because we're going to find nothing, aren't we?

'I can't remember. Late afternoon sometime. But I paid cash. It might have been the deli on Linlithgow High Street actually.'

'That's fine. We'll check there too. Was it good?'

'What?'

'The wine. Was it good?'

'I… It was OK, but I only had a sip because I was driving.'

'Very responsible of you, Ms Quinn.' His patience was beginning to outweigh his sympathy for the woman.

'So, you bought some wine that you can't remember the

name of, then drove to Mr Beauchamp's house to tell him you wanted to end your affair. He got angry and attacked you. You grabbed the bottle and smashed it over his head. You thought you'd killed him so you fled the scene. Does that all sound correct?'

'Yes.'

Malkie recognised the beginnings of a common interview stage where the suspect feels their lies start to unravel and decide the *Least said...* tactic might be wise.

'Why didn't you call an ambulance?'

She gaped at him, glanced from him to Gucci and back again. 'I panicked.'

'Would it not have been wise to call 999, from the house phone if you didn't want to identify yourself?'

'I told you. I panicked.'

'Yes, you said that. Did you check his pulse?'

'No.'

'Why?'

'I'm not a doctor; I wouldn't know how.' Her eyelids fluttered; even she knew her last answer was a stinker.

'Really? You've never seen someone do it even once? On TV, maybe?'

'Maybe I have, but as I said, I panicked.'

'Yes, you said that, too.'

He stared at her, hoped she'd take the hint that she was on a shoogly peg and something big was coming. He expected to hate doing this to her, but he needed her to buckle and cooperate, for Remi's sake as well as her own.

'So, if Remi's prints got on the bottle at your home and he was never at Beauchamp's house, did *you* inflict Mr Beauchamp's later, fatal injuries?'

He watched her struggle, aware that she had only two options now. Maintain her confession but extend it to include the multiple stabbings, or dump her brother in it. And both of them knew the second one was no real option at all.

He changed tack. 'Was Beauchamp blackmailing you, Ms Quinn?'

Her reaction was swift and dramatic. She stood, looked around her as if yet hopeful of an escape from the room. Then she howled and screamed and punched the side of her head. Malkie stood, took her hand and held it away from her. She stopped, stared at him.

'Yes. He was. And yes, I did. Kill him. Now charge me, for God's sake.'

She calmed as quickly as she'd erupted, looked bewildered, but allowed herself to be seated. Gucci passed her a handful of tissues, then she and Malkie returned to their chairs.

'You suggested otherwise, earlier. That Remi might have done it to protect you, Ms Quinn. Would you like to take a break? I would recommend you do.' He hoped he laced his voice with as much sympathy as he felt.

She shook her head.

Malkie sat back, gave her all the time she needed.

She sat in silence, her eyes dull and distant, and Malkie realised what was coming next, and that for the first time ever in his career, he would be glad to hear it from a suspect.

'Is it too late for me to ask for a lawyer?'

'A solicitor. No, Ms Quinn. You can change your mind at any time.'

'I want one now please.'

THIRTY

Back in the CID room, Malkie chased up the prints and the Tech Forensics on what he assumed would be burner phones from Beauchamp's secret stash.

'Nothing yet, DS McCulloch. Heavy work stack as usual. We told you that.'

'When? Never mind. Any idea on an SLA?'

'Prints won't take much longer, an hour or so. The techies are dumping everything from the phones. There was no security on any of them.'

Complacent fucker, weren't you, Beauchamp?

'OK, thanks. We have a vulnerable MisPer to locate and I'm hoping something on those phones might help us find him.'

'I'll do what I can, Detective.'

He thanked the woman again and realised he hadn't asked her name. Rude.

He headed for the café in the foyer of the Civic Centre for a double-shot latte and a muffin. He took them outside, sat on a bench in the landscaped grounds. It had rained at some time, and he had to wipe a spot dry with a handful of napkins he'd grabbed for that reason.

He watched people wander around the lawns. Some would be

council employees on their breaks, others anxious relatives of someone up before a beak in court that day. He sipped his coffee and picked chunks out of his muffin. A dozen pigeons appeared as if by magic. He decided his appetite wasn't what he hoped it would be, so he broke it into chunks to scatter on the grass behind him. Most of the birds scrambled for the crumbs, but one hobbled behind them, slow and clumsy, its feet little more than rotted stumps. It must have flown in OK, but on the ground it struggled, and he figured it wouldn't take long for it to starve to death or feed a fox or a bigger bird.

Fuck's sake. I could have done without seeing that.

He scraped scraps of muffin clinging to the paper, then dropped it on the ground near the poor wee sod. It leapt on the crumbs and got a few pecks in before the fitter beasts mobbed it and chased it away.

I hope it's quick when it comes, wee man. He knew as little about pigeon gender identification as anyone should, but his mind stubbornly assumed such a grubby specimen had to be a male.

The bird retreated. When the flock dispersed and flew away it picked at the ground, but Malkie doubted the others had left any. He considered buying another muffin, but that one bird would not know to wait, and besides, the same dirty scrum would happen again if he scattered more crumbs.

Sorry, mate. Life's shit, then you get eaten.

When his mobile rang he snatched it from his pocket, desperate for a distraction from the short, brutal life of your typical wild bird.

'Boss? Forensics came back. Need you here.'

'Coming, Lou.'

As he stood, the hobbled pigeon jumped away. It watched him with wary eyes, and Malkie felt worse.

Back in the office, Gucci had that look on her face. Something juicy.

'Hi, boss. We have numbers from every one of Beauchamp's

secret phones. He hadn't put any security on them for some reason.'

Arrogance? Oh, aye. And hubris like we can't imagine.

'Funny thing is, there's only one number in each of the phones, and always outbound, never received. No texts, no pictures, no emails or any media or internet. Just a single number on each.'

'He didn't want the owners of those numbers to know about the others.'

Rab spoke without turning. 'Seems Mr Beauchamp was paddling in a lot of pools outside of his marriage, doesn't it?'

Gucci rolled her eyes. 'Thanks for that, Rab. Do you learn these poetic turns of phrase at your writing classes?'

'Nope. Just naturally gifted, I guess.'

'Don't encourage him, Lou. It never ends well. What about the notebooks and the prints?'

'Oh aye, sorry. The prints are, indeed, Patricia Quinn's, but I doubt that revelation gains us much. She's already admitted being there.'

'Aye, but I don't believe her shite about buying the wine in Tesco and Remi touching it.'

He considered for a moment. 'Did we get the name of the wine from the label?'

Gucci scrolled further up the case notes. 'Aye. It was called Chateau de Melfont.'

'Expensive?'

She switched to a browser and ran a search. 'Good grief. Between £90 and £120. Who the hell pays that for one bottle of wine and drinks it alone?'

'Someone with exotic and pretentious tastes, Lou. And certainly not a single woman living in a sink-estate terraced home and caring for a high-dependency brother.'

'She didn't buy the bloody bottle at all.'

'Nope.'

'Meaning she didn't go there with any interest in dumping him.'

'Nope. And remember what she called him during her first interview?'

'Beauchamp. Not Sebastian. Beauchamp.'

'You call someone by their surname if you have no desire for any kind of personal connection with them, or if—'

'You hate them.'

'Or even just disapprove of, but yes.'

Gucci sat back in her chair and pinched her top lip as she concentrated. 'And the phones. One of those numbers will be hers, right? Damn it.' She scrolled some more and smacked herself on the forehead. 'Bugger. It is Patricia Quinn's number.' She opened another file, the Forensics report on Patricia's phone. 'Beauchamp called her but she never called him on that number, and it's not in her phone book.' She scrolled down the list. 'Whoa, hang on. Until last weekend. Four times in one day. Never answered.'

Malkie sat, couldn't believe their luck. He wanted to show off about how the phones were found but he'd been having some success in reducing his neediness and didn't want to derail his progress.

'Aye, was lucky the SOCOs found them; Forensics notes say they were hidden in a box, aye?' Gucci asked.

'Aye, under a false bottom, would you believe? And the notebooks?'

'Still being scanned and the pages checked for prints.'

'Bollocks.'

'Sorry, boss.'

'Not your fault, Lou. Carry on. Really good work.'

He heard Rab sigh, and Gucci patted him on the shoulder.

'Rab chased them twice today. Gave them a bollocking.'

Malkie patted Rab's other shoulder. 'Well done, mate. We'll make a copper out of you yet.'

'Hilarious.' Rab didn't bother turning to face them.

'OK, so we're getting the customer details on the other three numbers, aye?'

'Aye. Thompson's applying for the warrants now. You know what phone companies are like.'

'Aye, I do. So, apart from Patricia Quinn we don't know who else Beauchamp was calling and we don't know, yet, what he wrote in those notebooks. What *do* we know?'

'Patricia Quinn's confession is looking less and less reliable. Her brother's disappeared and none of the usual methods has turned up a scrap, which is highly unusual. Lin Fraser is ready for us to view Beauchamp's body any time this afternoon.'

Bollocks, I hate that bit.

'Let's get that over with first, shall we? Rab, you want to accompany me?'

Gucci had grabbed her coat but now looked at him in surprise.

Rab looked wary. He pointed out a nearby window. 'What? Like, out there?'

'Yes, Rab. We've all noticed how diligently you hammer away at that keyboard in your much-appreciated determination to mine the huge amounts of information we receive for patterns and outliers and that sort of thing.'

He paused, realised he was over-egging his act. 'It's only fair that you get to join me on a jaunt out into the sun and fresh air.'

Rab stared at him. He looked to have picked up on Malkie's sarcasm but still seemed torn between staying at his desk and exercising only his fingers or taking an opportunity to confound their beliefs about him.

'Fine. Let's go.' He huffed and grabbed his jacket.

Lou sat again, not quite managing to suppress a laugh.

THIRTY-ONE

When they arrived at the mortuary in St John's, Lin feigned surprise.

'It's Robert, isn't it?' Nobody could miss the gleam in her eyes.

'Rab, Ms Fraser. Just Rab.'

'Ah, I remember. Malkie, how lovely to see you. Are you well?' She made it sound like a glib social ritual, but she'd want the truth. Lin Fraser appeared severe and matronly, but she cared deeply for Malkie. And Steph.

'I'm OK, Lin, thanks. Steph's struggling but she'll get through it.'

'Yes. I heard. Poor Steph. Give her my best, won't you?' By which Malkie figured she meant *Look after her or I'll come for you.*

Lin led them to the main mortuary area. Beauchamp lay on a trolley, covered with a sheet up to his shoulders. Whatever Lin's knowledge or opinion of Beauchamp, she extended every dignity to every customer.

'Mr Beauchamp suffered two major injuries plus some minor ones.'

She pointed to the left side of his head. 'Someone smashed a bottle of red wine against his head, here.'

She took the corners of the sheet and pulled it down without warning. 'And these are the wounds which killed him.'

No shit, Lin.

The mess of slashed and torn flesh had Malkie swallowing the reflex to throw up. He'd attended hundreds of post-mortems over the course of his career, and all but a few had made him gag.

'What a bloody mess.'

Lin sighed. 'Indeed. Impossible to say how many individual wounds, the damage is so bad.'

Malkie didn't correct her on the sentiment behind his comment. He turned to Rab.

'Seen enough – maybe you should wait outside, mate.'

Rab swallowed, his face grey and sweaty, his eyes watering. He nodded and turned away. He walked towards the door to Lin's office in slow, halting steps, and Malkie was glad to see him make it through the doors without puking all over Lin's lovely clean mortuary. He just hoped he didn't redecorate her office.

'Hasn't Rab been in the job as long as you, Malkie?'

'He has, but he manages to avoid actual shouts more times than he's eaten hot and very fragrant curries at his desk. I suspect he cultivates an air of unreliability so none of us ever asks him to attend the so-called sharp end, so he also never screws up badly enough to risk his pension. He's actually an impressive phenomena, if you consider him that way.'

'Phenomen*on*, and you know it. Idiot.'

'Yes, Lin.' He grinned. 'Now cover him up again, will you?'

She did.

'You said he had some other, more minor wounds?'

'Yes.' She indicated three scratches on both of his wrists, probably angry and red before he'd turned that awful shade of grey that no funeral parlour ever managed to convincingly conceal.

'Defensive wounds?'

'Yes, I think so. Their spacing could suggest they were made by fingernails, and they were inflicted from the upper side of his wrists around to the underside of them.'

'Someone trying to pull them from their throat and losing their grip, for example?'

'Or shoulders, but you know I won't commit to any more than that, Malkie.'

'I have to try, Lin.'

'And you do, Malkie.'

'Skin under his fingernails?'

'None.'

'Bollocks.'

'Quite.'

She pulled her latex gloves off, disposed of them in a pedal bin, then headed for her office, sticking her arm through Malkie's as they walked.

'And Steph?'

'Ach, she's in trouble, Lin. It's gutting me to see her like that. I don't know what to do.'

'Just—'

'Be there for her? Aye I know that. She's got me well trained. But I don't know *how* to just be there for her. I mean, do I call her every day? Visit her every other day to make sure she looks after herself? Check she's eating? I'm no good at this kind of thing. I saw her last night and she looked terrible. All I could do was sit beside her and listen and let her rest her feet in my lap. When she leaned over I gave her a cuddle, but I don't know what else I can do for her.'

They had stopped short of the door to Lin's office, Malkie reluctant to let Rab hear too much. He lowered his voice.

'I'm a lousy friend to her, Lin. After all, in the immortal words of Tammy Wynette, *I'm just a man*.'

She chuckled. 'Oh bless you, Malkie. You're not just a man. You're a wee soul. Keep doing what you're doing. She'll let you know if and when she needs more.'

A mischievous twinkle appeared in her eyes. 'Trust me, I'm a woman.'

She pushed through the doors and left Malkie without a chance to respond, not that he could think of anything.

They found Rab perched on one of two chairs in front of her desk. Grieving relatives always seemed to come in pairs to identify their loved ones. Rab pushed a waste bin away with his toe, and Malkie did him the favour of pretending he hadn't noticed.

'Are you OK, Rab? Would you like a glass of water?'

'I'm fine.' Malkie flashed him a look for his tone.

'Thanks, Ms Fraser.'

'Malkie, off the record I'll admit that the balance of probability leans towards Mr Beauchamp's wrists having been scratched by someone with small hands trying to remove Beauchamp's from their throat. The position and angle of the scratches suggests someone shorter than him, but do not suggest many other ways he could have received them. However, that won't be in my official report.'

'I understand, Lin. And, as ever, thank you.'

Rab stood but still looked a tad grey.

'Let's get you some fresh air, Rab. Say *thank you, Lin.*'

'Thank you, Lin.' He managed a small nod and a smile.

Outside he sat on a step and heaved in huge volumes of cold, March air.

'You OK?' Malkie found himself genuinely concerned.

'Aye. I will be. You won't tell anyone, will you?'

Malkie suppressed an urge to take the piss. 'No, mate. I wouldn't do that.'

Rab stared at him.

'I wouldn't, mate. I promise.'

They sat in silence for a while.

'Is that why you try to avoid going out on first-response shouts?'

He hung his head. 'Aye.'

'Ah.'

'Most PMs I can handle, after they've been cleaned up. But that... Fuck's sake.'

'I know. Made me wince, too.'

Rab laughed and Malkie patted him on the back of a shoulder. 'I was struggling in there, too.'

Rab looked at him. 'Seriously? You never showed it. I nearly chucked my lunch all over him.'

'I have to work at it, to not retch. But the difference between you and me, mate, is that I always feel like that. You say you're fine at most PMs?'

'Aye, I am. You honestly struggle every time?'

'Aye. What, you think I'm an unfeeling clod?'

'You're anything but unfeeling, Malkie.'

'Bollocks.'

'No. Everyone knows you have a good soul. We just get monumentally pissed off that you never seem to give yourself a break.'

'Does it upset people?'

'No, it pisses us off something rotten.'

He seemed to realise how candid he'd been. 'Sir.'

Malkie roared with laughter and had to wipe tears from his eyes. 'Oh, Rab. We don't appreciate you enough.'

'And don't I know it.'

Malkie's chuckles died. How often had he cut Rab off or diminished his contributions?

Fuck's sake. Have I been an utter bastard to you, mate?

'Sorry, Rab. Really. And thanks for confiding in me.'

Rab stood. 'Oh, I've moaned to everybody about you, sir.'

Malkie had to wait a full three seconds for a triumphant grin to split Rab's face.

'I'm kidding.'

Malkie checked his eyes for a lie and found none.

They climbed into the pool car and started the engine.

'I only moan to Steph and Lou about you.'

Malkie let him have that one.

Back in the office, Gucci had that look on her face.

'You've got something?'

'Yes, boss. A belter. The prints off the wine bottle. Patricia Quinn's right enough. Forensics said it took ages because it broke into so many shards, but there's something else.'

She made him ask. Steph had a lot to answer for.

'Well?'

'Patricia Quinn's prints are around the body of the bottle.' She grabbed a water bottle from her desk. 'Like this.' She held it as if about to drink from it. 'Remi's prints are like this.' She turned it upside-down and held it by the neck.

'And if it was a broken bottle...'

'Like every bar fight in every bad movie you ever saw.'

Malkie sat.

'Well, bugger me.' He half expected Gucci to say *No thanks* like Steph always did, but she held her tongue this time.

This confirmed at least part of what Patricia Quinn had claimed; she had smashed a bottle over Beauchamp's head but didn't kill him.

Remi did.

Was he happy about this turn of events or not? Since Patricia's first interview he'd accepted that either she or her brother was guilty and would go down for it, but he'd found himself deeply unhappy at the prospect, and still did.

Gucci seemed to read his mind. 'I feel for the lad, too, boss. You know he'll get help, aye? Not a cell in Saughton or Addiewell.'

'Aye, I know, Lou, but I wonder if either of those will be as bad as the alternative for him. If he struggles as badly with life as his sister says he does. Poor sod could go under no matter how good the staff and his treatment are.'

Rab turned in his seat, his usual belligerent and stroppy expression dark with sadness.

'Rab?'

'I was thinking. Remi will struggle enough in even the best secure hospital unless his sister can visit him every day. But if she's banged up herself...'

All three sat in silence for a while. How could any of them be happy at this development? Either way, Remi – just about the most vulnerable and fragile person Malkie could ever remember meeting – would end up inside, a situation he simply might not survive.

He decided he needed Rab and Gucci focused, not hampered by dread. 'Let's not worry about that now. He'll get the best care possible, and I'm sure if his sister does do time, she'll still be an absolute harridan and make damned sure they spare no effort.'

Gucci nodded. 'Aye, I believe that.' After a moment she sighed and closed her eyes. 'When will we tell her?'

'No point putting it off, I suppose.'

Gucci picked up her telephone to request Patricia be moved to the interview room again.

Malkie rolled his chair over beside Rab's. 'You want to assist in this one, Rab? No, I'm not just indulging you, mate. I owe it to you to let you raise your profile a wee bit. After all, us forty-something under-achievers need to show we're not just malingering, right?'

Rab smiled. 'Thanks, boss, but to be honest I think watching Patricia hear this new information might upset me even more than Beauchamp's shredded tackle did.'

Rab noticed that Gucci had finished her call. 'Lou, Malkie's offered to let me sit in on this one, but I'd rather not. You mind?'

'That's fine, Rab. She knows me now.' She looked like she'd happily pass the task to Rab, but Gucci was, and always would be, far too good for this job.

Malkie returned to his desk to read the latest Forensics update for himself. As much as he trusted Gucci's interpretation of the facts, he felt he owed it to Patricia to be all over the details.

Ten minutes later, Gucci's phone rang. She answered, gave a brief acknowledgement and thank-you, then hung up.

'She's ready. Duty solicitor was already on site.'

'Same brief?'

'Aye, Miriam Lawson.'

'Good.'

'Why?'

'Because as much as solicitors get right on my tits sometimes, Patricia Quinn needs saving from herself more than most suspects. She'll be charged with assault at least, but I'd prefer it if she stopped building a case against herself for perjury, too.'

Gucci studied him. 'You're *Good People*, you know that, boss?'

'Oh, shut up. Rab, can you get started on an application to the Fiscal for permission to charge her? But hang on to it until we give her one last chance to level with us. I think Beauchamp did threaten her, and if he did it as violently as his injuries suggest, then let's just say she may well have a shot at a suspended sentence if she makes a decent case for self-defence at trial.'

'Only too happy to, boss.'

Malkie and Gucci headed through to the interview room and found Miriam Lawson already seated beside Quinn, a signed form on the table in front of them.

'Are you ready for us Patricia? Ms Lawson?'

Lawson glanced at Patricia, who nodded. 'Yes, Detective Sergeant McCulloch. We're ready.'

He and Gucci sat, and while she did the same recording admin all over again, Malkie checked the signed form, a formal request from Patricia for legal representation.

When Malkie opened his mouth to start, he realised he had no clue what he wanted to say.

THIRTY-TWO

A more uncomfortable silence Steph could not remember.

Boswell twitched like a nun at a... Good grief, she had to stop picking phrases up from Malkie's so-called sense of humour.

Now that she was prepared for the meeting, unlike before, she noticed how old he'd become. Quick mental arithmetic told her he had to be in his late forties, but he looked a decade older. Guilt? Regret? Maybe just a general recognition of what a screwed-up life he'd led.

No matter. Nothing he could say now was likely to change the truth. Not his truth, which she could imagine he believed, but the objective facts which she now knew damned him.

She'd decided to stop thinking of him as Barry. She'd found herself uncomfortably close to believing his claim that he and her mum loved each other. Because the letters were convincing, a stubborn scrap of sympathy had crept into her. Those from him, in isolation, she could have discounted as the sad delusions of a desperate man, but the one letter from her mother to him had given Steph painful pause for thought. She'd compared the handwriting in her mum's letter to a sample from the signature on her primary school reports, and decided it looked genuine. And besides, even entertaining the likelihood that he'd faked her writing told her she was clutching at straws because of the stubborn suspicion she could not shake that Boswell was hiding something, or had made himself forget something.

'Thanks for agreeing to see me. I know it can't be easy for you.'

'I need to hear your side. I always need to hear both sides. Even yours.'

His eyes betrayed his disappointment, and possibly a fear that the hill ahead of him might prove too steep.

She wasn't going to have a meaningful conversation with him if she didn't calm him down and stop terrifying him. She'd scared the shite out of Lang towards the end, but that hadn't brought her nearly the same guilty satisfaction as if she'd taken a more active part in his demise.

She scolded herself. That wasn't her; she had to be better than that.

'I mean, I want to keep as open a mind as I can, even under these circumstances.'

'I can understand that. You were lied to for years.'

Yes, Uncle Barry. I was. 'Decades.'

'Aye.'

'I don't know where to start.'

Impatience made her throw him a lifeline. 'When did you and my mum first start your relationship?'

'When Dean moved Joyce – I mean your mum – in with him. You know you were looked after by your uncle for a while, aye.'

'My real uncle.'

'Aye. Your mum's brother. Raymond.'

'Why was that? I never found out before it was too late to ask her.'

Boswell sighed and stared out a window at pedestrians walking past on Leith Street. She'd agreed to meet him in Edinburgh because he lived there, but also so he didn't leave a stain on any of her favourite Livi coffee shops.

'When you were born, Dean made Joyce send you to your uncle Raymond to be brought up. He couldn't be bothered with a child. He could have dumped Joyce, but he was never the sort of man to let *property* go that he got a kick out of.'

'A kick? He got a kick out of brutalising my mum?' She felt her temper rise and reminded herself to keep her tone neutral for fear of Boswell clamming up again.

'He had no respect for her. For some time we wondered why he kept her around, until we realised he just enjoyed tormenting her. Your mum wasn't weak, but after you were born she was afraid what Dean would do to you if she left him. She tried once. Leaving him.' He took a sip of his coffee. Then another.

'It didn't go down well, I take it?'

'He punched her and kicked her, then refused to take her to hospital. I tried – I promise you, I did – but he beat the shite out of me too, and said he'd kill me if I ever tried to tell him what to do again.

'He enjoyed watching her get more and more hopeless. Like it made him feel the big man. The way he treated her, I don't think he'd have got any other woman to take it. He once called her his little punchbag, and I never forgot that.'

'So, you did nothing? Could you not at least have called the police?'

'Things were different back then, Steph. Domestic abuse wasn't so common. It—'

'It was just as common but it was under-reported compared to now. And just as despicable.'

He flinched. 'I agree. But nobody believed the police took it seriously twenty years ago. If I'd reported him, he might not have got arrested, let alone charged. And then he'd have hurt you and your mum even worse.'

'And you.'

'You'll not believe me, but that was the least of my concerns. I was too angry at myself for letting it get as far as it did.'

She nodded. 'I'll reserve judgement on that.'

'Fair enough. I would if I were you.'

She felt a wall go up in her mind; she mustn't let his expressions of regret cloud her objectivity, no matter how convincing.

'He used to say… Terrible things about your mum. He—'

'What things?'

Boswell looked trapped. 'Don't make me repeat them. Please. It's bad enough I let him say them.'

A line from her mum's letter to Boswell forced its way to the front of her mind. '*I wish you'd been stronger because I wasn't.*'

She leaned forward, her temper fraying. 'Nothing you've said persuades me you didn't rape my mum, so you really should start telling me the truth, not just what you're comfortable repeating.'

His face blanched, and it took a few seconds and another gulp of his coffee for him to get more words out.

'He used to say…' He stopped again, then saw her darken.

He sat back, ran his fingers through his sparse white hair and screwed his eyes shut. Steph found in herself not a scrap of sympathy for him.

'He said she was too much fun to let go and that he would dump her when she started to bore him.'

'And he wasn't talking about her sparkling personality and lively sense of humour.'

'No. The more unhappy and degraded she was the more he enjoyed it.'

Steph stood. She took both their coffee cups – his almost empty, hers untouched – and approached the counter. She ordered two more of the same and paced the shop floor, her breath heaving, her hands on her hips to stop them from shaking. When the barista announced her order was ready, the poor girl shrank from the look Steph turned on her.

'I'm sorry. Got things on my mind. Thank you.'

The girl nodded but looked like she hoped Steph wouldn't come back.

Boswell looked up when she placed his cup in front of him. His smile disappeared as she sat down.

'When did you and my mum first—'

'About a month after Dean made her move in with him.'

'Did she start it or you?'

He hesitated, had to swallow before continuing. 'Me. I did. Whenever Dean went out to top up on cheap drugs and shitty booze, I would try to talk to her. Like, real conversation where someone listened to her, you know? It took a while, because her mind was permanently scrambled and barely conscious most of the time, but she trusted me eventually. I only asked her once why she didn't just leave him. She lost the plot thinking about what he'd do to her. And you. So I held back.'

He took another sip, flinched because he didn't stop to think it had just been poured.

'You were a coward.'

'I was. And I wish I could have overcome that twenty years ago.'

She took a while to get her next words out, feared she wouldn't hear a truthful answer to this most urgent question.

'Did you kill him?'

He swallowed, and Steph knew she was about to get at least one of the answers she needed.

'Yes. I did. And I'm not sorry.'

'At least that sounds like the fucking truth.' She glared at a couple on a nearby table who scowled at her.

'Are you going to arrest me and charge me? I'll confess. Or do you want to do something more personal to me?'

She took a few seconds. 'No. Not me. I'll log it and a couple of Uniforms will come to drag your sorry arse in.'

His frown relaxed, it looked like disappointment warred with relief in him; at least she didn't intend to hurt him. That would make her the kind of copper anybody who knew her would never expect her to become.

'Go home. I'll go to the office and log your claim. My colleagues will be in touch. I can't be involved because we're—'

'Family?'

His hopeful look turned her stomach. 'Connected. Through no choice of mine.'

He looked long and hard at her. She saw his ember of hope flicker.

'You believe me about me and you mum though. Don't you?'

'Go home. Wait for my colleagues.'

He had more to say.

'What?'

'The evening I killed him. I wanted evidence. To leave no doubt I did it.' He reached into his coat pocket and produced a voice recorder, an old one with a micro-cassette. He placed his thumb over the play button, but Steph stopped him.

'I don't want to hear it.' She pulled a plastic evidence bag from one of her secret inside pockets that Malkie always found so amusing. She opened it, held it out and Boswell dropped the device into it. She sealed it then handed it back with a pen.

'Sign across the join where the flap is sealed down.'

By the book. Everything by the book. Even him. Even now.

He did so but looked crestfallen. Had he hoped she'd be eager to hear how much he wanted to make things right and what exactly he'd said to Lang before killing him? Was he determined to see himself charged and answer for his crime out of guilt or some scrap of hope that she'd actually believe him, and he might get to be a daddy after all?

She stood and walked out, her second coffee untouched.

He'd said nothing about the worst revelation in her mum's letter. The one that had Steph throwing up in an alleyway minutes later.

THIRTY-THREE

'Got them.'

'Got what?'

'Phone company sent the owners of those numbers, boss.'

Malkie and Gucci shot out of their chairs and hovered over Rab's shoulders.

'Christ, I'll never get used to you two doing that.'

'Shut up and show us the goods, DC Lundy.' Malkie emphasised the C in DC.

'I'm doing it,' Rab snapped but Malkie heard no real venom in it.

Gucci cast Malkie a look behind Rab's back and he spread his fingers to promise her he'd back off.

'OK, we have... a Teri Marshall, an Amber Balfour, our Patricia Quinn, and someone called Zoe Anderson.'

'Excellent. Take your pick. One each, and we get them all at the same time in case they do know each other after all. Good plan?'

Gucci nodded. 'Good plan, boss.'

Rab grunted, 'As good as any.'

Gucci went first. 'I'll take the first one. No reason to choose any other.'

'Rab?'

'Second one, I suppose.'

'Excellent.' Malkie clapped his hands together. 'Zoe Anderson for me then. Take a pool car each and wait outside their home addresses. You got them, Rab?'

'Way ahead of you, boss.'

'Expected nothing less from you, Rab. We'll keep in touch by messaging. When all three are home, we knock on doors, OK?'

'OK.'

'OK.'

Malkie beamed at them. 'Like a well-oiled machine. I'm proud of you both.'

They grimaced but Malkie cared not a jot.

Malkie stocked up on sandwiches and KitKats and coffee, filled an insulated beaker Steph had bought him for last Xmas's Secret Santa – a remarkably benign gesture for her – then hurried out to the garage to make sure he didn't get the pool car with the knackered entertainment system. He got it anyway. Gucci and Rab grinned at him as they drove past out into daylight.

Zoe Anderson's home sat mid-terrace in a suburb of Bathgate. A rainbow-coloured flag hung from an upstairs window, flapping slow and lazy in the evening breeze. Someone, or several people, had lobbed various manky and wet things at it so it was pockmarked with ugly spots. Such neglect suggested Ms Anderson might be more of a keyboard warrior than an activist.

He settled in to wait. People came and went. Some stared at him as they passed, nosiness a favoured hobby in neighbourhoods like this. Most of the gardens were kept tidy and some even pretty, but too many others had been concreted or block-paved. His dad often bemoaned the gradual eroding of bee-friendly spaces and said the council planning department should do something about it. Just one of many subjects on which his dad had proved to be prophetic.

His phone chimed. A message from Gucci.

Marshall is home.

He acknowledged and pinged Rab a question mark.

Not home yet.

Malkie let Rab's curtness pass. None of them would be enjoying this way of spending their evening.

He saw a gate open next to Zoe Anderson's property and a young woman – closer to a girl than a woman, he noted – wrestled a huge pram through it. He caught a glimpse of a lawn overgrown and strewn with junk: an old office chair, a stained mattress, numerous soaked and collapsed Amazon boxes. The pram was massive because it held twins, and his heart ached for her. She looked far too young to support one child, let alone two. The babies started to cry as her temper got the better of her and she forced the pram through the gap. He saw the f-bomb on her lips. He hoped she was just having a bad day, that she was otherwise happy and lived with a good man, but statistics rarely reflected that.

His phone chimed again. Rab.

Balfour is home. Swanky house, she must be worth a few bob.

Malkie acknowledged and resisted an urge to remind Rab to wait.

He settled back in his seat but couldn't relax. If Anderson took too long, one of the others might go out again. He wasn't sure how he would handle that. He reached for the dashboard but remembered he'd got the crap pool car, the one the mechanics had been promising to fix for weeks but providing entertainment for bored officers on stakeout came a long way down their list of priorities.

He tried to blank his mind and failed miserably. Eventually the boredom became too much and he dialled Steph.

'Malkie? You OK?'

Typical of Steph to worry about him despite her current problems. Or was it typical of him to bother her?

'I'm fine. How are you?'

He had to wait for her response, and again resisted an urge to repeat his question.

'I'm... Confused.'

'How?'

'I met Boswell today for coffee.'

Malkie's heart skipped. 'Was that a good idea?'

'It was the least stressful of two options, the other being to sit here and drink gin with George Clooney and Brad Pitt and let my mind paint the worst possible picture. My situation wasn't going to sort itself out. I needed to do something.'

'Knowing you as I do, I think that was wise, partner.'

'Net result is he confessed, Malkie.'

'To Lang's murder? Or to... The other thing.' He cringed as he said it, prayed he'd find the right words now, when it really mattered.

'Lang's murder. But I found something else. In my mum's only letter back to him. I don't know if he'd have buckled if I'd raised it or if he'd have lied through his teeth some more. Or maybe he believes his own lies. People do that: convince themselves of past credit they don't come close to deserving. He was petrified of me, so I can't know for sure.'

'You can't help that, Steph. You scare the shite out of everyone, even people you're trying to be nice to.'

'Piss off. I'm not that bad.'

He waited for it.

'Am I?'

'It's a useful trait to have as a police officer, Steph, so don't sweat it.'

'S'pose so. Anyway—'

Malkie cursed under his breath as a car parked outside Zoe Anderson's home. The driver entered the house.

'What?'

'Sorry, Steph. What were you saying?'

'Seriously, Malkie?'

'Steph, I'm on—'

'It's fine. The job again? I can't blame you for that. Anything juicy?'

'I hope so.'

'Fine. Don't tell me. Go and be a copper.'

'Sorry, Steph.'

'Oh, stop apologising. What kind of a copper would I be if I interfered with you doing your own coppering?'

'Coppering?'

'Oh sod off.'

She paused, and Malkie's patience stretched.

'I'll be coming in tomorrow. I have to. Got... stuff I need to do.'

Malkie was desperate to ask more, but if Marshall or Balfour left their homes again, his cunning plan might fall apart.

'I'm sorry, mate. I do really need to go. Coppering stuff.'

'Go.' She hung up.

Only now did it occur to him that he had zero chance, again, of seeing Deborah tonight. He needed to call her later, unless one of these three women said something that further knackered all their evenings.

He messaged Rab and Gucci the go-ahead, then got out of the car and stretched three hours of bad posture from his spine. The cracks and pops his vertebrae made worried him and he resolved, yet again, to make more use of the Civic Centre's staff gym.

Zoe Anderson's front garden was tidy and functional, and what looked like a brand-new Ring camera blinked beside the door. He pushed the button and waited. He heard movement but nobody answered, so he lifted his warrant card to the camera lens and waited.

The door opened and a short, stocky woman peered out. She had purple hair and more piercings than Malkie thought anybody could sleep with. She probably set off every airport metal detector she ever walked through.

Reactions to the sight of a warrant card or – worse – a uniform tended to panic most people. Only experienced mouth-breathers fronted it out when they found The Filth on their doorstep. Zoe Anderson looked terrified.

'What do you want?'

Fuck's sake, man. Concentrate or you'll lose all credibility.

'Ms Zoe Anderson?'

'Who's asking?' Her tone was more defensive than belligerent.

'Detective Sergeant Malcolm McCulloch, Ms Anderson.'

'Do you have some ID?'

'Didn't you see it through your door camera?'

'It's broken.'

He sighed and held his warrant card up again. She studied it for far longer than anyone should need to. 'What do you want?'

'Can we talk inside please?'

'Have you got a warrant?'

Oh for fuck's sake.

'No. Do I need one, Ms Anderson?' Over many years as a copper he'd learned to lace that question with the perfect flavour of suspicion. Menace, even. She buckled, closed the door, unfastened the chain and opened it again.

Malkie flashed his best professional smile and walked past her.

He found her living room to be as tidy and functional as her front garden. Her coffee table was strewn with sheets of paper, some printed with banner headings and columns of text, others with cuttings from magazines pasted onto collages with ransom-letter-style captions like *Fight* and *Resist* and – his favourite – *Anything you can do I can do bleeding.*

She appeared from behind him, shuffled the papers together as if hiding dangerous secrets and pushed them to the back of a shelving unit holding books titled in a similar vein.

'May I sit down, Ms Anderson?'

She nodded, barely, but remained standing.

He nodded at the armchair behind her and waited.

She got the message and sat first. 'What's this about?'

'Have you seen the news articles about Sebastian Beauchamp?'

'No. Who is he?'

Good grief, people never know when they're crap liars, do they?

'Mr Beauchamp has died. He never regained consciousness.'

She swallowed but managed to maintain eye contact. 'I don't know the man.'

He studied her, figured she wouldn't take long to crumble. 'He knows you, Ms Anderson.'

She said nothing. Given her apparent lack of surprise at hearing Sebastian Beauchamp was very much aware of her, he half expected her to start *No Commenting* him. Despite not being anywhere near being arrested. Yet.

'I don't know the man.' A pleading note had crept into her tone.

'Yes, you said that. But he had your number.' He left out the part about it being the only number in one of five obvious burner phones.

She shrugged, without much conviction.

'May I see your phone please, Ms Anderson?'

'Don't you need a warrant for that?'

And here we go again.

'I would need a warrant to *compel* you to produce it, but you're perfectly at liberty to voluntarily give it to me.'

He gave her little time to think.

'At the moment you're just a person of interest in the enquiry into Mr Beauchamp's death. If I need to obtain a warrant to seize your phone, it won't look good for you. And besides, in the interests of preserving potentially useful evidence, I'm authorised to seize it if I suspect your reluctance to hand it over might originate in some desire to obstruct my investigation. I'm not permitted to examine it or any of the data in it until I do get a warrant, but I can, and will, take it.'

Fuck's sake. I'm turning into one of those Senior Damagers we used to see on Crimewatch *who never used five words when twenty would do.*

'Ms Anderson?'

'I don't know the man or anything about who murdered him.'

Bingo. The very reason the cause of death was withheld.

'I didn't say he was murdered.'

'Why else would a police officer want to speak to me if he wasn't murdered?'

'Police Scotland have to investigate any sudden death that happens outside of, say, a hospital or care home, or where the deceased had a history of life-threatening disease or injury. Not just murders.'

'I heard it on the news.'

His patience ended.

'No. You didn't, Ms Anderson, because you just claimed not to know him, and we haven't publicly released the cause of Mr Beauchamp's death yet. Nobody outside of Police Scotland and the Scottish Police Authority Forensics Service knows that, and I didn't tell you he was murdered.'

She stammered. 'I... I assumed.'

'No, I don't think you did. Now, may I examine your mobile phone please, Ms Anderson?'

Go easy, you idiot. She's not a suspect, she's only a PoI, and one who's just learned her number was in a murdered man's phone.

He acknowledged his approach might have been a tad hostile, but the woman had been giving out *lying through her teeth* vibes from word one.

She took forever to nod and produce it from the back pocket of her jeans.

She held it out to him, but he had to tug on it to get her fingers to release it. He pressed the side button and saw four boxes.

'Your PIN number?'

She said nothing.

'Ms Anderson?'

Nothing. She crossed to the window, folded her arms in front of her, stood for long seconds chewing a fingernail, then sat again. She crossed her arms and her legs and stared at him but failed to mask her fear with a show of bravado.

Malkie sighed and pulled his own mobile out. He headed to the hallway but kept Anderson in sight, and dialled Gucci.

'Anything, Lou?' He was careful not to mention Teri Marshall by name, in case Anderson, Marshall and Balfour didn't already know each other, and he trusted Gucci to do the same.

'Nothing. She won't give me her phone.'

'OK. Warrant time.'

'Yes, boss. Shall I ask for two, aye?'

'Three, just in case. Better to have it and not need it than etc. etc.'

'Agreed. I'll ping you when they're issued.'

'Cheers, Lou.'

Back in the living room, Anderson looked about as miserable as anyone could. He was about to sit again when she mumbled something.

'I beg your pardon, Ms Anderson?'

'1913.'

Thank fuck for that.

'Thank you.' He'd made sure all three of them had taken evidence bags with them. He dropped the phone in, sealed it, wrote his name, her name, the date and time and her address on it and signed it. He handed it to her.

'Can you please sign under my signature.'

'Why.'

'It's called chain of custody, Ms Anderson, and it reassures PoIs like yourself that nothing untoward can happen while it's being processed. It's one of our strictest practices, for obvious reasons.'

'What's a PoI?'

He bit back an urge to snap at her; she had the memory of a goldfish. But then, he'd hardly treated her gently so far, which could only have added to the woman's stress levels.

'A person of interest, Ms Anderson. You're not under arrest and I didn't caution you.' He smiled, hoped to repair some of the damage his foul mood and frustration might have inflicted.

Too little, too late.

She started crying, miserable and heartbreaking tears, and Malkie – far from the first time – hated his job with a vengeance bordering on debilitating.

THIRTY-FOUR

'I don't like it, guys.'

'What, boss?'

'It was too easy, Rab. Balfour gave you hers without barely a word, aye?'

'Aye. She crumbled under my masculine charm.'

'Quite.'

'OK, she looked like a rabbit caught in a car's headlights and she cried a wee bit, but she handed it over without a word.'

'Do we need to check up on her?'

'I don't think so. She seemed more resigned than distressed.'

'OK. And Anderson folded when she heard me talking to you, Lou. Marshall held out though, aye?'

'She did. That's why I got back here an hour after you two. That was one of the most uncomfortable hours of my life. She even made me a cup of tea, but I couldn't enjoy it.'

'We have all three phones now, so let's get these off to the techies then go home and get some bloody sleep, shall we? We'll interview them tomorrow. We're no good to any bugger exhausted.'

Before either of them reached to switch off their monitors, he changed his mind. 'Actually. Sorry. Give me five more minutes.'

. . .

'Do the names Amber Balfour, Zoe Anderson and Teri Marshall mean anything to you, Patricia?'

She sat up, looked like she'd been sleeping.

'Have you found Remi?'

'I'm sorry. Not yet.'

She looked to the ceiling and released a long, shuddering breath. Malkie saw her eyes glisten.

'Patricia?'

She lay back down and closed her eyes. 'I don't know any of those names.'

For fuck's sake, woman.

'Patricia, who do you think you're protecting? We know you were being blackmailed by Beauchamp, and I'm sure we'll find those other three women were too. We found four payments of £200 every month into his account. We know one of them came from you and I'm damned sure the others will be from those three women. We have Remi's prints on the bottle. Yours confirm you held the bottle around its width, but Remi's show he held it by the neck, and not as if he'd picked it up to read the label. We're looking for Remi, and we *will* arrest him for Beauchamp's murder, but I need you to start cooperating. For Remi's sake as well as your own.'

Silence, but she screwed her eyes up and tears spilled down her cheeks.

'Patricia. Please. Help Remi even if you won't help yourself.'

She turned to face the wall. He listened to her cry quietly, and knew he'd get no more out of her tonight.

Back in the office he as good as fell into his chair.

'Boss?'

He took a moment to trust himself to speak without losing the plot completely.

'She will not see sense, Lou. I tried to get her to accept the best way she can help Remi and herself is to cooperate, but she won't listen. It's like she's holding out on us, hoping she'll pressure us into working harder than she thinks we are for Remi.'

'She's desperate. Nothing else matters to her.'

'No. She won't accept there's nothing more she can do to stop Remi from being charged. I need to get through her stubborn refusal to work with us to help find him.'

Gucci said nothing. Rab too. What could they say?

'Ach, fuck it.'

He dropped all three evidence bags containing the phones into a secure internal envelope with a preprinted routing label on it, then stood.

'I'll wait for the courier. You guys get away home.'

They left, and he waited for the call from reception.

He checked his watch. If the courier arrived promptly... He decided to risk it and dialled Debs' number.

'Hello you.' She sounded sleepy.

'Hello you. Good day?'

'No. My physio hurt like a bastard this afternoon. Rudy said that was a good sign, but I think Rudy might be full of shit. He's Belgian.'

'Rudy's your physio?'

'One of them. Did I never tell you that?'

'No. I assumed you didn't want me knowing anything about the big, strong, muscular men who handled bits of you for a living. Is he good-looking?'

'He's gorgeous. Tall and strong, fit, follows a skin-care regime, and never says a word wrong.'

'He's gay, isn't he?'

'Of course he is. Bloody shame.'

'I think I can pop round tonight, if you're up for it?'

He heard her sigh. 'Oh, I don't know, Malkie. You've had to cancel a few times. I'm not sure I want to get my hopes up.'

He fumbled for some response that wouldn't sound trite. 'I know. I'm sorry. Just got this—'

'Pig of a case?'

'I was going to say bastard of a case, but aye. That.'

She didn't laugh. 'Tell you what. Let's assume you won't make it tonight. I'll take my meds an hour late and if you do make it, it'll be a nice surprise.'

He wanted to say *I'll make it* but couldn't. 'OK. Sorry.'

'I know it's the nature of your job, Malkie, but...'

He waited.

'It's hard for me, you know? My life is pretty shit at times and you're the best thing in it, apart from chef's lasagne with red wine.'

If her words were intended to make him feel better, they failed.

'Let's not make any plans, OK? You know my bedtime.'

'I'm sorry, Deb.'

'Please, Malkie... Don't apologise.'

He imagined her following her plea with *It makes it worse.*

'OK. Sleep tight, Deb. Love you to bits.'

'G'night, Malkie.' She hung up.

He threw his phone on the desk. Why did he have to follow *love you* with *to bits*, and dilute the intimacy? Was he losing her? Had he cancelled on her or shut her out once too often, even though she understood the demands of his job?

Fuck's sake, what wouldn't I give to hear her say it back to me.

He placed his face on the desk, clasped his hands behind his head and wished the shite would just fuck off and stop raining on him.

'Sit up, McCulloch.' McLeish's voice, barked at him with zero awareness that a man face down on a desk might need something other than his uniquely *up-his-own-arse* management style.

Before he could stop himself, Malkie muttered an unwise but – to his mind – justified, '*Oh, for fuck's sake. What now?*' When he lifted his head to face the music, he hoped even McLeish would see a man in trouble and go easy on him.

'Talk to me like that again, McCulloch, and I'll have your warrant card, and you'll be lucky to find work as a supermarket security drone; you hear me?'

Malkie nodded, didn't trust himself to open his gob again. Not yet.

'I said did you hear me?'

'Yes, Detective Inspector McLeish. I heard you. Loud and clear.' He failed to keep the anger out of his tone.

McLeish stared at him. 'Your days are numbered, McCulloch. I'll make sure of that. Now, update me on the Sebastian Beauchamp case and do it in less than five minutes. I don't particularly enjoy your company at the best of times.'

Malkie had a word with his inner idiot and – as usual – lost.

'Do you want me to appraise you of every detail of every development today, or just the stuff that's tricky to find in HOLMES? Sir?'

McLeish bent over Malkie's desk. His breath stank more than his aftershave.

'Fuck off, McCulloch. Go home and get used to spending a hell of a lot more time there. You're a fucking disgrace to the job.'

He stomped off, threw the door to the custody suite open so hard it slammed against the wall. The sound reverberated the length of the office.

As he contemplated another in a long line of Malkie McFuckup classics, possibly his last, his phone rang and Stuart Laird, the second of the two regular custody sergeants, informed him that the courier had arrived.

He grabbed his jacket and the envelope containing the three sealed evidence bags, switched his monitor off and headed for the door.

He was relieved to find no McLeish in the custody suite. He handed the package to the waiting driver and signed the chain of custody paperwork, then smiled at the bloke and waited for him to leave.

'Is McLeish gone?'

Stuart grinned. 'Oh yes, Malkie. What the hell did you say to him?'

'Truth to power, mate. Truth to power.'

'You mean you told him to go fuck himself?'

'In more words than that, but yes.'

Stuart chuckled and shook his head. 'Been nice knowing you, mate. When's the retirement party.'

'Has anyone ever told you how hilarious you are, Stuart? No? That's because you're not.'

Stuart laughed again. 'Oh, Malkie. Mate. This place would be so boring without you in it.'

'Ha ha fucking ha. I'm glad I provide entertainment, at least.'

Stuart turned serious. 'Ach, fuck him, mate. Did you actually swear *at* him?'

Malkie replayed the conversation. 'No, I don't think so. I swore, but not at him.'

'There you go, then. Black mark for unprofessional behaviour, but he'll struggle to get even a formal disciplinary out of that, let alone an end to your illustrious career.'

'Illustrious? Seriously?'

'Legendary, mate.'

'Ach... Fuck off.'

'You too, Malkie. Home to bed?'

'That or Port Edgar.'

'Eh?'

'My dad's boat. Wrap the anchor round my neck and drop myself in the Forth. It's tempting.'

'Nah. We'd miss you too much. Go home and get some sleep. Come back in the morning and don't give McLeish any more rope.'

'G'night, Stuart.'

'G'night, Malkie. Take care, mate.'

Malkie clung to Stuart's tone, to the sincerity he heard in it.

As he exited to the rear parking compound, he dialled his dad.

'Another late one, son?'

Malkie heard an edge to his dad's tone, and knew another night was about to be wrecked.

'I'll come home now.'

'Good. We need to talk.'

Fuck.

THIRTY-FIVE

She's not here. Why not?

Where are you, Patty? I thought you'd be here.

Does she remember? We only came here once, but she knew I liked it here.

She took a photo. I still have it. In my scrapbook. In my bedroom. I wish I'd brought it with me. I nearly did, but there wasn't enough room in my rucksack.

Why couldn't I stay in my bedroom? I like my bedroom. My computer. My action figures. My books. My PlayStation. They never surprise me or hurt me.

When I get things wrong on my PlayStation, nobody shouts at me. Nobody blames me and says I'm bad to the core. I just go back and try again. Why can't I just go back and try again like in my PlayStation games?

But I can't go back. I know that. I'm not stupid.

It's because of him. He made me do it.

I remember a film Patty and I watched a hundred times. The one with the shark. When the boy says his brother made him do it. The trick they played on those people.

I felt sorry for the shark. It couldn't help what it was. It was just hungry. It didn't know it was hurting people.

Am I like a shark? They say I hurt people and I say I'm sorry but I never know why I say that because I never know what I did wrong.

Mum and Dad took me to see a man once. When I was young. A Trick Cyclist, Patty called him.

He was nice. He had nice eyes. I liked him. He didn't seem to mind that I couldn't look at him. His voice was nice. Even though I was rude to him by not looking at him. How do other people always know what's rude, but I don't?

There were sweets in a bowl, but I didn't take any because Mum was watching.

Mum told me to be honest and tell the truth even if they didn't like what I said.

I did.

Mum slapped me so hard in the car after that. Dad tried to stop her, but she shouted at him too. Patty cried.

Mum said I was bad to the core. Said the things I told the Trick Cyclist made her sound like a monster.

I was confused because she really was a monster. But she was my mum too.

Mums shouldn't be monsters, should they?

I was glad when Mum died but I shouldn't have felt glad about that. Am I a monster?

The people in the film thought the shark was a monster.

But he wasn't. He was just being a shark because that's what he was.

How could he be something he wasn't?

People are what they are, aren't they?

They killed it. The shark.

Are they going to kill me? For what I did? It wasn't my fault.

I just told him the truth. The man. Patty always told me, after the Trick Cyclist, to always tell the truth.

So, I told him the truth. The bad man. I told him how unhappy he was making Patty, and he was mean to me.

He got angry because Patty had already hurt him. He had blood on him. The floor was red too, but not the same red, a different red. He scared me.

Patty always talked about people triggering me, but I don't know what triggering is.

He hurt me and I hurt him back. I was so scared. I wish I could remember what I did to him.

He was bad, but I hope he's OK.

I hated hurting him even though he was bad to me and Patty.

Bad to the core.

Like me.

THIRTY-SIX

Malkie risked it. He called Steph before starting his car.

'Malkie? Are you OK?'

'Aye. I'm fine.'

'Two calls in one day. Are you telling me the truth?'

Busted.

'No. I just gave McLeish a load more ammunition to see me crucified.'

'Oh, Malkie. You twit.'

He thanked her, silently, for going easy on him. Her favoured approach to educating him on the numerous errors of his ways was to give him a merciless verbal kicking, then remind him that she loved him despite himself, her uniquely no-sugar-coating approach to supporting a pal.

'What did you say to him, and don't leave anything out.'

He related as much of the cosy chat as he could remember, his temper having ensured that some of his comments might not have been quite as he now recalled them.

'Idiot.'

'Aye.'

'No change there, pal. You didn't actually swear *at* him, no?'

'I don't think so.' He doubted that would constitute the strong defence Steph and Stuart the custody sergeant seemed to think it would.

'You might be OK then.'

He didn't expect better from Steph. Her non-negotiable respect for truth in all things made her at the same time the best copper he'd ever worked with and the most intimidating copper he fully expected to work *for* one day. Unless he handed his arse to McLeish before that day came.

'How are you? And don't leave anything out.'

'Never quote me to me, Malkie. Pisses me off and I don't enjoy being pissed off at you.'

Malkie took that as the closest he'd get to affection right now.

'I'm OK today. I watched the video and read the letters again, and I believe Boswell has been lying to himself all this time. I don't feel any better, but more settled. Aye that's the word.'

'What video?'

'I thought I told you. I found a birthday video of me and my mum. Boswell was there, and Lang. Left me in little doubt that Boswell hated him as much as I did. That coupled with the letters – I think he believes his own shite. He'll answer for Lang's death, which is good, and I think he was only culpable in Lang's behaviour through his cowardice and inaction, but he has much worse to answer for.'

'And what's that?'

'Something I suspect he'll never go down for. I don't feel up to talking about it right now.'

'Is that why you're coming into the office tomorrow?'

She didn't answer.

'Steph?'

'Yes. Please don't ask me now. Tomorrow, aye?'

'Where is he now?'

'Home, I guess.'

'You guess? Has he done anything that might make him a flight risk? He confessed to murder.'

Again, no immediate answer.

'Steph, you're worrying me.'

'He won't run. Please don't ask me how I know that. You know I never bend the rules much. And I'm not now. I just need some time.'

'For what?'

'Nothing dodgy.'

'You promise?'

'Maybe a bit.'

'Fuck's sake, Steph. You're asking a lot.'

'You mean like when you made me drive down to South Lanarkshire to look for Elizabeth Dunn after the station nurse ordered me to take you to A&E? You mean that kind of asking a lot?' Her tone had hardened, and he felt a heavy ache eat at his heart.

'Is that where we are, Steph? Calling in favours?'

'No. Nothing like that. I'm sorry. I just have to do this a particular way, and I need you to trust me.'

He knew he would, but he couldn't allow her to disappoint herself.

'OK.' He heard her sigh of relief down the phone line.

'Thanks, Malkie. I don't think I can fully explain right now, but the way I see things between him and me panning out, it's going to get ugly, so I need to do it a certain way.'

'This isn't like you, Steph, and it scares me.'

'It scares me too. But I need to do it right. Can you trust me?'

'Of course I can, you daft mare.'

'Thanks, arse.'

'Daft cow.'

'Love you too.' And she hung up.

What the hell was she doing?

What the hell was *he* doing?

Malkie reached the cabin long after his dad's usual bedtime, but he found him on the deck, wrapped in a puffer jacket and with coffee on the table. Not just their favourite two mugs. A full pot, too. Not a good sign.

'Sorry, Dad. Hell of a day.'

'They all seem to be bad days lately, Malcolm.'

Tommy's tone stopped Malkie with one foot on the step up onto the deck. He looked at his dad; made it clear he wanted to know how he'd meant his comment. Tommy said nothing, just nodded for Malkie to sit. He poured himself a coffee, took his time adding milk and sugar. This late in the evening, the air bit right through his clothes, so he went inside for a thick fleece and didn't hurry. When he finally sat, his dad looked ready to lose his temper.

'What are you not telling me, Malcolm?'

It took him a second to switch his mind to his mum's death, and Ballantyne's reopening of the investigation into it.

'Damn it. Sorry, Dad. My mind is all over the place. I have this woman in custody who—'

'I don't care.'

Malkie cast his dad a wounded look, felt himself prickle, defensive at what sounded like unfair criticism from the one man he'd always thought he could depend on. He reminded himself that Tommy's world was a hell of a lot smaller than his, even more so since their lives were ripped apart after they both lost his mum. He wanted to relate how much he feared for Patricia Quinn's future and that of her brother, but his dad didn't care about all of that. Actually, that wasn't quite true. He would care if he wasn't being torn apart by the lack of information coming from his son.

Malkie leaned forward, elbows on the table, hands wrapped around the heat of his coffee mug.

'I told you our Forensics people lifted a print off a lighter that Callum Gourlay found in the mud outside the house. Well, we got an ID back on it.'

He hesitated, afraid of what the revelation would do to the frail and fearful old man across from him.

'It was Liam Fielding, Dad.'

Tommy's eyes widened and now he leaned forward too. 'The man whose father framed Walter Callahan?'

'Walter, aye.' Again, the vicious and negative part of his mind asked him when he last visited Callahan's grave at the Lothian Ex-Services Outreach Centre, the LESOC. The same place Deborah lived.

'Fielding killed your mum?'

Only now did it occur to Malkie that Liam's father, Jake, wouldn't be above planting evidence to implicate his own boy. After finding out his big, strong, tough son was gay and then disowning him for refusing to *get help*, the old bastard had been thrown out of his own home and Liam's partner moved in. The damage to The Jakey's reputation among the Edinburgh and Glasgow criminal communities would have humiliated the old bastard, but not as much as what he considered to be his son's *illness*. All of which suggested that Jake Fielding could easily have tried to send his own son down for murder.

'It looks that way.'

'It *looks* that way?'

'Aye. We resist forming opinions too early, Dad. Dangerous. Confirmation bias has caused more than a few investigations to fail to secure a conviction. Lawyers love to call out confirmation bias whenever they can.'

'Who else could have done it? Had the lighter definitely been there since that evening?'

'We think so.'

'Who's we?'

'Me and Callum Gourlay. Possibly DS Pamela Ballantyne too, but she'll keep her cards close to her chest, for now.'

'Who's she?'

'A colleague. Another DS, like me.'

'Is she good? At the job?'

Malkie considered this for a moment. He harboured no doubt that she was as good as any other DS, maybe better than most, but he wasn't used to admiring her. Partly her own fault for being so prickly in the past, but he knew now that much of that came from her mistaken decision to tie her career to an arsehole like McLeish. He couldn't blame her for carrying an immense grudge for that.

'She has a different style to me. More methodical and logical. I tend to make instinctive leaps, listen to my intuition a lot, before sorting through what I've found. Has caused me problems but sometimes produces results we might have otherwise missed.' He could only wonder how differently his current case might now be going had he not noticed Beauchamp's boxes and had a unique familiarity with exactly that brand of international travel guide.

'She'll get to the bottom of it, Dad. She's too good not to.'

'Do you think Liam Fielding did it?'

Malkie cast his mind back to Callahan, something he hated doing because he considered it his greatest failing, allowing Callahan to end up with three AFO rounds in the chest for a crime he didn't commit. Malkie doubted he'd ever stop feeling responsible for that.

'Malcolm?'

'Sorry, Dad. That case... It did me a lot of damage.'

'I remember.

'Do you still visit Callahan's grave at that place?'

'The LESOC?' *Not nearly often enough, Dad.* 'Aye, sometimes.'

'So, you think this DS Ballantyne will get to the truth?'

'She will. I'm certain of it.'

'Whatever that is.'

'Whatever that is, Dad.' He found himself leaning towards the idea that The Jakey planted the lighter. He'd misjudged Liam before. No, he hadn't misjudged the man. He was an animal: a chauvinist and an abusive husband to a woman he brutalised so much she'd played Malkie like a horny schoolboy out of sheer desperation to escape her marriage. He couldn't blame her for that.

They reverted to silence. Malkie turned his chair to look out across Harperrig Reservoir. He studied the massive, sweeping outline of the Pentland Hills, faintly silhouetted by town lights on their far side, and told himself, yet again, that he needed to haul his lazy arse up there more often. He used to hide up there on days when he felt his youthful awkwardness most keenly. He smiled at a memory of jam sandwiches, banana milk and comics and wondered if he might benefit from doing so again. He didn't read as much as he used to and maybe he'd find some dead zones where his bloody mobile couldn't get a signal.

'We should go hill-walking again, Dad. Would do us both some good. I miss it up there.'

His dad followed Malkie's gaze to the hulking shadow of the hills. 'Aye your mum liked dragging us up there, didn't she? Never missed a chance to remind us we needed more exercise.'

They smiled at each other, and Malkie decided that Ballantyne's investigation, no matter what it uncovered, would not stop him and his dad from living the best lives they could, as his mum would have wanted.

They sipped their coffee and shared the calm night air, as if it had an ability to heal them.

Until Tommy decided to remind Malkie of his old, embarrassing self.

'Is Pamela Ballantyne the one you called *Nippy Tits* once?'

'Aye, and I'm not proud of that. Even before I learned that she's not as bad as she comes across as, that was a crass thing to say. I should have been better than that.'

'I thought so but didn't want to make you feel bad.'

'You should have told me. Might have taught me a lot earlier that I wasn't much better than some of the apes I work with. Still embarrasses me, the lazy opinions I used to have.'

'Ach, we all learn, son. Your mum tore a strip off me once for saying that being a stay-at-home mum is a full-time job.'

'Isn't it?' Malkie felt another uncomfortable re-education coming as soon as he spoke.

'It is, but her point was why should it be? Did you know she always wanted to be a social worker?'

'No. I didn't.'

'Don't feel bad about it; I only found out after you were grown up and started your career.'

They sat in silence for a while. Malkie felt like an idiot; not a new experience for him. So much he never knew about his own mum.

THIRTY-SEVEN

[Zoe] We're fucked.

[Zoe] Teri?

[Teri] I'm here. Try to stay calm. We've done nothing wrong.

[Zoe] Yes we have.

[Teri] How?

[Zoe] We should have told the polis *what we know as soon as Patricia told us she'd killed him.*

[Teri] Shit. You're right.

[Zoe] Of course I'm right. As you helpfully reminded me, I've had more experience of the polis *than you.*

[Teri] I apologised for that, Zoe. And I meant it.

[Zoe] No, I'm sorry. I should have told you when I asked to join the chat.

[Teri] Let's move forward, aye?

[Zoe] We need to. They're going to see this chat, aren't they?

[Teri] Yes, they are.

[Zoe] We should tell them now. It'll just get worse if we don't. She only just told us so we can say we were scared? If we offer to help surely it'll be better for us than if they have to come for us?

[Teri] We'll get charged. For obstructing the investigation, something like that. Will you be OK, with your record?

[Zoe] No idea. I think so. My probation ended nine years ago. I don't think what I did will make this worse than it'll be for you. I wish I knew.

[Teri] But if the two of us don't go voluntarily, it'll definitely be worse for both of us.

[Zoe] Aye. Oh, fuck's sake, Teri. What will they do to us?

[Teri] I have no idea. But I don't think I can risk it. I want to hand myself in, but that'll look even worse for you if I do and you don't, won't it?

[Zoe] They'll see what we planned to do to him.

[Teri] And that was nothing illegal.

[Zoe] I suppose so. But will they take our plans as meaning we might have helped Patricia kill him?

[Teri] No. Why would she have announced it like she did, if we were in on it?

[Zoe] Oh aye. I didn't think of that. I'm not thinking straight today.

[Teri] Me neither. That's why we need to hand ourselves in. We both agree this can only get worse, aye?

[Zoe] Well, if they don't put us away, it won't change much for me. I'll just have two things on my record, and this will look like nothing compared to my previous conviction.

[Teri] Good. I'm glad. Really.

[Zoe] What about you?

[Teri] It'll be embarrassing but I'm not sure I care about that at my age.

[Zoe] How old are you?

[Teri] I'm sixty-two Zoe.

[Zoe] Really? Wow.

[Teri] What, you think only young women get catfished and blackmailed by misogynistic monsters like Beauchamp?

[Zoe] We've never said his name out loud in this chat, have we?

[Teri] No. I always assumed we were all too ashamed. I'm a self-employed financial adviser. Had my own company for decades. When all this leaks out, my credibility will be shot. I mean, who would trust their money with someone who allowed herself to be catfished and then blackmailed?

[Zoe] Fuck. Sorry, Teri.

[Teri] Don't be. Like I said, I've realised I couldn't care less what people

will say about me. I've thought about retiring for a while. This might be the push I need. Bit perverse though.

[Zoe] I run a newsletter called Fuck The Patriarchy. *No money in it, but I get by. Only job I was able to get with my record was in a café near where I live.*

[Teri] You know, this might actually help you, reinforce your qualifications to engage in feminist activism? If you can handle it becoming open knowledge, I mean?

[Zoe] I'll admit I'm going to struggle, Teri. Women like us shouldn't get taken in by fuckers like him, should we? People will think we're stupid. It's going to be humiliating, isn't it?

[Teri] No, Zoe. It really isn't. You've seen that documentary on Netflix, yes?

[Zoe] About the American woman?

[Teri] Yes. She was a really senior executive in some company, like board level. And she became a victim.

[Zoe] Aye, I remember thinking if someone like her can be fooled…

[Teri] Exactly. People like him are devious bastards. They have an instinct for how to manipulate people. And they think us older women are more stupid than the younger ones.

[Zoe] I'm only thirty-four.

[Teri] Oh God. Sorry.

[Zoe] Don't be.

[Teri] How much do you know about Patricia and Amber?

[Zoe] Hardly anything. I thought that was the rules of the chat. Names only.

[Teri] Well, I ran checks on all of you, to protect all of us, you understand?

[Zoe] Aye, you said. Makes sense. Sorry for going off on one at you, before.

[Teri] It's fine. To be expected, maybe. We're all about to get to know a lot more about each other than we ever meant to. You know about her brother already. I had to remind her about sharing too much personal information the day she told us about him.

[Zoe] I remember that day. She really needed to talk about him, didn't she?

[Teri] Yes. Maybe I made a mistake that day by letting her say so much?

[Zoe] What kind of person would it have made you if you'd shut her down when she so obviously needed friendly ears?

[Teri] Thanks. Really.

[Zoe] And Amber?

[Teri] She's a vet with her own practice. Amber Balfour. She took over the company from her dad. It has been in their family for generations. She was terrified the damage it would do to her reputation would mean she couldn't face her customers anymore. That it would damage the family brand.

[Zoe] How did Beauchamp get his manky claws into her?

[Teri] Zoe, that's the one chat rule I still don't want to break. I hope you understand.

[Zoe] Aye. Of course. Sorry.

[Teri] So.

[Zoe] Aye.

[Teri] First thing tomorrow morning?

[Zoe] Aye.

[Zoe] Teri. Can we have a wee coffee together in the Almondvale first? Before we go to the police station?

[Teri] Aye, I'd like that. Starbucks at 10:00?

[Zoe] Sure. One more thing though...

[Teri] What?

[Zoe] What do you look like?

[Teri] LOL. I'm tall and annoyingly skinny and I never go anywhere at this time of year without my woolly hat with the most ridiculously massive red pompom.

[Zoe] OK. I'm the opposite. Rampant, militant lesbian. Short and fat and scruffy. But I don't wear dungarees and I shave my legs once a month whether they need it or not. I'll be in jeans and a black hoody, so I'll find you.

[Teri] Hah! I think you and I could have been friends in better circumstances, Zoe.

[Zoe] There's still time.

[Teri] Yes. There is. See you tomorrow.

[Zoe] Before you go, have you heard from Amber? She should come with us.

[Teri] No, and that worries me.

[Zoe] Do you have her address?

[Teri] No. Just her number. It's going to voicemail. I left her a message.

[Zoe] You think she's OK?

[Teri] No. I don't.

THIRTY-EIGHT

'DS McCulloch. A word, please.'

'Sir.'

Malkie doubted anyone would be fooled by his and McLeish's feigned civility to each other, and he didn't care. However much trouble McLeish intended to make for Malkie, he was confident he'd committed no transgression bad enough to earn a charge of gross misconduct, so his pension should be safe. Selling the land on which their home used to sit would keep both him and his dad comfortable, if not exactly rolling in it, for the rest of Tommy's life, which was as far as Malkie's concern went.

He followed McLeish to the meeting room he'd designated as his office.

'Close the door.'

Malkie did, then remained standing.

'Sit.'

Malkie sat.

McLeish made him wait while he fiddled with his cuff links and pretended to pick fluff from his trousers. When he deigned to make eye contact, Malkie was ready for a fight.

'I've put in a complaint about your unprofessional behaviour yesterday and the day before, as well as your phenomenal cockup with Remi Quinn. I intend to have you suspended at least. Do you have anything to say?'

Malkie resisted an urge to call the fucker out about just who ordered him to bring Remi Quinn in for questioning without waiting for an Appropriate Adult with professional mental health qualifications. McLeish's continued failure to record his order in HOLMES plus several reliable witnesses to his assurance he would meant Malkie had a strong defence against that accusation. He'd keep that in his back pocket for later.

'I do.'

He sighed. 'Well?'

Malkie sat up, crossed his legs and clasped his hands in his lap. He pretended to consider his response. McLeish waited, but his lips pulled tight and thin and his eyes took on just a tad too much of an impression of disinterest.

'I think, sir, given the dynamic between us, currently and historically, that... May I speak candidly, sir?'

'Get on with it.'

Malkie waited him out.

'Oh, for fuck's sake. Fine. Anything you say for the next five minutes is off the record and not actionable in any way. Now fucking spit it out.'

'I think any action that will remove your inept and revolting carcass from my life, permanently, will bring me and others nothing but joy. You've shown yourself, repeatedly, to be completely lacking in empathy, good judgement or professional competence and have endangered at least three investigations that I'm aware of. I believe you are more of a disgrace to our profession than I will ever be, and that the Service, as a whole, would benefit from your sorry, lazy, self-important and arrogant arse being booted out for good.'

He waited a full two seconds before delivering one more, perfect, satisfying, 'Sir.'

McLeish turned a dangerous red and opened his mouth, but Malkie barged on. 'In short, sir, you're a complete wanker and a twat of the worst kind.' He didn't raise his voice and made the entire speech as if commenting on a junior detective's yearly performance review.

He smiled at McLeish, watched his temper boil over in glorious and unforgettable slow motion.

McLeish stood. 'Get the fuck out and go home, you fucking waste of space. I'll see your job and your pension fucked and I'll enjoy a glass of champagne at your retirement party if you have the brass neck to have one and if anyone bothers to turn up.'

'Will you be documenting the grounds on which your formal disciplinary request will be based, sir? Because as far as I can remember, apart from a few harsh words I may have uttered to you in the presence of witnesses but not actually directed at you, I believe I've conducted this specific investigation strictly according to procedure and have made significant progress despite the obvious demands other matters have made on you and prevented you from contributing as much as you'd no doubt prefer.'

McLeish exploded out of his chair. 'Get out. You're fucking finished. I intend to make damned sure of that.'

Malkie stood. He pulled his mobile from the inner pocket of his jacket and stopped the voice recorder.

McLeish's face, far from indicating any worry, turned apoplectic.

Malkie feigned surprise. 'Odd. Most coppers wouldn't fall for that one. Decent coppers, I mean.' He beamed at McLeish, more pleased with himself than would be good for him.

McLeish screwed up a form and threw it at him. It failed completely to reach Malkie and instead fell to the floor. Malkie picked it up and scanned it.

'You dropped this, sir.'

The door opened and Thompson appeared, her face white and her eyes blazing. 'Would you gentlemen care to join us for morning briefing?'

She lowered her voice. 'And dial down the fucking testosterone. Half the office heard you, you bloody idiots.' She stormed away, shaking her head and muttering more expletives.

'Sir.' Malkie smiled and left. Knew when he'd already gone too far.

He took his seat in the main office space. Gucci had, as always, saved him a seat next to her. 'Been nice knowing you, Malkie.' Was that the second time someone had said that to him in the past few days?

Morning briefing passed without an appearance from McLeish. Malkie updated Thompson, who said nothing until she nodded for him to sit down so she could move on to the next agenda item.

As soon as the gathered audience had dispersed, he tried to talk to her.

'Not now. Later.' Her voice promised physical harm or worse.

He returned to his desk. His phone rang. Bernadette Stevens at reception, another colleague who he'd only recently managed to stop irritating.

'I have two young ladies wanting to talk to you, Malkie.'

'Thanks, Bernie. I'll be there in a moment.'

'Was that shouting I heard? Sounded angry.'

'I've upset McLeish again, Bernie. He wants my head this time.'

'Did you give him enough rope?'

'I don't think so. Nothing actionable. Some choice words but I recorded his agreement to go off the record.'

'Ah. That'll be legally inadmissible if he didn't know you were recording him, but I guess Senior Management will listen to it anyway.'

'Let's hope so.'

She hung up, and Malkie headed for the door through to the foyer.

He nodded at Bernie as he passed the area from which she controlled everything that came and went in the station. She winked at him as she pushed the door release button.

Fuck's sake. Even Bernie thinks I'm saveable.

Two ladies stood as he entered the reception area. He recognised the shorter one as Zoe Anderson, but he detected none of the belligerence she'd shown the previous evening.

The taller one spoke. 'Are you a detective?'

'I am. How can I help you?'

She swallowed and glanced at Anderson, who nodded at her.

'I'm Teri Marshall. My friend Zoe and I have information which might... Which is pertinent to your investigation into the death of Sebastian Beauchamp.'

Well, fuck me.

THIRTY-NINE

Malkie signed Marshall and Anderson in, then showed them through to the custody suite and sat them in different interview rooms. They shared a look of dread as they were separated.

Malkie fetched Gucci. 'Lou, with me please. Rab, can you take a Uniform and ask Amber Balfour to come in for an interview please?'

'Will do.'

'If she refuses, tell her we're talking to Teri Marshall and Zoe Anderson. If she still won't come in, arrest her.'

'You sure, boss?'

'Aye.' He really wasn't.

He headed for the interview rooms. 'I'm not going to caution Marshall and Anderson, Lou. I'm still tempted to believe they're victims of Beauchamp, like Patricia was. Have we got the names of those account holders back from the banks yet?'

'Not yet. I'll chase them.'

'After we talk to these ladies. I have a feeling we may not need the bank to confirm them anyway.'

'Let's hope so. Which one first?'

'Marshall. I pissed Anderson off last night. She may not feel like opening up to me unless we get something from Marshall first.'

'Sounds like a plan.'

'Aye, let's hope this moves us forward before McLeish has security escort me from the building.' He grinned, but Gucci stared at him, hard, then shook her head and entered the interview room.

'Good morning, Ms Marshall. I'm Detective Sergeant Malcolm McCulloch and my colleague here, as you already know, is Detective Constable Louisa Gooch.'

Marshall nodded at Lou.

'You can call me Teri.'

'Thank you, Teri. We'll record this conversation but you're not under caution at this time, OK?'

She looked less than happy but nodded. 'Yes. That's fine.'

Malkie thought he detected an unspoken note of *Really?* in her voice.

When Gucci had started the recording, Malkie turned to Teri.

'So, Teri. What would you like to tell us.'

'Can I get a glass of water please?'

'Of course.' Malkie nodded to the Uniform by the door, who left. Malkie hadn't locked it, considered anyone who offered themselves up for interview shouldn't constitute a flight risk.

'I started a chat group, last year, after Sebastian Beauchamp... After he threatened to post a video he took of him and me...'

Malkie waited. He didn't enjoy the woman's discomfort, but he couldn't lead her.

'We slept together.'

She slumped in her seat. 'No. We didn't. We fucked. No, not that, either. He fucked me. On a table in the Scottish Parliament. It was after a dinner for independent financial advisers. I run my own company, TM Financial Ltd. When I met him, I found him charming and handsome, and thought I felt something.' Her mouth twisted in distaste. 'I'd rather eschewed personal relationships while I grew my company. I had a few drinks with him, then... I was told afterwards that I became ill and he took care of me. They said he took me to reception to call me a taxi.'

She took a moment. 'I'd really like that glass of water please.' Her voice was dry and broken. Gucci left to hurry it along.

Malkie smiled at Teri. 'Please. Carry on.'

'I woke up on a desk in a conference room at four in the morning. I was dressed but... But I knew. Please don't make me say it.'

He tried to soften his expression, which was not as hard as he expected because he already felt for the woman. 'Just once, for the recording please, then I won't ask again.'

She opened her mouth then closed it again, swallowed, and tried again. 'Sebastian Beauchamp raped me, DS McCulloch.'

'Thank you being brave, Ms Marshall.'

'Teri.'

'OK, Teri. What did you do when you regained consciousness?'

'At first I wanted to call the police, but I looked around me, at the conference room, the huge mahogany table and the leather chairs and the massive video-conferencing screen, and knew I couldn't.'

The door opened and Gucci appeared with two cups of water. Teri downed the first before Gucci handed her the second.

'In my industry, reputation is everything, DS McCulloch. And my word against even a junior SPAD to a cabinet minister... I would never have come out of that with my business intact.'

She dropped her eyes to her hands, clasped the table.

'As much it shamed me to let him get away with what he did, my pride wouldn't let me ruin my achievements by getting my name plastered all over the media in a case I couldn't hope to win. He'd have known that.' Gucci handed her the box of tissues. It would need replacing before the week was over.

Malkie's inner idiot itched to take her hand across the table, damsel-in-distress syndrome never far from his mind, but he resisted. He couldn't help her if he compromised his professional integrity.

'So, I went home. I showered and scrubbed myself raw. Then I did it all again. I threw up until my stomach was empty. I tried to swallow a bottle of sleeping tablets, but I couldn't keep them down. The next day, I managed to displace my shame with anger, enough to back off from letting that vile man do any more damage to me.'

Malkie wanted to tell her how much he admired her but stayed quiet. He noticed Gucci's hands clasped in her lap. Her knuckles were white.

'Over time, I rationalised it to a place I could deal with it, constantly reminded myself my only mistake had been to trust a man I thought was respectable and had integrity. I remembered afterwards how he'd shown me the artwork that lines the parliament corridors. He'd already drugged me by then, so it only came back to me later, in scraps and fragments.'

Malkie recalled the days and months following his failure to rescue his mum from her burning home. *I know how memories come at you, Teri.*

'Then, a few weeks later, I got a WhatsApp from him. He wanted money, or he'd post the video online. I panicked and paid him. Then he asked for more. And more.'

'We saw the transactions on his account. DC Gooch?' Lou opened her notebook and showed Teri the sort codes and account numbers she'd copied from Beauchamp's statement. Teri pointed to one. 'That's mine.' She looked even more ashamed than Malkie thought possible.

'Why only ever £200 Teri? He must have known you're a high earner, and he's wealthy too.'

'I don't think he did it for the money. He did it for fun.'

'For fun?'

'Yes. The things he said to me when he called me once a month. The money was just the mechanism he used to humiliate me. He often asked me if I wanted him to stop. He made me beg, then carried right on.'

She took a moment, stared down, then lifted her eyes and straightened her back.

'Last year, I was browsing an online chat group that supports women who have been victims of toxic masculinity and misogyny in any way. And someone called Amber had commented on how she'd been abused by a man known to many but who she couldn't risk naming. I felt certain she'd been a victim of someone like Beauchamp too. I posted back to her and put as much detail as I thought I could get away with under that group's rules. Amber contacted me. I have no idea how she found me, but she messaged me two letters and I knew.'

Malkie knew what she was about to say but couldn't lead her.

'What were the two letters, Teri?'

'SB.'

As far as Malkie was concerned, that breached a threshold. To allay his own irrational worries, he glanced at the recorder and confirmed it was still running.

'Teri. Was Patricia Quinn a participant in your group?'

'Yes.'

'And did she say anything in your chat about Sebastian Beauchamp?'

'She said she killed him. In self-defence though.' She looked directly at Malkie, her eyes pleading. 'Is she OK?'

'She's in custody, helping us with our enquiries, and she's unharmed.'

Teri relaxed, but her expression remained suspicious, falling far short of trusting.

'Do you know she has a brother, Teri?'

'Yes. Remi. He's... Troubled.'

'We know. Do you have any information that might help us find him?'

'He's missing? You don't think Beauchamp hurt him, do you?'

'I can't tell you why we're looking for him, Teri, but we have to find him.'

'I'm sorry. I knew he existed, but Patricia never said anything about him other than that he was a handful sometimes.'

'Are there any other members in your chat group?'

'No. I rejected three last year, then gave up and made it a closed group.'

'Why?'

'I didn't want anyone too volatile joining.'

'For the sake of the others?'

'That and...'

Malkie waited.

'We were planning to expose Beauchamp. Publish the video he sent of him raping me, and another one of him doing the same to Amber. He was careful to edit himself out of them, even made it look as if we were conscious and consenting. They wouldn't have fooled your experts, but they didn't need to. There was nothing that could identify him, but they would have ruined us.'

'I know you feared for your reputation, but Amber Balfour?'

'She owns a veterinary practice, it's been in her family for decades. She was terrified of ruining their reputation and losing their customers. We both tried to believe Beauchamp would never release the videos in case your guys could trace them back to him, but we were terrified. And ashamed. We couldn't take the chance.'

'Women who fall victim to sexual predators never deserve it, Teri. You say you were about to expose him. I thought you were afraid of losing your business and everything you worked for?'

She thought for a moment.

'I was. But the chat made me realise there was more than myself to think about. I have enough stashed away for a comfortable retirement, but I knew I wouldn't enjoy it as long as I thought he was out there doing what he did to me to other women. I can live with the shame of being labelled a stupid old woman, but not that.'

Malkie smiled at her and meant it. 'I think that's enough for now, Teri. Please get yourself a coffee or something. There's a café in the atrium of the Civic Centre. I'll come and find you after we've spoken with Zoe and Amber, OK?'

'You're letting me go?'

'Yes. Anyone who voluntarily comes to us and admits to minor offences isn't likely to constitute a flight risk.'

This triggered something in Teri. 'Thank you.' She let out a long breath, and Malkie saw her gather herself for a new subject. 'I'm worried about Amber. Amber Balfour. She's not joined the chat since Patricia told us what she thought she'd done.'

'A colleague of mine saw her just last night, Teri. She was fine. But I've sent someone to ask her to come in for an interview.'

'Good. She's not been answering her phone.'

He nodded to Gucci. As she reached to stop the recording, an earlier scrap of info jumped to the front of Malkie's mind.

'Actually, one last question, Teri. Did you know that Patricia remortgaged her house recently?'

Teri thought for a second, then closed her eyes and groaned. 'Oh, Patricia. You silly, silly, girl.'

'Teri?'

'I think she was trying to pay Beauchamp off, to get him off all of our backs. She was never convinced by our plans to expose him.'

'Thank you, Teri. You've been very helpful.'

For once, he meant that.

FORTY

'You lead on this one, Lou. She probably hates my ample guts already. I was less than polite to her yesterday. I know, I know. Must do better.'

As they entered, Zoe Anderson stood, her eyes fixed on Malkie.

'Detective. I'm sorry about last night. I was scared and in shock. Please forgive me.'

Malkie resisted an urge to glance at Gucci.

'No problem, Ms Anderson. It can be intimidating finding a police officer on your doorstep and people react in all sorts of ways. Let's say no more about it. Please, take a seat.'

She nodded, her relief obvious, and sat.

Malkie performed the recording admin and was stupidly pleased that Gucci didn't need to remind him of anything. He nodded to her to begin.

'Ms Anderson, I'm Detective Constable Louisa Gooch and this is Detective Sergeant Malcolm McCulloch. We appreciate you volunteering to assist us with our enquiries. What prompted you to come here today?'

'Eh? You took our phones. I figured it was better to hand ourselves in than wait for you to come for us.'

'Hand yourselves in? For what, Ms Anderson?'

'Eh? I just meant come to talk to you voluntarily like.'

'About what?'

She took a few seconds. 'Patricia told us she killed Sebastian Beauchamp...'

'Patricia Quinn.'

'Aye. She told us she killed him, and we didn't believe her.'

Gucci held Anderson's gaze. It took only a second.

'OK. We were too scared to report it.'

Malkie resisted an urge to roll his eyes. *Fantastic. Book her, Gucci. Case closed. Job done. Everyone to Nando's to celebrate.*

Gucci cast him a look and he realised he'd breathed a long-suffering sigh, anyway.

Gucci turned back to Anderson. 'Thank you for that, but can you elaborate?'

'Not really. We've not heard from her again. When we saw the news we realised she was probably telling the truth.'

'And you believed her, after that?'

'Aye, we did. But you know, we were in a state of shock.'

'Yes, that must have been a nasty experience when you realised she'd been telling you the truth and reaching out to you.'

'Aye. It was a shock. We were shocked.'

Fuck's sake, I'm glad I asked Lou to lead.

'So, what exactly did she say?'

'She said she murdered him with a wine bottle.'

'Nothing more specific than that?'

'No, just that she murdered him with a wine bottle.'

'Did you wonder how exactly she did that?'

'I assumed she lamped him with it. That could kill someone, couldn't it?'

'It could, Ms Anderson.'

Malkie noted Zoe's expression, hoping for more info, then disappointed when Gucci didn't elaborate.

'And she said nothing more than that?'

'Oh, wait.'

Malkie had to bite his tongue. *You remember something else? Again? Really?*

'I remember now. She said she smashed it over his head.'

'OK. And she was sure she killed him?'

'She sounded pretty sure all the way through the chat.'

'Do you ever delete the chat, Ms Anderson?'

'No. I never thought I'd need to.'

'Then we can check exactly what was said when we get the report on the contents of your phones, hopefully this morning. Do you feel up to telling us why you joined the chat?'

She looked sheepish. 'He caught me kicking the shite out of a guy.'

'Who did?'

Zoe scowled, as if confused. 'Beauchamp.'

'And what did he film you doing?'

'I hospitalised a man I saw hassling a girl in the car park down the lane from Linlithgow train station. She was crying and trying to walk away, but he kept pushing her back against a wall and asking her why she was being so unfriendly. He didn't know I'd come up behind him until I grabbed him by the hair and hauled him off the girl. She ran away and I attacked him. I got a bit carried away. Angry, you know?'

She swallowed. 'I lost it. I think I nearly killed him. As I made myself walk away, Beauchamp got out of his car. He'd been filming the whole thing on his phone. He had this fucking – sorry – evil grin on his face, and he laughed when I noticed him. I was so surprised I stood there while he walked up to me and got a good, clear close-up of my face. Then he took my phone out of my hand and made me unlock it. He pushed me up against the same wall and leaned all over me. It was fucking disgusting – sorry. He took my number. I hoped I'd never hear from him again, but that was really bloody naive of me, wasn't it?'

Gucci didn't react. Zoe looked disappointed but continued.

'He messaged me a week later. Said if I didn't deposit £200 in an account he'd post the video on social media. The fucker had found me and knew I had a record and said the *polis* would bang me up in a second if he posted it. I didn't know what to do, except pay him.'

She deflated as if relieved to have got the worst over with. 'Then he demanded more money from me a month later, and he's been doing it ever since. You know I've been in prison before, aye? Never again.'

She slumped, rested her arms on the table, and shrugged at them as if to say that was all she had.

'Thank you for your candour, Ms Anderson. That can't have been easy for you.'

'No.'

Malkie nodded at Gucci. She opened her notebook and laid it in front of Anderson, open at the list of accounts. Anderson grimaced and sighed, then pointed to a number. 'That one.'

'Did you know that Patricia has a brother?'

'Aye. Handicapped, isn't he?'

'Well, he's on the autism spectrum. How much do you know about him?'

'Not much, just that he's a nightmare sometimes.'

Good grief, I hope this woman never has kids of her own.

'You never heard Patricia talk about him?'

'No. I told you.'

'He's missing, Ms Anderson. If there's anything you know – anything – that might help us find him, you need to tell us.'

She glanced from Gucci to Malkie and back again, looked cornered. 'I don't know anything about him. There's nothing useful I can tell you. Patricia hardly ever mentioned him.'

'OK. Relax, Ms Anderson. What was the purpose of the chat group that Ms Marshall started?'

'How do you mean?'

'I mean, was there an agenda? A reason beyond just mutual support?'

'You mean the videos? Well, Teri's video. She wanted to publish hers, even though it might ruin her. The fucker kept his face out of it, but he made sure hers was front and centre. Teri decided she wanted to give it to the *polis* in case you could identify him. I knew from publishing my blog and my newsletter that techies can get all sorts of information out of videos. She said she was prepared to take the chance if it meant he might get exposed for what he did.'

'So, none of you wanted to hurt him? Or kill him?'

'I wanted to. Hurt him *then* kill him. But I would never have done it. I couldn't risk going inside again.'

'Did the others ever suggest hurting him?'

'No. None of them. We just planned to release the videos.'

'Not Patricia?'

She snorted. 'Patricia? She was even against us releasing the videos. She kept saying maybe he could be negotiated with. She was so bloody naive. All she cared about was protecting her brother. She would never risk doing anything that might get her put away because Remi can't survive without her.'

'So, you don't believe Patricia could have killed him? Despite her saying she did?'

'No chance. If she was there, she went there hoping she could reason with him. Patricia, hurt someone? Never. She couldn't—'

She was cut off by a knock on the door. Thompson appeared and nodded for them to join her outside. Her face had Malkie dreading the reason for the interruption.

Gucci closed the door behind her but Thompson led them down the corridor, away from the interview rooms.

'Amber Balfour has committed suicide. Same blue stuff in a syringe a vet used to put my dog to sleep.'

'Aw fuck, no.' Malkie braced his hands on the wall to stop himself from punching it.

'Rab just called it in. She didn't answer her door, so he looked through the letter box and saw water pouring down the staircase. Uniforms forced entry and Rab found her in the bath with a syringe in her arm. SOCOs are on their way there now.'

'Poor woman. Fucking Beauchamp as good as killed her even after he was dead. This is sick.'

'It is. Question is, do we inform Quinn and Marshall and Anderson?'

'I think we tell only Quinn for now.' He glanced at Gucci.

She gave it some thought then nodded. 'I agree. It might give her the push she needs to see sense and cooperate, but yes – it's too soon to share it with Marshall and Anderson.'

Thompson nodded. 'OK. Do it.' She wandered back through the door to the CID desks.

Malkie rubbed his eyes. This was turning into one of those days that made him question his career choice. 'OK. Let's wrap up with Anderson, then go and tell Quinn, see if it shakes anything out of her.'

They returned to the interview room, neither with any great enthusiasm. Malkie stayed quiet, and Gucci led, again.

'Ms Anderson, I only have a few more questions. You've said you don't know Patricia Quinn very well personally, and we assume you know Teri Marshall a bit better. What about Amber Balfour? How well do you know her?'

Zoe perked up. 'Have you heard from her? Is she OK? I thought she'd deserted us, but Teri doesn't think she'd do that. Is she OK?'

'I can't talk about her at the moment, Ms Anderson. How well did you know her?'

Gucci's mouth clamped shut and Malkie had to resist an urge to step in too obviously.

'What do you mean *did*? Where is she? Is she OK? What are you not telling me?'

Gucci could not recover from this, so she didn't try. 'I think we've covered all we can for now, Ms Anderson. Thank you.' And she was gone. Malkie performed the end-of-interview recording formalities.

'Thank you, Ms Anderson. This gentleman will see you out and we'll be in touch if—'

'Where's Amber? Tell me.'

He couldn't. He wanted to but couldn't.

'I can't discuss any more with you for the present, Ms Anderson. This constable will—'

She pushed past him through the door Gucci had left open. 'Teri? Are you here, Teri?'

'Teri was shown to the foyer. I suggested she wait for you at the café in the atrium of the Civic Centre. She's probably waiting for you there, Zoe.'

The Uniform took her gently by the arm.

'Get your hands off me. Where's Teri? Where's Patricia and Amber?'

Malkie stood in silence. She glared at him for a moment, then spun on her heel and headed back the way she'd come in, the Uniform close behind her.

He headed straight for the ladies' loos, pushed the door open a few inches and heard Lou crying.

'Lou. Come out. Talk to me.'

The noises stopped, but she took a while to appear. Her face dared him to say anything, but he had to.

'Interview room three. No arguments.'

She walked ahead of him, even her footsteps furious.

The instant he shut the door, she started.

'How could I be so bloody stupid? I'm better than that. What the hell was I thinking? Damn it.' She kicked a chair.

He waited. She looked at him, her hands on her hips, her breath heaving in and out, her eyes wild.

'Sit, Lou.'

She dropped herself into a chair and propped her head in her hands, her elbows on her knees. 'I'm sorry, boss. I'm so, so sorry.'

He pulled another chair in front of hers and sat. He didn't risk any physical gesture of reassurance because he'd never seen her this furious with herself, had never known her to cock anything up. This was a first for her, and she was obviously livid with herself.

'Lou. You're talking to the recognised king of fuck-ups. My HR record has more black on it than white. I've been officially classified as a threat to national security because of my gob.'

She snorted. 'Rubbish. You're not that bad.'

'I am. But you're not. You're tired. We all are. I've been pushing you and Rab too hard. How much sleep have you had in the last seventy-two hours?'

Her brow furrowed.

'See? You have to think about it. Says it all. Everyone screws up, Lou. Even a Police Scotland all-star like McLeish got something less than correct once, I heard.'

She snorted again. 'Funny. Really. You can't stop me feeling terrible for this, boss. It's going to have to go on my record, isn't it?'

'Aye. I could have stopped the recording in a hurry, but that itself would have led to questions. You made a mistake, Lou. We all do. What matters is that we learn from it and grow.'

'You sound like an HR guidance document.'

'Aye, well. Even HR talk sense sometimes.'

'Steph never screws up, does she?'

Sore point right now, Lou.

'Rarely. It's only one of her multitude of annoying traits.'

Lou stood. 'Sod it. I screwed up, and I'll take the kicking for it. Thanks, boss.'

'No problem, boss.'

'Eh?'

'Just practising for the future, Lou.'

As Gucci headed back to her own desk, the young bloke with the hipster beard appeared again.

'DS McCulloch?'

'Yes, son.'

'Edward.'

'I apologise. What can I do for you, Edward?'

Malkie thought he sounded unconvincing and the lad looked less than impressed, but until he lost at least the hipster beard, Malkie would be unable to take him seriously.

'There's been a sighting of someone who might match the

description of someone you've flagged as a MisPer. A... Hang on.' He checked the piece of paper in his hand and Malkie resisted an urge to grab it from him. 'A Mr Remi—'

Malkie snatched it anyway. Gucci and Rab turned to listen, their eyes eager for any break they could get, the messenger ignored.

Malkie noticed the lad was still standing there, looking aggrieved. 'Thanks, Edward. We've been seriously worried about this guy. I didn't mean to be rude.' He extended his hand. The bloke looked at it but took a second to take it. 'No problem. Sir.' He walked away, shaking his head.

'OK, what do we have? Possible sighting of person matching description of MisPer Remi Quinn, jeans, white trainers, white T-shirt, hoodie under black puffer jacket. Reported by driver of number 918 bus. Disembarked in a village called Creagan. Driver was concerned by the boy's behaviour, tried to talk to him, touched his arm, and he claimed the boy attacked him and ran away.'

He noticed a paperclip in the top corner, skipped the rest of the paragraph and turned the note over. He found a grainy still from what looked like a driver's eye view of a bus door. As rough as it was, Malkie thought the figure turned half to the driver could be Remi.

'Time to talk to Patricia Quinn again. Hopefully she'll confirm that her brother was still alive at...' He checked the paper again. '18:52 yesterday.'

He scowled, confused. 'What the hell was he doing so far from home?'

FORTY-ONE

They didn't come. My friends who Dad said live in the trees. He said they were always watching us. He said they were friendly and helped people who got lost.

I thought they'd be here.

Did they forget me too? It was eleven years and a hundred and thirty-two days ago. Four thousand, one hundred and fifty days.

I'm cold.

I wish I'd got some fish and chips. Maybe those people wouldn't have looked at me.

They always look at me.

People looked at me before. Those girls at the bus stop. Then they stole my money and laughed at me. Why are people like that?

Is it because I hurt people?

Because I'm bad to the core?

Is that why Mum left us?

Then Dad?

I liked Dad. But he left too.

No. They didn't leave. They died.

Was it because I was bad?

I thought my friends would be here. It's their bridge.

They must think I'm bad too.

I am bad. I hurt that man.

I don't remember hurting him, but he was shouting at me and hurting me then he was on the floor and there was lots of blood and the other red stuff and he wasn't moving and I had something in my hand, and I dropped it and ran away.

Why did Patty go there? He was bad. He hurt her. I saw him hurt her. Through the window.

She was being nice to him, but he hurt her.

I was scared she saw me through the window. I wasn't supposed to be there. She would have been angry. I make her angry a lot. I don't mean to.

She was frightened all day before she left the house, so I hid under the blankets in the back of the car where people put their feet. It hurt my head and it scared me a lot, doing something like that without planning it and preparing for it. I was brave, but I didn't like hiding from her, but she was leaving and I couldn't let her leave me alone at home again. Not when she was so scared too.

I was bad. The man hurt Patty then he hurt me, but I shouldn't have been that bad.

I sneaked back into the car while Patty was crying. I heard her. Crying in the dark. She said bad words.

The man hurt her and he made her cry and say bad words that she never says.

He hurt me too. My neck. But I don't remember it. It still hurts. I tried drinking some water, but it hurts too much.

Where are you, Patty?

I thought you'd come.

I don't think they're here. Maybe they were never here.

I'm so cold, Patty.

And I'm tired.

Of everything.

FORTY-TWO

'Ms Quinn. We've had a possible sighting of Remi. He was fine, at the time.' Malkie handed her the printout of the bus CCTV photo.

She grabbed it and stared at it, then fell apart. She flopped over to one side clutching the photo to herself, buried her face in her blankets, and howled.

He waited.

After a few seconds, she stood and approached him, the photo still held to her chest. She placed one hand on his arm and looked up at him, her eyes red and wet.

'Thank you, Mr McCulloch. That's Remi. I'm sure of it. I'm sorry for giving you a hard time, but...'

'No need to apologise, Ms Quinn. I get used to being the bad guy until I'm the good guy again.'

She studied him. 'I doubt there's much bad guy in you, Mr McCulloch. Remi liked you, I could tell, and he's a superb judge of character. Allow yourself some credit.'

He wanted to believe her, wanted to accept the compliment, so he nodded to her and poured all the warmth he could into his eyes. 'I appreciate that, Ms Quinn. Now, let's find your brother, shall we?' He nodded down at the photo and she refocused.

'Where was it taken? Is he OK? Are you bringing him here?

No, you mustn't. You need to release me so I can take him home. He'll—'

She stopped and studied him. Her excitement and her relief evaporated. 'What are you not telling me?'

'Please sit down, Ms Quinn.'

'No. Tell me.' Her voice started to fray again.

He placed his hands on her arms, made her look at him. 'Sit down, and I'll tell you what we know.'

She sat, her eyes fastened to the photo clutched in her lap.

Malkie sat beside her. He realised he still held the rest of the MisPer sighting report, so he folded it and slipped it into the inside pocket of his jacket, in case she grabbed it.

'First, when that was taken at 18:52 last night, he was alive and well and didn't seem to have been hurt or injured. He just seemed... Frightened.'

Her tears flowed again. 'Oh, Remi. I'm so sorry. I let you down.' She leaned forward with her arms folded in front of her and rocked and moaned. Malkie couldn't help but remember the night his mum died and feel for her. He took her arm again, didn't lift her back into a sitting position, just pulled her from her self-recrimination, brought her back to their conversation.

'Remi was reported to Police Scotland by a bus driver who thought he looked lost. He tried to talk to him, and...' He feared how she would react to this. 'Remi fled when the driver touched his arm.'

Patricia lifted her head to the ceiling as if to stop yet more tears from spilling. 'He'll have freaked out. He hates anyone but me touching him. Where was this?'

'That's the odd thing, Ms Quinn. You said he never leaves the house?'

'No. He doesn't. Not on his own.'

'Then how did he end up over a hundred miles away in a village called Creagan?'

She frowned. 'I have no idea. Dad took us on holiday to Oban a few times, to give Remi a break from Mum, I think. I remember we always stopped in Tyndrum on our way up to the highlands, and Remi always kicked off if we didn't have fish and chips. Loads of people stop there before heading further north. But that was years ago, he could only have been nine or ten years old. How the hell did he get that far? He never leaves the house without me.'

'Never? Not once in all the time you've lived in West Calder?'

'No. Yes. Once. I found him at the Livingston bus stances outside the Almondvale shopping centre. He said he wanted to visit his *little friends in the woods*. It was an odd thing for him to say. He doesn't have any friends, not here in the central belt or anywhere else. I never got him to tell me who he wanted to visit, and he never tried again. Some girls waiting for a bus laughed at him and stole his money.'

'He has money?'

She cast him a stern look. 'Of course. He's not an idiot, Mr. McCulloch. I give him pocket money every week. I keep hoping he'll ask me to take him shopping to spend it on something other than books and his PlayStation. He asks me to buy new games for him, but he spends weeks on the internet beforehand researching them and watching YouTube reviews, like he even needs to know a game inside out with no surprises before he'll play it. Then I can't get him down for dinner some evenings, he loses himself in it so much.'

'And some girls stole it from him?'

'Yes, they asked him where he was headed. Making fun of him of course. He said he was going to visit his friends up north. They asked if he had enough for his bus fare, and Remi being Remi and knowing nothing about how rotten people can be, pulled all his savings, hundreds of pounds, out of his pocket, scrunched up in his fist. They took it. Then they pulled his trousers down and ran away laughing. The people that called the police for him, every time they tried to help him he just screamed harder and lashed out at them.'

She sighed, wiped her eyes. 'He never left the house without me again, and even then, not without planning it and talking every detail through, then never changing anything about what we agreed. He never forgot that experience. He has an incredible ability to remember the smallest details of things that happened to him, even years ago.'

She stood, stepped away, turned back to him with her hands on her hips.

'We need to go there, Mr McCulloch. Now.' She returned her gaze to the photo. 'We'll come for you, Remi.'

Malkie also stood, and held his hands out as if to fend off her demand. 'It's not that simple, Ms Quinn. You're about to be charged with assaulting Sebastian Beauchamp. Even if I can persuade my superiors and the Fiscal to allow you bail or RUI—'

'What's RUI?'

'It means Released Under Investigation, like being on bail but much less restrictive. But considering Beauchamp was murdered, it's by no means certain I'll get authorisation for that.'

'You have to. If anyone else tries to approach Remi, I don't know what he'll do. He could hurt himself or someone else. Do you want that to happen?'

'Please calm down, Ms Quinn. I want to help.'

'Then start by understanding. Do you have a brother, Mr McCulloch? Or a son?'

His temper broke but he managed to keep his voice to a low and dangerous rumble. 'No, but I am a son, Ms Quinn, and my mum was every bit as protective of me as you are of Remi.'

Her anger evaporated and her shoulders slumped. He figured she hadn't missed his use of the past tense. She looked shamed by her own words. 'OK. Then go with me. Handcuff me if you have to. Tag me. If you don't get me to him he'll hurt someone or he'll hurt himself. Either way, you're going to have some hard explaining to do, Mr McCulloch.'

Malkie held his hands out; she'd started to approach him again, her eyes frantic.

'Please. I'm not doing anything until you sit and calm down.'

With a supreme effort she sat, but on the edge of her bed and looking ready to launch herself at him.

'I need to talk to my superior about this. I promise I'll update you as soon as I can.'

She started to protest, but Malkie spoke over her.

'That's the deal, Ms Quinn.'

She closed her mouth again and Malkie turned to leave the cell. At the door he remembered the other news he'd been lumbered with delivering to her.

'Patricia?'

Her eyes told him he'd failed to keep his tone neutral.

'Amber Balfour is dead. I'm sorry. She took her own life. Drugs from her veterinary practice.'

Patricia said nothing. Tears spilled again. She leaned forward and hung her head, let her tears pour and fall to the floor. Malkie heard a strangled and anguished moan from her before he left, hating himself for – even he knew – no valid reason.

He returned to the meeting room that Thompson called her office.

'I need to take Patricia Quinn on a road trip.'

'You have got to be kidding me.'

'I'm serious. Her brother was spotted near Oban today, and she believes if anyone but her approaches him, it'll end badly.'

Thompson stood, stepped past him and pushed her door closed.

'I can't, Malkie. Despite how our understanding of Beauchamp's behaviour is shaping up, she's going to be charged with assaulting him or worse, so it's not happening.'

'She didn't kill Beauchamp. Her prints were only around the body of the bottle. Remi's are around the neck and in a position that shows he held it exactly as if he used it as a stabbing weapon. That backs up the theory that Patricia lamped him on the head with it, but then someone else... Did the rest. And the only other person whose prints are on that bottle is Remi.'

Something snagged on his mind, and he had an uncomfortable feeling that something he'd missed earlier – and shouldn't have – was about to take on a whole new and significant meaning.

'Give me two minutes, boss.' And he was gone.

He returned to Patricia's cell.

'Show me your neck.'

'What? Why?'

'Just show me, or do I need to get a warrant to see your neck? I'm trying to help you, Patricia.'

She looked confused and wary, but she pulled the top of her police-issue sweatshirt down.

Malkie stepped forward and reached towards her. 'May I?'

She nodded but didn't look happy about it.

He pulled the fabric down an inch more at the front and to the left and right sides of her neck.

'Damn it. I'm an idiot.'

'Why?'

'I can't tell you yet. Bear with me.'

As he left, she raged at his back. 'No. We have to find him.'

He pulled the MisPer sighting report from his pocket as he re-entered Thompson's office and read it again in more detail. He'd been in such a desperate rush to ask Patricia to ID him that he'd only scanned it.

The same way as he'd only skimmed Callum Gourlay's Fire Investigation report into his mum's death and missed the key observation that suggested she was murdered.

Bloody stop that. Deal with now.

He reread the final paragraph and swore under his breath.

'Fuck.'

'Malkie?'

'Bruises, boss. Patricia's neck. No damned bruises.'

'Meaning?'

'Lin Fraser told me that scratches on Beauchamp's wrists could suggest someone tried to pull his hands from their neck or shoulders. Patricia Quinn has no bruising around either.'

'It's a bit thin, Malkie,' Thompson said.

'Except that the bus driver said Remi had no obvious injuries but might have had the flu or a sore throat because his voice sounded raw and painful.'

She frowned. 'Still a bit thin.'

'I agree, but other than the Beauchamps we found only two sets of prints on the bottle or elsewhere in Beauchamp's study, and Patricia's neck is unmarked. Also, both Marshall and Anderson are adamant that she does not have it in her to attack Beauchamp. Finally, the fact that she was in the middle of remortgaging her home suggests she might have been trying to buy him off. Stupid, I know, but she was – is – desperate. Teri Marshall agrees that's the kind of thing Patricia would try to do.'

'I'll talk to McLeish. He'll need to agree to taking her anywhere.'

'Aye. I'd ask him myself, but...'

'Indeed.'

She shook her head as she left to consult him.

She appeared two minutes later and looked stunned. 'He said yes. No argument. He asked who would accompany her. When I told him it would be you, he agreed in an instant.'

'He'll be hoping she escapes or we find Remi too late or I fuck up in some other spectacular way.'

Thompson pretended to consider this then shrugged in the most unconvincing way Malkie could imagine.

'Can we apply for Release Under Investigation while we try to find Remi and hope it gets approved? I'll make sure she stays secure until and if it does.'

She scowled at him. 'Good God, Malkie, you don't half pick them.'

'You assigned me this one, boss.' He grinned at her but her expression wiped it from his face.

She thought for a while then stood. 'You keep her cuffed to you at all times. She's never detached from you, right? Not for a second.'

'Yes, boss.'

'Actually, take Gucci with you so Quinn can use bathrooms, etc.'

'Yes, boss.'

'And a Uniform.'

He nodded.

'Fine. Do it. But for fuck's sake, Malkie. Do not screw this up. McLeish will have my arse as well as yours.'

'Ye—'

'And don't you dare say *Yes, boss*.'

He gestured as if locking his lips with his fingers then held up a Boy Scout salute.

Thompson leaned forward and looked up at him. 'Piss. Off.'

'Yes, boss.' He almost ran out of her office and heard the door slam behind him. He noticed McLeish standing in the doorway to his temporary office, arms folded and legs crossed at the ankles, every inch the pompous prick Malkie had come to know and loathe.

'Good luck, McCulloch.'

Malkie leaned close. 'Fuck you very much. Sir.'

If he hoped to see McLeish lose his cool, he was disappointed.

McLeish grinned. 'Fuck you back, you disgraceful excuse for a copper.'

Malkie returned to his desk but didn't sit.

'Gucci. Fancy a wee trip up north?'

FORTY-THREE

'Ready, Lou?'

'Ready, boss.'

'I hope this isn't screwing up your day?'

'A wee bit, but nothing I couldn't rearrange. I want to find him.'

'Aye. Me too, Lou. As much as we're always told not to get personally involved...'

'You'd need to have a stone for a heart not to want to bring this one to a happy conclusion, wouldn't you?'

'Well said. You got a change of clothes, etc. in case it turns into an overnighter?'

'Aye. You?'

'Aye, nipped home to the cabin. Theresa Carmichael went to Patricia's house and packed a bag for her. She dropped it off five minutes ago.'

Gucci looked uncertain. 'Is this OK, what we're doing, boss?'

'I think so. As long as we keep her secured, she's still technically in custody. If we get the authorisation, Thompson will put the paperwork through and we can uncuff her en route.'

'Fair enough. Ready when you are.'

They found a Uniform, Davie Semple, waiting with Martin Reid outside the charging booth.

'Hi, Davie. You were told how far we're going? How long we might be?'

Semple stepped to one side and nodded at a holdall on the floor. 'Aye, boss. All good to go.'

Malkie nodded at Reid, who headed for the cell corridor to fetch Patricia. He reappeared with her looking impatient. Reid had already fastened one cuff on her, and he let Malkie fasten the other to his wrist. Reid handed Malkie the key.

Malkie turned to Patricia. 'You understand you're still in custody, yes?'

She nodded.

'I can release you only to use a bathroom, in which case DC Gooch will go with you. Is that clear?'

'Yes. Can we go, please?'

Malkie studied her, saw a woman for whom nothing mattered more than seeing her brother safely back in her arms. He couldn't imagine what might make her risk him being taken away from her, and he felt himself make the decision at last. This woman hadn't murdered Sebastian Beauchamp.

With one more nod to all, he led them out the back door to the car park and a waiting patrol car, to head north to find the man who had.

Malkie and Patricia sat in the back. She stared out the window as Davie Semple navigated the roads of North Livingston to the M8. Once they reached cruising speed, Malkie leaned forward.

'Are the locks on back here, Davie?'

'Aye. Why?'

Malkie pulled the key from his pocket and removed the cuffs from his wrist. He left Patricia's on. Gucci cast him a look.

'She's not going anywhere, Lou. That's why I asked for a patrol car.'

Gucci gave him another few seconds of hard stare, then faced front again. He saw her shoulders lift then drop and knew she was sighing.

She's right, you idiot. This could come back to bite you.

Patricia smiled. 'Thank you, Mr McCulloch.'

He nodded but said nothing. He needed Patricia to remember that despite this small show of trust, he was still the police officer who would have to charge her with assault.

The journey passed slowly. Gucci produced her phone and asked Davie to plug it into the USB port, then played some music. Sounded like middle-of-the-road guff, but it would mask the uncomfortable silence.

Malkie slid down in his seat until the back of his head was supported and closed his eyes.

'Wake me at Tyndrum, aye?'

He heard someone tut from the front but pretended he didn't.

FORTY-FOUR

'Steph?'

'Boss. Need to talk to you.'

Thompson started toward her office but changed her mind.

'Coffee, I think, and not the muck from the vending machine.'

As they neared the door between the foyer and the CID area, Bernie Stevens spotted Steph and stood. A huge grin on her face turned to concern.

'Steph? You OK?' She wrapped her in a hug. Steph nearly disappeared into Bernie's ample bosom and enthusiastic arms. She cast a *Help me* look at Thompson, who suppressed a smile but only just. When Bernie released her, Steph straightened her jacket and Bernie returned to her seat.

'You know *he's* back, I presume?' She glanced toward the office space with a sneer on her lips.

'Aye. I've seen him, Bernie.'

'And?'

'It's not me he needs to worry about. It's Pam Ballantyne.'

'Hah. Good point. Hell hath no fury like a DS who backed the wrong horse, right?'

'Well said, Bernie. Sorry, but DI Thompson and I need coffee and a chat.'

'Go. Leave me to my solemn duty as gatekeeper to the hallowed sanctum of the Livi cop shop.'

'Very theatrical, Bernie.'

Bernie waved them through with an exaggerated and dramatic flourish.

In the Civic Centre atrium, they ordered a latte each and found a table.

'What's up, Steph? I can't take you off desk duty yet. Sorry. Or are you on gardening leave?'

'No idea. I just needed a day or two.'

Thompson seemed to pick up on Steph's tone. 'What's happened?'

Steph took a moment to line her thoughts up.

'Barry Boswell killed Dean Lang.'

Thompson's cup stopped halfway to her lips. She put it back on her saucer.

'And you know this how?'

'He told me.'

Thompson sat back. 'I hope you're not about to ruin my day, Steph.'

Steph related the whole story: Boswell turning up at her home, the letters, coffee and confessions, the Xmas video, she laid it all out for Thompson, then sat back herself. She felt the clichéd weight lift from her.

A lift of Thompson's eyebrows told Steph the tale had made the impact she'd known it would.

'And you're sure of all this?'

'Yes, boss.' She reached inside her jacket, into what Malkie called her bottomless pockets because of the way she always carried a supply of shoe covers and evidence bags and other first responder paraphernalia. She pulled out an evidence bag holding the letters, replaced in their envelopes. From another pocket she produced a second bag containing the videotape and a third with Boswell's voice recorder. She hated to hand over the video but knew she'd get it back, the only real memento of the mum she lost far too soon.

Thompson considered for a moment. 'The letters and the videotape I get, you told me about them. What's on the recorder?'

'Boswell claims he recorded it. Him killing Lang.'

'Seriously? Why?'

Although Steph understood what Boswell wanted, what he hoped might yet mitigate his guilt in her eyes, she filed his historic crime against her mother into her mental to-do list.

'I think he wants to atone. He wants to pay for what he didn't do rather than what he did. He hopes he and I can salvage some of our relationship for whatever years he has left after he serves his time.'

'And what didn't he do?'

'He didn't stand up to Lang. He didn't protect my mum. Lang was vicious and violent, so I almost understand Boswell's fear of him. But he never even tried.'

She took a moment before she could get more out.

'But there's another matter. A personal one, not anything we can pursue him for officially. I believe every word and sentiment in those letters, but I also believe he did rape my mum, boss.'

Thompson's lip curled in disgust. 'Let me guess. He raped her but he doesn't see it as rape because they were in a relationship? Not so long since that wasn't even a crime. Fuck's sake we're a loathsome species, aren't we? We know it happens and we know how hard it is to secure convictions for it, but to know it happened to...' She tailed off, couldn't finish the sentence but Steph didn't need her to.

'I think he fucked my mum when she was incapable of providing informed consent. Something she said in the one letter she sent him from prison. I'll deal with that between him and me, personally, but for now, let's get him arrested for Lang's murder before I change my mind and just drop the bastard's corpse in a reservoir.'

'Of course. But please don't even joke about that in front of me, Steph.'

'Shit. Of course. Sorry, boss. I wouldn't, ever. I'm better than that.'

'Yes, you are, Steph.'

They sipped their coffees and watched people come and go across the atrium. Some would be council employees, some would be the public, perhaps attending the sheriff court either in the dock or in the jury, or supporting their loved ones and wondering whether they'd get to take them home that evening. Boswell would go down for premeditated homicide, and for a long time. Steph figured he might still get out with a few years left to him, and she had to hope she could let go of her fury toward him before that happened.

The letters had suggested he'd given her mum what little happiness she'd enjoyed during her otherwise ugly adult life. He'd certainly given her mum a daughter she'd been proud of, despite Lang's poisonous attempts to make Steph think she contributed to her mum's descent into squalor and degradation. But none of that changed what he was. A rapist. No ifs and no buts.

'I'd like to come back to work please, boss.'

'Of course. If you feel up to it.'

'I'm my mother's daughter, boss, and she was the bravest woman I ever knew.'

They returned to the CID area. Thompson disappeared into her office but left the door open. Steph sat at her usual desk.

She logged in, but hesitated. Was what she was about to do completely legal? She'd never had even an informal reprimand before this year and now she was on gardening leave or whatever people called it. Her personal connection to a man who deserved to plummet four floors onto a parked car had messed her life up.

'Sod it.' She started accessing databases she believed would not be logged as closely as more sensitive ones, and hoped she'd be able to plug the hole in her understanding.

The time had come for her to cut through Lang and Boswell's

shite and confirm once and for all whether she understood correctly what had happened and when, and whether her *Uncle Barry* had been one hundred percent honest with her or was still either lying through his teeth or deluding himself.

Could she be reading too much into one small comment in her mum's only letter to her then-lover?

Did it simply imply the understandable fallibility of her mum's drug-addled memory? Or had she known Boswell didn't always wait for her consent?

The words rattled around in her head. They damned Boswell as much as they shamed her mum. She had known all along but – until the day she died alone and confused in a prison shower – she still wanted to stay with him.

'*I wish I could remember the night we conceived her.*'

FORTY-FIVE

They made a comfort stop at Tyndrum.

Malkie secured Patricia's wrist to his own before Semple opened the doors to let them both out, and released her only long enough for Gucci to accompany her into the ladies. When they came out he saw Patricia glance around in shame as people watched Malkie replace the cuffs on her. He felt for her but the thought of McLeish hoping he'd screw up meant he took no chances.

They ate in the famous Green Welly Stop, and Malkie asked Patricia to try to recall any small detail or comment from Remi that might help find him. She related stories of their childhood trips up through Glencoe, around Fort William, down to Oban then south to the Trossachs, but she claimed nothing sprang to mind that Remi might have remembered in the area around Creagan. She apologised, and cried, and berated herself for her failure to deliver. Malkie and Gucci reminded her that their last holiday – her and Remi and their dad – was over a decade ago, but she refused to forgive herself.

She scanned a maps app, hoped something would leap off the screen at her, but it had been too long. She remembered only vague details of places they'd walked or camped, no specifics and no location names.

Malkie called Rab, who said he'd taken photos of everything he thought might be relevant and would send them. Patricia had told Malkie to look for Remi's scrapbook and Rab had reported with bad grace that it was filled with dozens of photos of hills and mountains, ancient monuments and ruined bothies, and crumbling stone bridges across babbling streams and rivers. He'd tried to send them by email but there had been too many, so he'd start sending them in batches.

The four of them took enough drinks and provisions to the car for an extended journey. Malkie removed the cuffs again as soon as the rear doors were closed and locked.

As they recommenced their journey, Malkie checked his mobile and nodded to himself.

'Paperwork has gone through. You're now released under investigation, Ms Quinn, but I advise you to remain with us even though you're no longer in custody.'

Patricia rubbed her wrists and managed a sad smile. 'Thank you. Definitely a good guy, Mr McCulloch. Remi seemed to think so.'

He saw Gucci cover her mouth with her hand in the front seat and knew she would take the piss out of him with enthusiasm, later.

Was it about time he started accepting credit where it was due, instead of irritating the tits off people with constant self-flogging? He promised himself he'd start appreciating himself more. A New Year resolution for next Hogmanay.

He watched hills roll past as Semple drove the winding A85 north and west. Malkie and his dad used to walk this terrain often but they hadn't been this far north in years. He missed these bleak but beautiful regions of Scotland, clad in Forestry Commission plantations of conifers in myriad shades of green and brown that seemed to glow as the sun dipped to the west. He'd already worked out that dusk would be imminent by the time they arrived, but waiting until morning had not been an option. Every year too many people underestimated the danger of even low-lying hills in winter, when temperatures plummeted as darkness fell quickly. If Remi was up here, they needed to find him without delay. But until Patricia came up with some idea of where he might be, they couldn't focus any mountain rescue efforts because the highlands are simply too massive and too rugged.

The first of Rab's emails arrived as they passed the easternmost end of Loch Awe. Malkie saved the images to his phone and passed it to Patricia. She scrolled through them, stopping for a while on each and casting her mind back, trying to trigger memories of childhood holidays. She recounted stories of trips they'd made, but none stood out to her, none recalled anything other than Remi's apparent indifference. He always seemed less distressed by the unknown on a forest walk than he did amongst crowds of people in more urban surroundings, but that meant that every holiday tended to merge in her recollection. None stood out to her because Remi had ambled through every ramble without ever seeming to enjoy any one location more than another.

By the time they reached Ardmucknish Bay and turned off the A85 onto the A828 and north past Oban Airport, Rab had sent three batches of photos, and not one had jumped off Malkie's phone screen to give Patricia any kind of eureka moment. The atmosphere in the vehicle became bleaker as they neared the tiny village of Creagan and the unavoidable acceptance that they had nothing to focus their search on. Patricia grew morose and irritable. She cried again and slammed the palm of her hand against the window. Malkie imagined McLeish's delight if he returned empty-handed, regardless of what that might mean for the missing Remi.

When they arrived, Davie parked outside the closed and boarded-up Creagan Inn. Malkie and Davie did a circuit of the building, checked none of the boards over the windows had been loosened or removed. Davie produced a torch and they peered through any gaps they could find, but found no entry points large enough to suggest Remi might be inside. They were going through the motions. Anything to avoid telling Patricia they had no other plan.

They returned to the car. All inside sat in silence, miserable and frustrated.

Patricia had started again from Rab's first batch of photos. She lingered over each one, her eyes scanning every square centimetre of every picture, desperate to spot something, anything, that might produce a spark of inspiration.

Gucci checked her phone, looked up how long after official sunset time Creagan would become completely dark; they had ninety minutes.

Patricia tugged on the door handle but Davie hadn't released the locks. By the time he did so, she was yanking on it and screaming and sobbing. Malkie placed a hand on her shoulder to distract her, but she shook it off. When the locks released, she threw the door open and fell out onto the road.

Malkie exited too and ran around to her, now on her hands and knees and sobbing. He crouched and laid one arm across her back, the other on her arm. She rose to her knees and fell into him. She buried herself in him, her shoulders heaving and her breath juddering as grief racked her. Eventually, exhausted, she quietened, but Malkie held on to her. When she looked up at him, he helped her to her feet and they returned to the car. She sat with her legs drawn up to her chest and her arms around them, and stared out of the window. Malkie thought her desperate that Remi might just walk past and unable to accept the pity in the eyes of the three officers.

Malkie called Rab's phone. 'Anything?'

Rab sounded as dejected as Malkie felt. 'No. Sorry, boss. I sent you every photo I could find.'

Malkie turned to Patricia. 'Can you think of anything else my colleague can look for in Remi's room that might help us? Anything? Even something you might not consider important?'

She shook her head.

'Patricia. You need to think. As far as we know, Remi is here somewhere, and another night in the open... You know how cold it gets here after dark. You have to concentrate.'

Malkie's last words seemed to penetrate her despair. She looked at him, then at Gucci and Davie Semple, turned in their seats to watch her.

She ran her hands through her hair then rubbed them down her face. She closed her eyes and took a steadying breath.

'Did your man look through the drawers in his desk?' Malkie relayed the question to Rab, who replied that he had.

'Patricia, take my phone. His name is Rab. Help him.' He enabled the speaker and handed it to her.

'Hello, Rab. Yes, I'm thinking.'

All waited as she agonised, her forehead furrowed in concentration.

'Did you look under his bed and under his pillow?'

'Yes I did, Ms Quinn.'

'Did you check the pockets of his coat? He always takes some kind of security object with him if he has to go outside. Usually one of those fidget things or his old Nintendo DS. What about his bookcase? Are any of his books sticking out? He always has the spines of his books perfectly aligned.'

'Hang on. Ah...'

The atmosphere in the car turned electric. Patricia's hand reached for Malkie's.

'There's one book sticking out.'

Four people sat in tense silence, in a car surrounded by the failing light of a highland dusk, and held their breaths.

'There are a few photos in between the pages. Hang on.'

The four minutes it took Rab to scan the photos and send them were some of the longest of Malkie's life. Patricia rocked backwards and forwards and moaned quietly to herself. Davie Semple faced forward and closed his eyes. Gucci stared at Malkie, and he read the same terrified dread in her eyes that he felt.

This was not about closing an investigation anymore. It wasn't about refusing McLeish the pleasure of seeing Malkie fail so he could nail him and see his arse booted out of Police Scotland. It wasn't even about Malkie's habit of defining every effort he made to protect or save someone as a measure of his entire worth as a human being.

This was about nothing more than one frightened and vulnerable human being who needed his sister.

The phone pinged and Patricia fumbled with the buttons. Malkie took it from her, opened the message and clicked on the first of four new images.

She shook her head, looking increasingly frustrated and despondent. She grabbed the phone back and swiped past the first two pictures, but stopped on the third, her eyes wide, her mouth hanging open, her hands shaking.

'Patricia?'

She stared at Malkie but seemed unable to form words.

He looked at the photo, a tiny stone bridge built from ancient boulders, with thick spikes of rough-cut stone which looked like miniature menhirs, spaced a foot apart along the low walls on both sides.

'Do you know this place, Patricia?'

She nodded. Her mouth opened but she had to swallow before she could try again. 'I think it was our first holiday, so I would have been only twelve and Remi six. I can barely remember it, but he forgets nothing.'

'Yes, you told me.'

She handed Malkie's phone back to him. 'Do you have a maps app on there?'

'Aye, sure. Use it all the time. Hang on.' He swiped sideways, pressed on an icon and Google Maps came up.

She snatched it back from him, pressed the current location icon, the slid the map north and east. She studied it, swiped over a wide range around Creagan, her temper and her patience fraying. She swiped too hard and the map shot off hundreds of miles into the Atlantic. She threw the phone down and screamed her rage.

Her hands shook violently and she shifted in her seat as if unable to decide whether to sit there or exit the car.

'Patricia. Please. Try to calm down. We know we're probably within a few miles of him now. Let's try to concentrate. You can do this.'

She fixed her eyes onto his, slowed her breathing. 'Yes. I need to find him before nightfall.' She looked out the window to the darkening sky and moaned. 'We're too late. Oh God, we're too late.'

'No. We're not. Patricia. As soon as you confirm he must be somewhere near here I can call out Mountain Rescue. I just need you to be confident he has some reason to want to return here. Think, Patricia.'

She picked the phone back up, zoomed out, re-centred on Creagan, then zoomed out again in increments, scanning left to right and top to bottom in a widening circle.

As she searched north-east of the village, she frowned.

'Patricia?'

'Loch Creran. We camped on the shore of Loch Creran. I remember Remi wouldn't stop going on about it for weeks after, until Mum snapped at him for being so obsessed with a specific place. A bridge. He was fascinated by it. He kicked off so badly when we tried to leave it, we had to sit there an hour until Remi decided they were not going to come and play with him.'

'Who, Patricia?'

'The fairies.' She followed a single-track road, barely a thin grey line on the map, further north and west and zoomed in. 'There it is. That's where he'll be. Looking for them.'

She pointed to the screen as she handed the phone back to him, and he saw it.

Fairy Bridge of Glen Creran.

'We need to get up there.' She grabbed the door handle but Davie had locked it again.

'Let me out. I have to go to him. Let me out.' Her voice rose to a furious screech.

Malkie nodded at Davie and he unlocked the doors. She fell face first onto the tarmac in her hurry to get out.

Gucci had read the situation and was waiting for her. She caught her and helped her to stand. Patricia stared at the palms of her hands, scratched and scraped and bloodied. She wiped them on her trousers, faced the hills to the north and screamed. 'Remi. I'm here, Remi. I'm coming.'

Malkie joined her and Gucci, took Patricia by the arm and made her look at him. 'Patricia, he can't hear you from here. That spot is at least four miles through dense forest. DC Gooch is going to call Mountain Rescue. We can drive up the road but... Look at me, Patricia. If we do that, you stay in the car until they arrive. That's the condition, OK?'

She took long seconds to respond, her eyes frantic, but she nodded.

'OK.'

Gucci stepped away to call in Mountain Rescue from Glencoe. Malkie led Patricia back to the car and made her sit inside. He left the door open but stood to block her exit.

Gucci returned a minute later. 'On their way, ETA thirty to thirty-five minutes.'

Malkie looked to the sky; they were going to cut it fine. He ordered them all back into the car and Davie took it slow up the B-class Invercrenan road. As they neared the village of Fasnacloich, Malkie spotted a rough track on the satellite view in his maps app that wasn't marked on the terrain map.

'Davie, about a quarter mile the other side of here, there's a private track that forks off to the left. It looks like it heads up the hill towards a private residence, but it'll take us much closer to The Fairy Bridge than the public car park at the start of the signed walk to it.'

Gucci dialled her phone. 'Hello. It's DC Louisa Gooch again. We're en route to... No, we won't go up there on our own. We spotted a private track to the left of the road about a quarter mile after... Aye, you know it. OK. We'll wait for you at the bottom of that track. OK, good. Thanks.'

'They said they were already planning to start there given the urgency. Good instincts, boss.'

'Aye, I can be right about things occasionally.'

Gucci smiled at him, but it fell away as Patricia sat forward.

'Really? Jokes at a time like this? Seriously?'

Malkie held his hands up. 'We apologise, Patricia. The job makes us... Not insensitive, but prone to compartmentalising, for the sake of our mental health if nothing else. But that was stupid of me. I'm sorry.'

He met her eyes and was relieved beyond measure when they softened and she sighed. 'No. I'm sorry. You need to do that like I need to joke with Remi's social worker. We do that or we go nuts, right?'

'Gets us through the days, Patricia.'

She reached across and squeezed his hand, then turned back to the window.

FORTY-SIX

'You ready?'

'Aye. Ready as I'll ever be.'

'You don't look ready.'

'He's still lying to me, to himself. It's eating me up inside, boss. I need to hear him admit what he did was—'

Her phone rang. Bernie at the front desk.

Steph jabbed the speakerphone button and stared at Thompson for support.

'Hi, Steph. There's a man at reception says he's your dad?'

They shared a look of disgust. Thompson raised her eyebrows at Steph, and she held a hand up to confirm she could handle this.

'Two minutes, Bernie.' And she disconnected.

Together with a Uniform they grabbed from his desk on the way past, they pushed through the door to the foyer. Steph stayed back and pointed Boswell out to Thompson.

Thompson strode forward, a woman on a much-relished mission. 'Barry Boswell?'

He nodded at Thompson but glanced at Steph. A disgusted sneer curled her lip before she could stop herself and his face turned white.

When Thompson read him his rights he nodded his understanding, his lips clamped shut, his eyes frantic, begging Steph for support. The Uniform cuffed him, then Thompson led him back through the office area to the custody suite. Boswell looked back for Steph, but she stopped beside Bernie.

Steph caught a confused look on her face. 'My biological dad, Bernie. And a piece of shit.'

She squeezed Bernie's hand and they shared a smile, then Steph headed for the custody suite too.

Boswell had his prints taken, his identity confirmed and was arrested on a charge of first-degree murder, to which he nodded, then was taken to a cell. Steph returned to her desk, laid her head back and closed her eyes. She craved a tall, cold gin and tonic and had a stern word with herself.

'You want to talk to him?'

Susan Thompson stood before her.

'Is that allowed? Him being... My...'

'You know the score. Don't ask him anything we'd need to strike from the record.'

Steph couldn't decide if she did or not. The single, remaining question had been rattling around her mind all morning while she waited for him to hand himself in. Now, she wasn't sure she wanted to ask him, was afraid he'd still not see the extent of his culpability for what he did to her mum.

Thompson pulled up a chair from an adjacent desk and sat. 'You OK?'

Steph took a moment to be sure of her answer. 'Aye. I think I am, boss. Monumentally pissed off that Boswell pushed Lang off his balcony before I got a chance to beat seven shades of shite out of him. Yes, I'm joking. But aye, I'll get through it in time. What was it that German philosopher said?'

'Nietzsche?'

'Aye, him.'

'What doesn't kill me...'

'Makes me stronger?'

'That was it.'

Thompson laughed. 'He must have had someone just like you in mind when he said it.'

Steph smiled, but not for long. 'He'll go down for years. His brief will tell him he might get a sentence reduction for handing himself in and saving us, the Fiscal and the courts a load of cash, but he knows there are no guarantees.'

'And what about years down the line? When he's eventually released?'

'Depends.'

'On what?'

Steph stood, pushed away her reluctance to face him. 'On how he answers just one personal question, boss.'

'And that is?'

Steph lined up her thoughts before answering. 'I found it easy to believe the worst of him because Lang's conviction in what he said seemed complete to me, even from him. Boswell was my Uncle Barry most of my life and I adored him. We lost touch when I grew up and became a copper, but I had no reason to believe Lang's pack of lies that Boswell raped my mum. But I did. He was weak and let my mum down appallingly, although I couldn't blame him completely for what he didn't do. She who is without sin, etc., right? But now...'

Thompson waited in silence.

'Now, I do. Believe what Lang said, I mean. Just because my mum made love to Boswell willingly sometimes didn't make it OK the times she knew nothing about it. That shit still goes on and it has to fucking stop. Sorry for the language, boss, but...'

'No problem.' She leaned in close. 'You're completely fucking right and I completely fucking agree with you, Steph.'

Steph smiled her appreciation, even as both acknowledged the appalling truth they had both just agreed on.

'I need to hear from him that he realises what he did, boss. He needs to be made to see how wrong it was.'

Steph started toward the custody suite and Thompson had to run a few steps to keep up. A Uniform unlocked the door to

Boswell's cell after a nod from Thompson. Boswell stood but the Uniform barked at him. 'Sit down, please, and remain seated.'

Boswell did, looked like a naughty schoolboy trying his damndest not to get in more trouble than he already was.

Steph stepped inside and leaned against the cell wall, her hands clasped tight behind her to stop them from damaging Boswell again. Thompson nodded to the Uniform to wait outside, then stood with her back to the closed door.

Steph stared at him until he squirmed, drew his feet up onto the bunk and wrapped his arms around his shins as if he needed a barrier between him and his own, admittedly ferocious and monumentally pissed-off, daughter.

Steph dug deep and found strength to ask her question, and to hell with the consequences.

'This is off the record. My DI has been kind enough to give me a few minutes with you, daughter to father, as it were.' She enjoyed his appalled reaction to the vitriol she laced her words with. Then she hated herself for wanting to torment another human being, even him.

'When did you and my mum begin your relationship?'

He stared at her as if composing his response to minimise further damage.

'It was in March before your second birthday, Steph. We started writing those notes to each other around then. Why?'

'And when was I conceived, Mr Boswell?'

He couldn't answer.

'Unless I was born over two months prematurely, which I'm sure I'd know about, I was conceived at the same time Lang was serving time in Saughton, wasn't I?'

Thompson stepped between them. 'Steph. Be careful. Please.'

Steph ignored her and sidestepped her. Boswell cowered against the cell wall. Thompson took up a position beside her but held back for the time being.

'And that was also two years before you claim your relationship with my mother started, wasn't it?' Her voice rose now, her fury leaking out despite her best intentions to remain calm.

Thompson laid a hand on one arm, but Steph shook it off and lunged toward Boswell. He screamed but she stopped short of his bunk.

Thompson grabbed her arm again and called for the Uniform to return. Steph had seconds, no more.

'We messed about a bit when Dean was away, just a couple of times. I promise that was all.'

Steph's rage breached her normally rigid self-control. 'No. My mum's only letter to you from prison said, "*I wish I could remember the night we conceived her*". I thought that meant she couldn't recall it because her memory was fucked up by all the drugs Lang kept giving her. But it didn't mean that, did it *Barry*?'

Boswell looked sick. Either because he'd been found out or because he only now faced up to the reality and immensity of what he did to a woman he claimed he later fell in love with.

'She couldn't remember it years afterwards because she didn't even remember it the day it happened. You had sex with my mum two years before you started a relationship with her, and she was completely unaware of the fact. Was she even awake? Was she off her face on Lang's shit narcotics? Did you think it was OK as long as she was at least partly conscious? Did you rape my mum when she couldn't say no, you filthy fucking piece of shit?'

Stronger hands than Thompson's clamped around her from behind, even as the fight drained from her to be replaced by a desolate and debilitating exhaustion.

'You did conceive me, but while Lang was in prison. And my mum had no fucking idea, did she? You fucked her while she was in no fit state to consent, you fucking animal. Then you lied to her and gas-lighted her to make her forget about it. You got away with the woman you claimed you loved never realising what a piece of utter shit you really were.'

She saw Boswell's eyes fill and spill over and knew she was right.

She allowed herself to be led away out of the cell, bereft and broken. She heard Boswell say something about '*only one time*' but she'd lost the will to fight her way back in to kill the bastard.

Back in the CID area, Thompson pulled Steph into her office and closed the door and window blinds.

'You OK?'

Steph knew her face would tell Thompson just how OK she really wasn't, but what else could her senior officer and friend say?

She sat, rubbed her eyes, heaved a huge, settling sigh, before she could speak.

'I will be. I can't get over him saying "*only one time*" as we left his cell. He really believes he *let her down a bit* just that one time, and that the rest of whatever relationship they had makes that OK. He deserves to go down as a convicted rapist and he deserves what other cons do to people like him, and...'

She needed a deep, steadying breath to continue. 'I won't feel the smallest scrap of compassion if I hear he's been shivved in the shower, like my mum was.'

Thompson reached across the desk and squeezed her hand.

'You'll survive this. Anyone who knows you even a wee bit, knows you'll survive this, Steph.'

'Yes. I will, boss.'

FORTY-SEVEN

Mountain Rescue arrived in their Land Rover Defender twenty minutes later. Gucci had mentioned the possible optics of a vulnerable person with level two autism spectrum disorder dying on their watch.

A woman climbed out and shook everyone's hands. 'I'm Fiona Brooks and my colleagues are Alan Webb and Clare Weir. You said you suspect a young man might be at The Fairy Bridge and may have been there through last night already?'

'Aye. This lady is the man's brother, Patricia Quinn. She believes she remembers her brother having a particular fascination with the spot.'

Patricia shrugged, looked like she hated to bother them. 'I can't be a hundred percent certain, but Remi, my brother, has never shown a specific interest in any other place we ever went.'

Malkie stepped in, saw Patricia had started to fret again. 'A bus driver reported a man fitting Remi's description disembarking at the Creagan roundabout. Ms Quinn has seen a still from the vehicle's CCTV and confirmed the ID.'

Brooks nodded to Malkie then took both of Patricia's arms. 'Ms Quinn. We're the experts, so we need you to wait here with Clare.

It's only a short hike up there, but Clare and I will maintain contact via high-band radio and keep you informed, OK?'

She tailed off because Patricia had started shaking her head. 'No. I need to come with you. Remi is afraid of strangers, and he has serious problems with anyone in uniform. If he sees you two arrive in all your hi-vis clothing and your rescue gear, he'll hide. And he's very good at hiding.'

'We're the experts, Ms Quinn. If he's anywhere near The Fairy Bridge, we'll find him.'

'No. I'm coming with you. I have decent boots on and I'm wearing thermals, so I'll be safe.'

'It's a short stroll, Ms Quinn. We'll be back—'

'I'm going with you.' She turned to Malkie. 'Unless you're prepared to handcuff me again, I'll just follow them. Besides...' She swallowed. 'If Remi gets hurt...' She didn't finish.

Malkie agonised. Protocol said she could not be allowed to endanger herself on a steep forested trail in near darkness in falling temperatures, even accompanied by the experts. But he believed her; she would kick up an almighty fuss if they tried to leave her behind. He recalled the state Remi got into when he spotted the Uniforms outside his home. How much more distressed and frightened would he be in the middle of a dark forest, having been without his sister for two days?

'I'll go too, and I'll take full responsibility for Ms Quinn.'

'No, you won't,' replied Brooks. 'Neither of you. This might be an easy wee quarter-mile jaunt through—'

Patricia turned on her. 'A quarter mile? You didn't say it was that close!' She started toward the trees, but Malkie caught her. She tried to pull away, but his greater strength held her.

'Remi? Are you there? Remi? It's me, Remi?'

Malkie turned her to face him. 'He may still not hear you, Patricia. Those trees are dense.' He didn't believe it himself, but he needed her calm, to allow the professionals to do their job without having to worry about her running off.

Brooks faced her. 'I was saying, the walk up there is easy

during daylight, but the paths are rough and washed away in places, and will be icy soon. If we have to bring one of you down with a sprained ankle or worse, there'll be hell to pay, and we might not get to your brother in time.'

Malkie faced her. 'And if you don't take Ms Quinn you'll not find Remi if he sees or hears you first and panics. And Ms Quinn is not going up there without me. I know you outrank me while we're on this hillside, but it has to work this way, Ms Brooks.'

Brooks opened her mouth but Malkie cut her off. 'I promise you, Ms Brooks. This *is* necessary. I've seen him when he's been triggered, and I fear for his safety and all around him. The poor lad is seriously troubled. Ms Quinn and I will go with you.'

Brooks seemed to consider arguing again, but Malkie's warning seemed to persuade her. 'Fine. Do you have suitable clothing?'

Malkie noticed only now that he'd packed his hiking boots and a fleece, but nothing more substantial. 'Sorry.'

Brooks blessed him with an unimpressed lift of her eyebrows; Mountain Rescue's intolerance for idiots climbing Ben Nevis equipped with trainers, T-shirts, Irn Bru and KitKats was well known to all except the idiots themselves.

Brooks produced two well-used jackets from the back of the Land Rover and tossed them to him and Patricia. 'Put these on.'

After another few minutes checking equipment, Brooks looked at Malkie and Patricia. Both nodded.

'Gucci, update Rab and Thompson, will you?'

She nodded but looked less than happy about any attempt by Malkie at demanding physical exercise.

'I'll be fine, Lou. I'm not a complete wreck yet.'

Five minutes up the steep track, he was knackered. He refused to slow down, with Brooks needing to repeatedly pull Patricia back from forging ahead of them, but his legs ached and he felt sweat break out on his forehead and in more intimate places. He tripped twice, over rocks and other natural hazards, his vision not perfect in the failing light.

'You OK?' Brooks asked him in a polite and professional voice, but laced with amusement.

'I'm fine. Stop asking.'

She continued, but not without a grin at her colleague.

A minute later, Brooks stopped. 'It's about a hundred metres ahead. Ms Quinn, do you want to go ahead? I'll follow close behind you?'

Patricia looked up the path. It bent to the right. She seemed at a loss.

Brooks touched her arm. 'The Fairy Bridge is around that bend, Ms Quinn. If you insist on proceeding alone—'

'I do.'

Malkie stepped around Brooks, but Patricia held a hand up. 'Just me, Mr McCulloch, please.'

He relented but let his face show how bad an idea he thought it to be.

Patricia stared at him. Her lips trembled and her eyes glistened. He gripped her arms. 'Go get your brother, Patricia.'

Brooks added, 'If he's not there, call us and we'll carry on searching, OK?' Her voice was low and warm, comforting.

Patricia nodded at both of them, then walked up the path.

'Remi? It's me, Remi. Are you there, love?'

She disappeared around the bend. Seconds stretched out. Malkie could hardly believe less than a minute could feel like such an eternity.

Patricia cried out, distraught and terrified. 'Remi? No, no, no. Remi.'

Malkie and Brooks and the other rescuer, Alan Webb, took off after her, adrenaline fuelling Malkie's tired calves. He kept up with them easily. They rounded the bend to find Patricia on her knees in the mud, holding a pale and slack Remi in her arms. He sat with his back to the inside of one of the sides of the bridge topped with short stone spires. She looked up at them, her face soaked and her voice breaking with grief.

'He's dead. He's dead. Oh God, he's dead, Mr McCulloch.' Her words, screamed with so much fury that Malkie took a step back, reverberated around the small clearing in which The Fairy Bridge sat. It looked just like the photo Rab had sent, would have seemed quaint and magical in any other circumstances but these. Malkie sat on a rock and felt all hope drain from him.

Another one. Another one I didn't save. Christ, how much longer can I do this?

'He's alive.'

Malkie's head snapped up. Brooks crouched beside him with two fingers on Remi's neck.

Patricia leaned in to watch. 'Can you feel—'

'Shh.' Brooks sounded harsh, but Patricia nodded and sat back.

Brooks nodded to her colleague. 'There's a pulse but barely.'

Webb had already dumped his rucksack on the ground and was rummaging, pulling various pieces of equipment and arranging them on the ground. Malkie saw rolls of foil, a first-aid box, an oxygen bottle and mask, even what looked like a portable defibrillator.

Brooks pushed Patricia gently away and laid Remi on his back. Patricia moved to stand beside Malkie, close but not quite touching him. He felt useless but also glad Remi's survival didn't now rest in his hands.

Brooks grabbed a foil blanket, shook it out and wrapped Remi in it. She fastened an oxygen mask to him, connected a bottle and turned the valve. She checked his pulse again and shone a penlight into his eyes.

Malkie prayed to a god he'd never believe in that the lad survived but remained unconscious throughout the ordeal.

Brooks pulled her radio from a clip on her belt. 'Clare. Ambulance, please. We've found him. Severe hypothermia, but no obvious injuries. Over.'

Malkie heard her confirm and Brooks returned the handset to her belt.

Brooks pulled an electronic thermometer from the first-aid box and inserted it into Remi's ear. It seemed to take an eternity to beep but she displayed none of the impatience that had Malkie pacing in frustration.

Brooks checked the display and scowled. 'Thirty-three, Alan.'

'Fuck.' Alan pulled a thick roll that looked like a sleeping bag from his rucksack and opened it out. They wrapped Remi in it without removing the foil sheet, then zipped it up to his neck. Alan unfastened another package, large and bulky, secured to loops on the back of his pack, opened it and pulled out a mass of nylon fabric and poles; it reminded Malkie of the tent he had stuffed somewhere in the spare room of the cabin. Alan constructed a portable stretcher in a minute, then both he and Brooks lifted Remi onto it. They strapped him in, then after repacking and hoisting their rucksacks, they turned to Patricia and Malkie.

'Ready?'

Both nodded. Neither spoke.

Brooks took her radio from her belt and thumbed the button. 'Beginning descent. Over.' She handed Malkie and Patricia two head torches she'd pulled from her pack, then she and Webb lifted the stretcher and, without a further word, started walking. Malkie found the power button on his head torch and switched it on, placed it around his head then helped Patricia do the same.

The hike down was slower and more careful than the outward journey for obvious reasons, and Webb led. Malkie assumed this was because the downhill load would be heavier; Brooks looked fit but Webb towered over her and out bulked her by a wide margin. It took a full twenty minutes, so careful were Brooks and Webb, examining the ground with care before each step.

When they reached the cars, Gucci and Davie Semple were out and waiting.

'Is he OK, boss?'

'I don't know, Lou.' He glanced at Brooks. She glanced at Patricia, who cast a worried look at them both.

Brooks checked Remi's vitals again. 'His pulse is still weak and his temperature will take a while to recover, so it's too early to tell, I'm afraid.'

Malkie felt Patricia lean on him. He placed a hand on her back to hold her upright.

'An ambulance is on its way from Oban. He should be in A&E in a little more than an hour. He'll get the best possible care there, Ms Quinn.'

Malkie got the distinct impression that although Brooks might feel at home on a cold and windy mountainside with one or two colleagues, she didn't excel at people skills.

They loaded Remi's stretcher into the back of the Land Rover. It stuck out the back but sheltered him from the worst of the now-freezing night air. Gucci and Davie returned to the car and ran the engine. Patricia refused to leave Remi, and Malkie refused to leave her.

They stood in bleak silence and watched her brother. His face held no colour and looked slack. The thick layers of insulation hid any sign of his breathing. Patricia sniffed and Malkie saw she was crying. He moved a few inches closer and she leaned toward him. Not enough to need his support, just close enough that he felt her jacket and she felt his reassuring presence.

'You have to charge me with Beauchamp's murder, Mr McCulloch.' She spoke barely above a whisper. Brooks looked preoccupied with monitoring Remi. If she heard, she pretended otherwise.

Malkie felt misery swamp him. 'I can't, Patricia. As much as... I just can't. I'm sorry.'

She moved away from him again. 'Then he'll die in prison instead of here. We might as well have let him die up there, on his Fairy Bridge, in peace. He was already unconscious, so the worst was over for him. Now it's all still ahead of him.'

Malkie wanted to scream, to kick something. She was right.

He'd saved a woman from killing herself before but he also knew she'd find a way to do it later, after suffering a court case and conviction and an unbearable period of pretending to be stable to get herself removed from suicide watch. Should he have let her die? He remembered hearing about some poor bastard in Texas who had suffered a heart attack on his way to the electric chair. He had been treated and made a full recovery, only to be put to death six months later.

Was that what he was doing? Saving Remi from one death so the poor sod could go through hell in a psychiatric hospital without his sister, and maybe kill himself eventually anyway?

'No. Fuck that.'

'What?'

'Eh?'

'You said *No*, then something else.'

'I said that out loud? Sorry.'

'No what?'

He couldn't lie to her, but she needed something.

'There's every chance you might receive a suspended sentence, maybe even an acquittal. If Beauchamp did attack you and you did hit him with that bottle in self-defence, then you've actually committed no crime. Well, you might be charged with obstruction, but it seems to me there's nothing you could have told us under caution that would have helped anyway. So, you may walk away without any punishment or even a record.'

She watched him and waited. The hope in her eyes broke his heart, so he reminded himself to keep her feet on the ground.

'Remi, though... He'll be charged with Beauchamp's murder. He's unlikely to go to prison though, more likely a secure hospital. I know, I know – he'll struggle there too, but he'll be cared for, treated. They won't put someone as vulnerable as him in prison. They can't. Remi has rights regardless of what he gets convicted of.'

Patricia folded her arms and leaned on the side of the Land Rover. 'Will I be stopped from seeing him?'

'I can't see them being able to do that. I can't imagine what measures can be put in place to give you more access than is standard, but I would hope the authorities will do all they can, if only to protect themselves from accusations of putting a vulnerable man with mental health issues at greater risk than he needs to be.'

'Will I be able to care for him at home?' Her tone suggested she already knew the answer, but Malkie guessed she was reaching for any possible shred of hope.

'No. He murdered someone, Patricia.'

'I know.'

Her voice nearly broke him. He'd played a major part in getting to this situation. He'd investigated the case correctly and with as much care as his job allowed, but the fact remained that he'd always know he helped put Remi away, and regardless of right or wrong, it felt brutal and cruel.

They both heard the ambulance seconds before they saw the blue strobes.

Brooks and her colleagues pulled Remi's stretcher from the back of the Land Rover and laid him gently on the ground. The ambulance pulled up and two paramedics climbed out. They conferred in calm and quiet voices with Brooks, got her to sign some paperwork, then opened the back doors to load Remi.

Patricia climbed in and sat beside him. She loosened the hood around his face and held the palm of her hand against his cheek. 'He's so cold, Mr McCulloch. I wish he would wake up.' Tears appeared, and Malkie wondered just how much one woman could cry in a single day.

He squeezed her fingers, then left her with her brother.

Gucci and Davie stood by the patrol car. Gucci smiled at him. 'Well done, boss.'

'Eh? I didn't do anything. I just take the credit for what you and Rab do. Sorry, and you, Davie.'

Gucci and Davie shared a look, then Davie climbed into the driver's seat. Gucci sat in the passenger seat and Malkie stretched out along the rear seat.

Gucci turned to face him. 'Where to, boss?'

'Oban. Place called the Oban Bay Hotel, or something like that.' He pointed in the direction the ambulance had gone. 'Wake me when we get there.'

FORTY-EIGHT

Malkie made it to the hotel's dining room for breakfast with only minutes to spare before they started clearing everything away. He grabbed a couple of Danish pastries and a coffee then joined Gucci and Davie Semple at their table beside a picture window.

'Morning, boss.' Gucci's beaming grin irritated him, but he said nothing. It was hardly her fault he'd spent the entire night sleepless and dreading a call from Oban Hospital.

'Did you sleep well, boss?' Davie didn't beam at him like Gucci had, but Malkie decided to be irritated with him too. No sleep and a constant fear of his own mobile had a way of bringing out the worst in him.

He grunted, then started spooning sugar into his coffee. He sipped it and grimaced. It tasted fine – good even – but his foul mood needed something to fasten on to.

'Any word from the hospital, boss?' Lou's concern sounded genuine, more than just professional curiosity.

'No. Nothing.'

'That's good.'

Is it, Lou?

He wondered if Remi Quinn might be better off never waking, then loathed himself for the thought.

'Aye. It is.' He managed a smile that felt completely unconvincing, but he wanted her to think he was making an effort.

Davie Semple drained his coffee cup and stood. 'I'll get properly dressed, then.'

Lou leaned forward and propped her arms on the table. 'You OK, boss?' He felt a pang of guilt at how genuine her concern seemed.

'Ach, I'm sorry, Lou. It's Remi. And Patricia. Both of them have gone through hell, and the bastard who made them suffer so much will never face justice for it. He deserved to be shamed, publicly humiliated. He got off lightly. Nae justice.'

'Bleeding to death from shredded wedding tackle was getting off lightly?'

Malkie snorted into his coffee and got brown spots all down the front of his shirt.

'Sorry, boss.'

'Don't apologise, Lou. I needed a laugh. Still, public shaming would have made the fucker suffer so much more. Well, not more, but for much, much longer.' He stared out the window, across Oban Bay to the Isle of Kerrera. The sky was virtually cloudless and the sun brilliant. He watched morning ferries heading off to the Western Isles and wondered if he could just board one at random and worry about accommodation and requesting the leave later. But he knew he couldn't. Wouldn't. As much as he wished it, he wouldn't put his life on hold and hide. He and his dad needed to discuss the troubling new discovery in Ballantyne's investigation into the house fire that killed his mum. Steph wouldn't need him, but he wanted to be there for her anyway. McLeish would need to be dealt with; Malkie couldn't go on dreading every serious crime that came his way in case it brought him into confrontation with that idiot.

He sighed, a long, slow and miserable exhalation that had Gucci frowning with concern.

'Boss?'

'Ach, ignore me, Lou. This case, you know? Brutal.'

She considered this. 'Yes. It has been. But we can only do what we can do, can't we?'

Malkie felt tears well. Gucci had echoed his own mum so much, he felt an almost physical longing for her.

'Malkie?'

He waved a hand at her. 'I'm fine, Lou. Just tired.'

Her look told him she believed none of it, but she knew when to leave him alone. They sat and drank their coffee in companionable silence until Davie reappeared.

'Ready when you are.'

Malkie smiled up at him. 'Cheers, Davie.'

Gucci fetched her bags from their rooms and joined Davie in the car park. Malkie explained that he'd need to stay in Oban until Remi could travel, then crossed to the side of the shore road. He took another long look at the view. He and his dad had resolved to tour the coast in *The Droopy Goose*, Tommy's twenty-foot sailing tub, an impulse buy and money-pit now moored at Port Edgar, but like other plans they'd made, it hadn't yet happened. Malkie suspected his dad couldn't bear to enjoy anything without the girl he'd loved since their schooldays, but life has to continue, and those left alive have to do more than just survive.

He hauled in a huge lungful of sea air and turned back to the waiting patrol car.

He climbed into the back seat. 'Right. Oban Hospital please, Davie.'

He decided he liked Oban Hospital. Or The Lorne and Islands Hospital, as the sign at the entrance informed him. No drab grey or brown brick here, only plain white walls and tiled roofs, almost like a hotel from the outside. He remembered his dad telling him that so many houses in the highlands were painted white because of a centuries-old tradition that marauding giants would mistake them for sheep and pass them by. He missed the old man and found himself impatient to return home.

Davie Semple found parking spaces in plentiful supply, but he dropped them at the entrance before heading to the far corner of the car park, overlooking a patch of open land surrounded by trees. Maybe Malkie wasn't the only one of them who hadn't slept well.

He and Lou asked at the reception desk and were directed to Intensive Care, where a nurse checked their warrant cards then led them to a private room. They nodded to a uniformed officer seated outside and found Patricia Quinn inside, asleep. Seated beside her brother's bed, she had rested her arms on the blankets and her head on her arms.

'Ms Quinn?' Even though Malkie pitched his voice low and gentle, she sat bolt upright and gazed, dopey and bleary-eyed, around the room until she spotted Malkie and Gucci.

She looked to Remi who lay still, his eyes closed and his arms by his sides. The absence of any tubes or masks or any other hospital gadgets suggested he might be past the most dangerous stage. He noticed bruising around Remi's neck, as if he needed any more evidence of the poor wee sod's ordeal. And his guilt.

Guilt, my arse. What a fucking world we live in.

'How is he?' Malkie pulled a chair up and sat beside her.

Patricia spoke to Malkie but kept her eyes on her brother. 'Doctors are optimistic. He hasn't regained consciousness since he was admitted, but you can see he doesn't seem to need much in the way of monitoring.'

Malkie looked closer and saw nothing except a simple blood oxygen clip on one forefinger.

'My colleagues will return to West Lothian. I assume you'll want to stay here until Remi regains consciousness?'

She nodded, her eyes still on her brother.

'Will you be able to afford a hotel or a bed and breakfast? Some fresh clothes and toiletries?'

'I'll be fine. I have savings but thank you.' Malkie could believe she'd sit here in the same clothes for days rather than leave Remi's side. While he felt for the boy and his probable lifelong issues, he envied him the unconditional love his sister so obviously held for him. Would he come, in time, to feel such absolute and non-negotiable love for Jennifer? Was it too late for that father-daughter bond to grow and deepen to such a level? He hoped not, but it depended on Jennifer too.

'Mr McCulloch? Malkie?'

'You know there's a local constable posted outside, yes?'

He saw her lower her head for a moment. 'Yes. I know. Will Remi be taken back to Livingston to be charged?'

'Aye. He will. He'll be in custody though. Local Police Scotland are aware of his volatile nature, but I'm afraid you'll not be allowed to travel with him.'

She turned a look on him that he feared he'd take an age to forget. 'You realise he might not even survive that journey without hurting himself?'

He held his hands out to the sides. 'I'm sorry.'

For a second, he hoped she'd let him know she understood and didn't blame him, but whether because she'd been through too much and it had broken her, or because her concern for her brother's welfare left no room for any understanding of his position, she left him feeling as if the blame for the ordeal yet to face them both lay partly with him.

Not for the first time, he wondered if early retirement might soon become too tempting to ignore.

'I'll be staying until Remi is well enough to travel, and I'll accompany him back to West Lothian. Can I suggest you introduce me to him and do what you can to help me earn his trust for that journey?'

She nodded. 'If he hurts himself or anyone else…'

She didn't finish, and Malkie didn't need her to. He looked to Gucci who nodded, her face solemn and sympathetic.

They left her to wait for her brother to regain consciousness and face the ordeal to come.

Fuck's sake. Why does doing the right thing so often feel like the opposite?

Outside, Malkie lifted his face to the bright March sunshine, but he felt no warmth from it.

'Lou. Who said that any society can be judged by how it treats its elderly and its sick?'

'No idea, boss. But yes. Point taken.'

'Aye.'

'Will they be OK, do you think?'

He dropped his gaze from the cold sun to Lou's troubled face. 'We have to hope so, Lou. We all know the Criminal Justice System is on its knees and having to push more people through the grinder faster than ever, but we have to hope there's still room for compassion in the system.'

'I suppose it'll depend on how good a brief they get.'

'Aye.'

'Do you think she'll be up to it? What's coming for them?'

He smiled. 'I think Patricia Quinn is about to discover she's stronger than she never knew.'

'Goes without saying.'

'Why?' He scowled, wondered what he was missing.

She grinned at him as Davie Semple drove up. 'She's a woman, boss.'

'You, Detective Constable Gooch, are a cheeky sod.'

But yes, you're bang on, too.

FORTY-NINE

It took Remi Quinn until late the next day to regain consciousness. Predictably he'd kicked off when he woke in a strange place and a hospital room, at that. Patricia had been there for him, as Malkie suspected she always would be, and managed to calm him down, explain that doctors and nurses would be coming to check he was OK.

She had asked the local Uniform to remain out of sight until she explained to Remi what was going to happen to him and why, then she'd brought Malkie in and introduced them. To Patricia's great surprise he remembered Malkie and decided they could friends.

He had asked his sister if he'd done wrong, and she could find no answer. He knew, anyway. He told her he couldn't remember attacking Beauchamp, or what he actually did to the man, because he was nothing but terrified. He said he'd never before felt fear like that night, which coming from a person like Remi, defied all comparison with even the worst ordeals of *normal people*, whatever that meant.

He kept repeating that Beauchamp was *bad to the core*, and that whatever Remi did to him that he still couldn't remember, Beauchamp must have brought it on himself. Malkie noticed

Patricia had to choke back tears when he said it. She didn't explain and Malkie didn't ask. Remi also said something about sharks, but he muttered it quietly as if he doubted anyone would understand, then refused to elaborate.

Remi struggled to lie still when nurses wrapped blood pressure cuffs on him that inflated and squeezed his arm. He looked to Patricia when they had to fuss over him. She held his hand and smiled, and he seemed to accept that if she trusted them, he could too.

Patricia told Malkie afterwards that Remi's two nights alone at The Fairy Bridge had changed him, seemed to have forced him to do a lot of growing up she'd never been able to help him with. She thought the fairies failing to appear to him, something he asked her about repeatedly in the hours after waking up, had forced a long-overdue realisation on him that the world outside his home wouldn't always be as he hoped. He'd never understand why, though; he seemed to possess only a limited capacity for self-analysis and would always be unaware that he was adjusting the best he could to a world that would only ever make limited allowances for him. Both agreed he was lucky to live in an age where treatment was an option. Being banged up would have caused him more meltdowns and made him fair game for any nutter looking for an excuse to hurt people.

Davie Semple had driven up from Livi to fetch Remi. He was plain-clothed and brought a secure but unmarked pool car. No van, no cage on wheels. When the time had come to leave the hospital and sit in the back of the police car for the journey home, Patricia had cried when he climbed into the car and – with an effort – said hello to *the man*.

'I could never have hoped, and it sounds perverse, but some good might come of this.' She stopped and considered her words. 'No, that's not right. But maybe Remi and I can come out of this in better places?'

Malkie squeezed her arm. 'What is it people say, Patricia?

When we can't control what happens to us, we can at least decide how to respond? Something like that?'

We do what we can, as his mum always told him.

'Mr McCulloch, are you OK? You drifted a bit and you looked so sad. Sorry, not my business.'

'I'm fine. As you'll be. Both of you. Eventually.'

'Aye. We'll survive. We have to.'

To her obvious surprise and relief, Malkie ushered her into the back seat beside Remi, after all, and closed the door. He sat in the front beside Davie, and made sure Davie saw him appraise his lack of uniform.

'Nice one, mate. Really.'

Davie nodded. He said nothing the whole three-hour return journey, except to share Remi's delight at two highland cows, Honey and Hamish, in a field beside the Green Welly Stop in Tyndrum. They did, of course, have to stop for fish and chips, which Davie fetched and they ate in the car. Way outside of protocol, but Davie was old school, like Malkie, and could be trusted.

When they reached St John's in Livi, Remi panicked. Waiting Uniforms apparently hadn't been briefed on how to handle him and had pulled cuffs from their belts, but looks from both Malkie and Patricia stopped them, and a discreet wave of Davie's hand made them back off.

Patricia and Malkie walked with him to a secure private room, Patricia explaining everything to him in Remi-friendly language, then sat with him. When Remi asked his sister to invite Malkie to join them, Patricia nearly broke down.

Malkie had called ahead and Rab had fetched Remi's comics and his ancient Gameboy from his bedroom.

McLeish came to satisfy his curiosity, but Malkie saw Remi's reaction to the big man and sent DI Arsehole packing.

'You're an excellent judge of character, young man.' Malkie reached out and patted his arm without thinking. Both he and Patricia glanced at each other as if they expected World War Remi to kick off, but he surprised them both by adopting a serious face, turning to Malkie, extending his arm and giving him a weak handshake. It felt like holding a wet fish, but Malkie nodded seriously at him. Remi laughed like a drain, laid back in his bed and flapped his hands in uncontainable glee, and Malkie decided that yes, he and his sister might well be fine, in time.

Malkie promised to return as often as he could, and the smiles they blessed him with lifted his heart like few things could.

Back at the station, his debrief with Thompson confirmed that Remi would be charged with manslaughter mitigated by self-defence and the mother of all cases of diminished responsibility. He'd need to be admitted to a secure hospital, but he'd be treated as a patient to be helped rather than a prisoner to be 'rehabilitated'. Further forensics had confirmed Patricia's version of events: Beauchamp had attacked her when she'd gone to his home to offer him tens of thousands of pounds, raised by remortgaging her home, to leave all four women – Teri Marshall, Zoe Anderson, Amber Balfour and herself – alone. Malkie suspected Balfour's suicide would haunt Patricia for life, despite there being nothing she could have done to prevent it. She was to be charged with obstructing the police, but the Fiscal declined to authorise any further action. Her assault on Beauchamp had been credibly in self-defence, and the post-mortem had revealed that although he'd bled profusely and passed out, that injury would not in itself have resulted in his death. A suspended sentence for obstruction of justice was almost inevitable, but nothing that would stop her from supporting her brother through his difficult recovery.

A long and difficult journey waited for both of them, and Malkie resolved himself to add them to Walter Callahan's grave for regular and non-negotiable visits.

Thompson also filled him in on Steph's *difficult day*. When he asked which cell Boswell was in, Thompson ordered him not to set foot in there, even once. Another DS, possibly from another station, would pursue the case against Boswell for homicide, although both agreed even the best prosecution would struggle to secure a conviction for the historic rape charge.

When Steph failed to answer her personal and work mobiles Malkie dropped by her flat in Linlithgow but saw no signs of life through the letter box. Eventually he got a voicemail from her. Three words. *I'll be fine.* He believed her, and he'd never stop being amazed at the sheer bloody-minded resilience of her. She'd been through enough to crush any mere mortal and yet Malkie harboured no doubt she'd grow from it, come out of it stronger, if maybe a tad more cynical.

He needed to hear Deborah's voice. She answered her phone before he even heard the ring tone.

'Are you OK?'

'I'm fine. Well, I am now, Debs.'

This seemed to panic her more. 'You're fine *now*? What happened? Are you hurt?'

'No, nothing like that, I promise. Just an emotionally bruising case. Long hours and a two-day trip to Oban.'

'Oban? What the hell were you doing in Oban?'

He considered how to start the story but couldn't muster the energy. 'I'll tell you all about it when I see you. I promise.'

'And when will that be? No. Sorry. That wasn't fair of me. I know what your job's like.'

Not all of it, Debs. Not all of the ugly bits.

'It's fair. I've been neglecting you, I know. I'll make it up to you.'

He suffered through a pause that lasted only seconds but tortured him.

'OK. I'll hold you to that. Dinner. Somewhere swanky.'

'Where?'

'You choose, but I want tapas. There's a fantastic place on George Street in Edinburgh.'

'Done. So. We're OK, aye?'

Another agonising pause. 'Of course we are, you numpty. Where else will I find a Dirty Old Man with standards low enough to—'

'Stop that. I'm punching way above my weight bagging a wee cracker like you. Everyone thinks so.'

'I'll take your word for it.'

Fuck's sake, Debs. You're the best thing in my life. Why can't you believe that?

'And stop calling me a Dirty Old Man. You don't know who might be listening.'

'Your fault, old man.'

He cast his mind back to his feeble joke about being an undercover pervert the day they met. 'Fair enough.'

'So, when will you be round next?'

'Tomorrow night, I hope. I have a shitload of paperwork to do from this case, and I need to spend an evening with Dad. We have some serious talking to do.'

'Pam Ballantyne's case? I mean your mum's?'

'Aye. New information.'

'What?'

He couldn't start that conversation now, not without some major scene-setting. 'I'll tell you all about it tomorrow, OK?'

'Sounds ominous, but yes, of course. Get your police stuff done then see me tomorrow. I got myself a set-top box with a recorder and I've got loads of crap soaps we can enjoy together. We can go out for a swanky dinner some other time.'

'Enjoy?'

'If you know what's good for you. Call me tomorrow to let me know you're still coming?'

'I will. Love you, Debs.'

'I miss you, old man.' She hung up.

He heard a split second of a pause before *miss you* and dared to believe a different word had wanted to come out of her mouth. He could wait. She needed time, worried that no man could want her given the extent of her injuries. He'd tried to put her straight that he was going nowhere, but he knew the strength of the stubborn streak that ran through her and would never take any future with her for granted.

FIFTY

When McLeish reappeared with his overcoat on and a holdall clutched in one hand, Malkie had to suppress a career-limiting *Thank fuck for that.*

'Leaving already, sir?' He beamed his best gleeful grin at the man. A *shit-eater smile*, he believed American cops called it.

'Don't start, McCulloch. I'm reporting back to MIT HQ for a briefing and progress check, then I'll be back. I intend to be here when some fucking big chickens come home to roost.'

Malkie feigned incomprehension. 'Not sure I get your meaning, sir.'

McLeish turned red, always a win in Malkie's book.

'Let's see. Shall we start with your incompetence and complete failure to bring Remi Quinn in for interview? His subsequent escape and the danger you put him in, a poor, vulnerable, young adult, ill-equipped to handle even day-to-day modern life let alone going on the run from the authorities?'

Malkie mulled this over for a few seconds or at least pretended to.

'You make a very good point, sir. I agree.'

McLeish's mouth opened but his indignant glare faltered and no words came.

Malkie raised his eyebrows as if to enquire as to the man's hesitation to respond. *Can you see what's coming, you bloated and self-delusional turd of a man?*

'Exactly. It was remiss of you to handle his arrest so badly. He could have harmed himself or others.'

'And I would certainly have deserved every sanction Police Scotland could level at me for such blatant negligence in not taking a trained mental health professional with me on that shout. I'm sure you would agree, sir?'

McLeish glanced around him. Thompson, Ballantyne, Rab, Gucci, all watched the proceedings. None betrayed their awareness of McLeish's imminent car crash although Malkie would be disappointed in any one of them if they didn't see it coming.

McLeish faltered, then doubled down. 'So, you're aware how reckless your actions were and the damage that might have resulted?'

'Absolutely. Sir. Whomever ordered Remi Quinn brought in without the support of a trained mental health practitioner and professionally accredited Appropriate Adult when his extreme vulnerability and volatility was well understood in advance, should face serious sanctions.'

Finally McLeish's penny seemed to drop as he realised the magnitude of the shit storm about to rain on him due to his own legendary hubris. He turned and headed for the door to the front foyer, his stride quick and determined.

Malkie made sure his next question carried the length of the open-plan CID office.

'DC Lundy. Would you be so good as to confirm who logged the HOLMES action to bring Remi Quinn in against my advice, please?'

McLeish stopped but didn't turn.

Rab played along, a gleam in his eye, no doubt delighted to be taking part in McLeish's long-overdue dismantling.

As Rab tapped away at his keyboard, McLeish turned back, his face dark, like a cornered animal realising it has nowhere to run.

It's coming, fucker, and it couldn't happen to a more deserving arsehole.

Rab turned from his PC. 'Very odd, sir. I see my note about that conversation, but there's no SIO sign-off on the actual action.'

Malkie feigned disappointment in his colleague. 'That can't be right, DC Lundy. I clearly heard DI McLeish confirm his intention to record his verbal request in HOLMES.'

When McLeish's eyes bored into Malkie he refused to flinch, surer of his footing at that moment than he'd ever been.

'Sir? It must have slipped your mind, yes?'

Malkie watched McLeish realise he had two options. He could admit his own fuck-up and maybe even earn himself a scrap of respect for taking the hit where it was due. Or he could double down on his doubling down. Malkie harboured zero doubt about which way he'd go.

'You must have misheard me, DS McCulloch. I agreed with your appraisal of the required protocol at that time. If you decided to proceed without ensuring sufficient support was in place for Mr Quinn, I can only wonder why you didn't follow your own advice. I clearly remember qualifying my instructions to you, and I would have logged the action in HOLMES as soon as you'd assured me you had put all appropriate safeguards in place.'

Malkie turned away from McLeish and winked at Rab. 'DC Lundy. Why didn't we contact Mental Health before trying to bring Mr Quinn in?'

Rab floundered for a second and Malkie's arse puckered as he feared he'd asked too much of the man.

Thompson intervened. 'Speak up, Rab. We all want to get to the bottom of this unfortunate error.' Her eyes communicated her intention to back any of her team to the proverbial hilt, and Rab seemed to take confidence from her.

'My recollection is that you gave DS McCulloch a direct order, sir. Sorry, sir.'

McLeish's eyes cast about the gathered spectators, came to rest on Pam Ballantyne. 'DS Ballantyne. Is your recollection of that discussion more reliable than that of DC Lundy?' His emphasis on the S and the C was a cheap shot. All present would know it and expect nothing less from their supposed *Superior*.

Pam stood and strolled over to stand inches before McLeish. She took a few seconds, and Malkie could only guess at the amount of satisfaction she would squeeze out of McLeish's idiotic misplaced belief that she'd back him up after her long years suffering his patronage.

'My recollection is perfect, sir. You ordered DS McCulloch to bring Mr Quinn in and assured him you would record the action in HOLMES. When DS McCulloch expressed concerns about doing so without ensuring adequate metal health support, you told him to – and allow me to quote you verbatim for the sake of accuracy – "*Bring Remi Quinn in for questioning. Tonight. Just fucking well do it, McCulloch.*"'

Ballantyne stared up at him, eight inches taller than she was, and she reminded Malkie of Steph on her best day.

Thompson stepped forward. 'DI McLeish, I suggest you leave now, in the interests of not prejudicing the inevitable Professional Standards investigation I'll be obligated to request into this incident. I'm sure you'll agree that's for the best, given the obvious uncertainty around these events?'

McLeish stared from Thompson to Malkie and back, then with a look of pure venom towards Ballantyne he turned on his heel and stomped away. He rattled the door to the front foyer as if trying to tear it from its hinges before remembering the door release button on the wall beside it.

Goodbye, McLeish. Enjoy the monumental fucking kicking that's coming your way, you utter prick.

Malkie turned to Thompson. '*Obvious uncertainty around the events?* ma'am?'

Thompson sighed. 'I want to hear no more discussion of this until any investigation is completed. Is that understood? All of you?'

Rab and Gucci nodded. Ballantyne and Malkie just stared back. Malkie broke the uncomfortable silence.

'You will not hear one word about this from any of us, boss.'

From the way Thompson glared at him, he knew she hadn't missed his weaselly non-assurance. She headed back to her office and slammed the door behind her.

All heaved a sigh of relief, a collective release of tension following what all hoped would prove to be a career-ending self-implosion on McLeish's part, the likes of which they might never enjoy again.

Malkie headed for Thompson's office. She took long seconds to respond to his knock with a curt 'You have two minutes.'

He closed the door behind him and leaned back on it. And waited.

'You really pushed your luck there, old man. You know that, right?'

'I—'

'I'll grant you that he deserved it, has had that coming for years, but turning it into a spectator sport? Drafting Rab into your performance and taking so much bloody obvious pleasure in it?'

'He—'

'On paper he hasn't a leg to stand on and no grounds to discipline you other than for your stupid no-filter gob. He gave you an order. You advised against it. He repeated the order and left you no alternative but to obey or give him yet another bloody big stick to beat you with. And you have several enthusiastic witnesses to corroborate it all. He'll have no option but to drop his request for an investigation into you, but you do *not* treat a senior officer that way under any circumstances. You follow process and you stay professional. I can't believe I still need to remind you of such basic stuff. You're supposed to set an example, for fuck's sake.'

She ran out of wind. Or fury.

'Susan, I—'

'For the rest of today, even in private, it's boss, mate. Now bugger off and try to pretend you're an experienced and competent copper, at least for today please.'

She opened a file on her desk and seemed to study it, but her chest heaved with barely restrained anger.

Malkie opened the door. He knew this was one of the times Steph always suggested he should keep it shut, and he amazed himself by managing to do just that.

FIFTY-ONE

Malkie found both Teri Marshall and Zoe Anderson at Patricia Quinn's home when he arrived.

Patricia's welcome at her front door seemed genuine but by the time he entered her living room, both Marshall and Anderson looked tense. They stared at him as if half expecting him to arrest them.

He waved a hand at them. 'Relax. I'm not here for you two.'

They glanced at each other. Neither looked convinced.

He sat on an arm of the sofa, tried to make himself less tall and imposing. 'You'll both be charged with withholding information pertinent to the investigation, but I really doubt anything much will come from it, certainly nothing custodial. The cells in Cornton Vale are already stuffed to the gunnels with mouth-breathers who did far worse things than you two. I can't see any judge putting you away for being scared to go to the *polis*. But don't quote me on that.'

They deflated in unison. Anderson looked ready to vomit, Marshall resigned and less than happy but calmer than the last time he met her.

Zoe spoke first. 'I had a suspended sentence for attacking

someone years ago.' She looked like she'd decided a second strike would see her inside.

'I know. We did background checks on you both. We're the *polis*. That's our job. It won't be a factor.'

Zoe took a deep breath. 'Thank you, Detective Sergeant McCulloch. What about Patricia and Remi though?' She asked the question as if obliged to but dreading the answer.

Malkie clasped his hands in his lap and looked at the floor, wasn't about to enjoy this part of the conversation. 'I can't go into much detail except with Patricia, but you'll both be aware that...' He glanced at Patricia, who stiffened even though they'd already had this conversation. 'Patricia will likely only get a suspended sentence for her shenanigans in the interview room, given the obvious reasons why she was initially less helpful than she could have been. But Remi will face a custodial tariff, no getting away from that. He won't see the inside of a cell though. He'll do his time in a secure medical facility, probably Carstairs, where he'll get as much help as the state can afford. I know, I know. But that's the reality of the situation. He looked again to Marshall and Anderson. 'I can't discuss any more with anyone but Patricia, for now.'

They shared a look, then stood. They crossed to Patricia, who had been standing in one corner since bringing Malkie in. They hugged, heads bowed, close, hands rubbing backs. He heard sniffles and whispered words and Patricia nodded to them. When they separated their eyes were red and wet, and Malkie had to choke down a lump of emotion he couldn't afford to let them see under the circumstances.

As Marshall and Anderson put their coats on, Malkie stood. 'Will you two be OK? Patricia will need you.'

Anderson looked away, couldn't hold eye contact, and Malkie suspected her newfound care for Patricia hadn't always been so forthcoming.

Anderson crossed to Patricia again and whispered something. She nodded back, then squeezed both of Anderson's hands in her own. Marshall smiled at them both, then the two left.

Malkie sat and waited for Patricia to do the same. She seemed flustered, probably dreading the conversation to come.

'Tea, Detective? Coffee? Water or juice?'

Malkie held a hand up and smiled. 'Patricia. Calm down. Remi's safe and he'll get help now.'

She looked ashamed. 'I tried to get help for him. I did, Detective. But there were never any appointments when he needed them. The local medical centre did what they could but they're always so understaffed.'

'I know. Mental health services in this country are as underfunded as the CJS, Patricia. It's a crime. Which, stupidly, us *polis* can't collar anyone for.'

'CJS?'

'Criminal Justice System. Court appointments backed up, not enough judges or time, overworked solicitors, too many bad guys and not enough cells. It's tragic.'

She appraised him. 'Your job is difficult, isn't it?'

He looked down, couldn't bear the pity in Patricia's expression. With all she had on her plate at the moment, with her vulnerable brother and herself facing an uncertain future at the mercy of an often brutal and unfeeling system, she still made space to feel for Malkie and his like.

'It doesn't make our job any easier, no. But we do what we can do.' Memories of his mum telling him that on so many occasions pushed forward in his mind but he did his best to ignore them, along with persistent and demanding thoughts about Liam Fielding and his incriminating lighter. A time and a place. Fielding's time would come, and Malkie would be there for it.

'Mr McCulloch? Are you OK? I asked about Remi. Will I be allowed to support him, if I don't get put away I mean?'

Fuck's sake, I need to focus.

'Are you OK, Mr McCulloch?'

He debated how much to tell her, but decided he needed to start holding back, keeping his personal life personal and giving his work the focus it needed. The focus people like Patricia and Remi Quinn deserved.

'Sorry, Ms Quinn. Just some personal stuff that has me a bit distracted.'

She considered him. 'I won't pry, but I hope you sort it out OK. We owe you a lot more than I appreciate just now, so I hope you get some peace.'

He found he wanted to talk, needed to unburden himself if only to get his thoughts lined up and exposed to the cold light of day, but he refused. His load was his to carry, and Patricia Quinn had more than enough of her own.

'Thanks. I'll be fine. Has your brief spoken to you about how to approach your case? Your plea?'

'Yes, she has. She's been brilliant. She says the same as you, that there's a better than fair chance I'll avoid prison, because it'll harm Remi more if I can't see him regularly.'

'Good. Sounds like you have a good brief there. Unless you're very unlucky with the jury, she should be able to paint a convincing picture of you as a woman desperate to appeal to an evil man who caused brutal pain to you and who knows how many others, and your actions as self-defence when he attacked you. And we have character statements about him that will give credibility to your claim that he was violent toward you.'

'From whom?'

Malkie recalled a phone conversation with Francesca Beauchamp that morning. When he told her about her husband's activities, about the phones and the notebooks he'd kept hidden in his study, she'd taken all of two seconds to adopt a damage limitation strategy of claiming she'd been as much a victim of her husband's toxicity as anyone and would be happy to testify to his repugnant and vile attitude towards women of all ages.

'Someone whose opinion will be believed. You can trust me on that.'

'When will we know? What will happen to us?'

Malkie's heart sank. As much as he was only the messenger he felt sick at delivering the information. 'The date for Remi's mental health assessment will be *sometime in May*. I'm sorry.' The words sounded pitifully inadequate to his own ears.

'May? Seriously? He won't survive that long without me. No, there must be something you can do, Mr McCulloch. Talk to someone. Please.' She looked ready to unravel, and Malkie couldn't blame the poor woman one iota.

'Please, Patricia. I have limited influence on all matters concerning the CJS, but our reports and recommendations will be taken into account. A mental health professional will be assigned to assess Remi and his needs, and they tend to cover their own backs by taking no chances. I'd hope you'll at least be allowed to visit him on remand as long as someone sits with you to shut down any conversation that might be prejudicial to either of your cases.'

He took a breath. Was what he was about to say crossing a line?

'Successive governments have promised to increase mental health awareness, and to improve Police Scotland and CJS policies. Anything to minimise the trauma for vulnerable people caught in the system. But without funding, the people on the ground are fighting losing battles on every front, and I'm afraid' – *I'll get such a kicking if she quotes me on this* – 'people like Remi suffer. Those least able to defend themselves and withstand the processes get hurt the most. I wish it were otherwise, Patricia.'

He got little more from her. She leaned forward and buried her face in her hands.

'Patricia?'

Nothing. He stood for a few seconds, felt like a spare part, then let himself out as quietly as he could.

It took him a full five minutes of staring through his car windscreen before he started the engine and headed for home.

FIFTY-TWO

'Do you think he did it?'

Malkie dug deep, for his dad's sake, but couldn't find any answer he could believe himself.

'Fielding? I don't know. He's capable of it. So's his dad. They're as bad as each other and worse than most. Real bad news, both of them.'

'But you're not sure he did.'

'No.'

They sipped coffee and watched bats flit around the cabin in the half-light of early evening.

'What will Pam do next?'

'She'll follow procedure, Dad. It's all laid out in boring and long-winded documents. Every little detail of how we're supposed to do our jobs, so bad guys don't wriggle out of charges and we don't get our arses kicked by clever and ridiculously well-paid lawyers.'

'I used to think policing was exciting until you became one.'

'Hah. It can be, for short periods, but boredom and stupidly over-engineered process is always waiting to drag us back to tedious reality.'

'So, what will she do next?'

'Interview both Fieldings. Try to find out if either of them were near the house that evening, although after ten months that will be difficult. She'll ask door-to-door to see if anyone can remember anything. Although most of our old neighbours are your age, so...'

'Cheeky sod. Us wrinklies are sharper than you give us credit for, boy.' He affected a stern expression but couldn't disguise the twinkle in his eyes.

Malkie studied him. 'Aye, I do believe you are, Dad. If you were twenty years younger I'd suggest a career in the *polis*, but I fear you'd fail the physical.'

Tommy looked pointedly at Malkie's spreading waistline. 'They still make you pass a physical?'

'Ha ha. Funny.'

They lapsed into a companionable silence again for a while.

'How's Deborah?'

'Ach, I haven't seen her for a week.'

His dad stared at him.

'Leave me alone. I've been busy. Work's been stupid. Uniforms have it worse than we do; volume crime is through the roof.'

'Volume crime?'

'Low-level stuff that happens all the time. No glory in it but it sucks up time just as much as the juicy cases.'

'Are you two OK?'

He considered his answer. 'We will be. I think.'

'Good. You should invite her here for dinner again. She seemed to enjoy getting away from that place.'

Malkie grinned. 'Nothing to do with her needing to be accompanied by Dame Helen Reid, of course.'

'Nothing to do with that. I just think she's good for you, and you seem to be good for her. You need to hang on to a good thing when...'

He tailed off and lowered his eyes to his coffee cup.

Malkie couldn't think of any words that would sound anything but trite, so he didn't bother trying. He reached over and took his dad's hand. The old man squeezed back, his grip – as ever –

stronger than his frail appearance suggested. They broke contact after a few moments and nodded to each other, tacit agreement that no words were necessary.

'So, Dame Helen Reid, eh? Tasty for her age?'

His dad snorted, mid-sip, into his coffee. 'Can't say I'd thought about it, son.'

Malkie opened his mouth to land another dig, but Tommy held a hand up. 'You look after your love life, son. I'm happy as I am.'

Are you, dad?

'How's Jennifer?'

Malkie groaned. 'Damn it. I forgot to call her back too. We were supposed to have coffee in the Civic Centre, but you know? The case?'

'Was it a bad one?'

They all are, Dad.

'Upsetting. Young autistic lad killed a man he saw sexually assaulting his sister. He blacked out and claims to remember nothing about the attack, and he seems incapable of lying.'

'What will happen to him?'

'Treatment rather than a cell in Addiewell. His sister will visit him every day, I suspect, but he's being forced to grow up more quickly than will be good for him. Actually, that's not right. You can't apply terms like *grow up* to people like him. It's more a case of him being forced to adjust to a society that pays lip service to inclusivity but then fails to back its stated good intentions with money and action. Boxes get ticked and good people stand on doorsteps and bang pots and applaud other good people, then business as usual is resumed, and vulnerable people like Remi have to cope the best they can.'

He sipped his coffee, if only to stop more words coming out.

'The greatness of a nation can be judged by how it treats its weakest members.'

'Aye, that. I was saying that to Lou Gooch. Who said it?'

'No idea, but is that why you do what you do, son? To protect people from the injustice and cruelty that we inflict on each other?'

'Well, we do more catching and punishing and not enough preventing. People who hang flags on lampposts want bad guys punished and people who consider themselves more enlightened want them rehabilitated, but most people just don't want them walking their streets.'

'Lovely aspiration.'

'Aye, but they're being released as fast as the Criminal Justice System can lock them up. No room for them. Invade some old lady's home, terrify and brutalise her, bleat about your troubled upbringing and *survival of the fittest* and how the government isn't creating enough twenty-hour-a-week jobs that pay fifty grand a year, and be back on the streets a half hour after standing in front of a judge.'

'Good God, that's depressing. Why do you keep doing it, son?'

'Because if nobody does, then they win, Dad.'

'Doesn't sound like you're winning now?'

'True, but we have to try, don't we?'

Malkie stood and wandered down to the shore of Harperrig Reservoir. He ached for peace, longed for even brief respite. Was it time to think about retirement, just when – according to his colleagues – he seemed to be conquering demons both old and new and finally finding his feet as a grown man and an experienced copper? Did he owe anyone anything? Did he owe himself some time? To repair his life and his dad's?

He had a daughter now. And a partner. Was he ready to leave that behind?

First, those Fielding fuckers. Liam had turned out to be innocent of Walter Callahan's brutal and undeserved death, and Malkie had needed to adjust his thinking in light of how blinkered he'd been in his desire to nail the man. Now he worried he was heading for a repeat confrontation with him, and he harboured serious doubts as to what level of objectivity he'd be able to maintain in his pursuit of which Fielding had left that lighter at the scene of his mother's death, and was therefore guilty of her murder.

One of them needed to go down for destroying the lives of Malkie and his father. One of them had to pay, even if that failed to alleviate Malkie's or Tommy's grief.

Then he'd think about hanging up his cuffs.

Or would he? Could he?

Hadn't he achieved some measure of good for Remi and Patricia Quinn? Would another copper, a less compassionate one, have shown them less sympathy, compartmentalised and left them to the so-called mercy of a Criminal Justice System on its knees and more focused on boosting Home Office statistics than searching for true justice?

It was a strange word. Mercy. Rare in these modern times, he feared. Rare and fragile.

No, he couldn't quit. Not yet. Not while he could make a difference that others couldn't or wouldn't.

He chuckled to himself.

Steph would flog him alive for even considering it.

A LETTER FROM THE AUTHOR

Dear reader,

Thank you for reading *A Fragile Mercy*. I hope you enjoyed Malkie's story. If you'd like to hear about my new and upcoming releases, you can sign up for my author newsletter.

Also, can I ask you to be kind enough to leave a review of this book? Let me know what you liked and what you didn't like, what resonated with you and what really didn't.

www.stormpublishing.co/doug-sinclair

I got serious about my writing late in life, after my amazing wife made me get help for lifelong 'issues' and helped me believe I could do this ridiculous 'writing' nonsense. I owe her an amount of gratitude that modern science is currently incapable of measuring. And my old mum, who still says every one of my books is perfect even before reading them. Without them, I may have given up years ago.

In my youth, I read only science fiction and fantasy; I couldn't handle books about 'real life' because the world seemed to me to be unremittingly bleak and cruel. When a friend made me read my first crime fiction novel, I realised crime fiction is the perfect vehicle to explore what makes us tick, what scares us, and what terrible acts the best of us can be driven to by the worst of us. Modern life hurts people who dare to care too much. Writing my books reminds me there are good people, too.

2025 was a difficult year for me and mine. Working on this

book was a struggle and I needed much TLC from my editors, for which I will never stop being grateful. Thanks, so much, all.

I hope you enjoyed this, my fifth book. Malkie continues to try to be a better man in the face of what most of us, thankfully, rarely have to look at. I hope you find his stories contain some hope for better, even when Malkie annoys the hell out of you, as he does to me all the time.

Please check out my website at www.dougsinclair.co.uk for information on coming books and some free short stories.

You can connect with me on Facebook, or Twitter, and I'd love to hear your comments – the good, the bad, and the ridiculous.

Thanks again for being part of this amazing journey with me, and I hope you'll stay in touch – I have so many more stories and ideas to entertain you with!

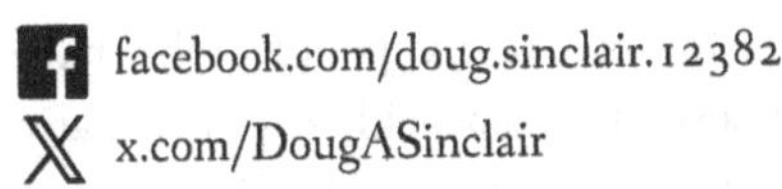

ACKNOWLEDGMENTS

The words 'book four' had me pinching various tender parts of me until they were bruised. 'Book five' has me reeling, if I'm honest. I've heard from numerous sources that imposter syndrome (a.k.a. the poison parrot) never, ever, fully leaves an author and that the blank page/screen/mind never stops scaring the *<insert own expletive here>* out of us.

I believe it.

I need to thank too many people who have supported and cajoled me and booted my backside over too many years to achieve my dreams despite the aforementioned parrot. Gordon Brown and Kevin Pocklington – thank you so much for seeing what I couldn't and helping me get my scribblings 'out there'.

I couldn't have finished this one without the stellar support of Oliver Rhodes, Claire Bord, Kate Smith, Naomi Knox, Laurence Cole, Shirley Khan, Alexandra Begley, and the awesome Angus King, who pretty much *is* Malkie in the superb audiobooks.

Thanks, also, to Craig Robertson, Caro Ramsay, Douglas Skelton, Mark Leggatt, Neil Broadfoot, Michael Malone, Carla Kovach, Zoe Sharp, Alex Gray, Graham Smith, Alison Belsham, Noelle Holten, Sharon Bairden, Jacky Collins, Kelly Lacey, Suze Bickerton – thank you so much for your patience.

Donna en mijn schoon-familie, lub lub to you all.

The Twisted Sisters of Dumfries – Irene, Fiona, Linda, Anne, Jackie – thank you for letting me become an honorary, er, sister.

Andy & Al, Rich, Dave T, Meesh, Wendy, Eleanor, Fergus, Rosie, Lorne, Kathy, Henbo, Colin – thank you for your support. I shall wear it, always.

Mother, Maaike – love you both more than chocolate digestives.

www.ingramcontent.com/pod-product-compliance
Lightning Source LLC
LaVergne TN
LVHW031335150826
845673LV00012B/2901

* 9 7 8 1 8 3 7 0 0 0 3 6 4 *